DEPARTMENT ZERO

DEPARTMENT ZERO

PAUL CRILLEY

an imprint of **Prometheus Books**
Amherst, NY

Published 2017 by Pyr Books®, an imprint of Prometheus Books

This is a work of fiction. Characters, organizations, products, locales, and events portrayed in this novel either are products of the author's imagination or are used fictitiously.

Cover illustration by Patrick Arrasmith
Cover design by Nicole Sommer-Lecht
Cover design © Prometheus Books

Inquiries should be addressed to
Pyr
59 John Glenn Drive
Amherst, New York 14228
VOICE: 716–691–0133 • FAX: 716–691–0137
WWW.PYRSF.COM

21 20 19 18 17 • 5 4 3 2 1

Library of Congress Cataloging-in-Publication Data

Names: Crilley, Paul, 1975- author.
Title: Department Zero / Paul Crilley.
Description: Amherst, NY : Pyr, 2017.
Identifiers: LCCN 2016045974 (print) | LCCN 2016050309 (ebook) |
    ISBN 9781633882010 (softcover) | ISBN 9781633882027 (ebook)
Subjects: LCSH: Space and time—Fiction. | Reality—Fiction. | Paranormal fiction.
    | BISAC: FICTION / Fantasy / Contemporary. | GSAFD: Fantasy fiction. |
    Science fiction. | Adventure fiction.
Classification: LCC PR9369.4.C75 D47 2017 (print) | LCC PR9369.4.C75 (ebook)
    | DDC 823/.92—dc23
LC record available at https://lccn.loc.gov/2016045974

Printed in the United States of America

For Bella and Caeleb. You guys are the reason I get up in the morning.

CHAPTER ONE

The polite term for what I do for a living is "biohazard remediation." That's what I say if anyone asks me at a dinner party. Not that I'm ever invited to dinner parties. (Megan got custody of all the friends in the divorce.) But it's what I'd say if I *was* invited, and if someone was actually polite enough to approach me through the chemical smell of industrial-strength cleaning products that cling to my body.

Another term for what I do is *Crime and Trauma Scene Decontamination*. Or CTSDecon, if you want to sound cool.

Which basically means that I clean up stiffs for a living.

All the stiffs. No prejudice in my line of work.

Murder? *Check.*

Suicide? *Check.*

Murder-suicide? *Check.*

Industrial accidents? *Check.*

Decomposition after unattended death? *Check.*

Infectious disease? *Check.*

Spontaneous human combustion? *Check.* (Not that I've ever had one of those, but I live in hope.)

The company I work for is called LA Cleaners. (*No matter the mess, we clean for less.* That's my boss's tagline. He's weirdly proud of it, considering it's a pile of shit. But then, my boss is proud of his son as well, so maybe it's not *that* surprising.)

I've been stuck in this dead-end (ha-ha) job for ten years now. Not bad, considering it was only ever meant to be temporary. Something

I could do to earn cash while I figured out what to do with my life. A decade later, and here I still am.

But that's me in a nutshell, as Megan always said. Big plans, no follow-through.

I yawn noisily and stare out the truck window. "What's the crime scene?" I ask Jorge. I should know this. After all, it was my contact at the LAPD who gave us the job. But the call came through at three in the morning, so I didn't stay on the phone to chat. Or to even ask what the cleanup would involve. I just swore at the guy for waking me up, gave him the office number, and told him to leave a message on the answering machine.

"Murder scene," says Jorge, yawning. Jorge is the aforementioned boss's son. Twenty-something, incredibly lazy, and addicted to his phone. He's partnered with me for a bit of "work experience" before he moves on to the offices where he will, in about a year, be my boss.

I relax. Murder scenes are our most common jobs. Not too difficult.

"Unattended," adds Jorge.

Crap. Unattended deaths are my least favorite cleanups. Messy as hell. And yeah, I'm aware that it's a bit tasteless to rank deaths by how hard it is to clean them up, but it's my job, so what do you expect? You do anything for a long enough period of time, it tends to lose its . . . uniqueness.

What an unattended death means is that somebody kicked the bucket but hasn't been discovered for a while. Could only be a matter of days. Could be weeks. Could even be months. But they're all bad. It still surprises me how quickly a human being can be reduced to a leaking bag of liquefied fat and grease.

I'm not looking forward to this. And the undercooked eggs and greasy bacon I had for breakfast? Probably not the best idea.

"Hey—did you watch it?" I ask Jorge.

Jorge is attempting to drive the van while checking out his cell phone at the same time. "Watch what?"

"The movie. The one I told you about."

"Nah, man. I tried."

"What do you mean, you tried?"

"Couldn't get past the beginning. Them sitting in a car talking about cheeseburgers? What's with that?"

I stare at him in amazement. "That's what makes it so good! That's characterization. Two people, traveling through LA in a car. Just talking. You see how each responds. Reveals who they are."

"Whatever, dude. It was lame."

"You obviously have no idea what you're talking about. You probably like Adam Sandler movies."

Jorge glances over at me with a grin. "Yeah. Sandler! He's funny. When he goes crazy and starts screaming and beatin' on someone? Gets me every time."

"You're a goddamn heathen. I don't want to talk to you anymore."

Jorge shrugs and carries on driving. Screw him. That's the last time I try and bridge the generation gap with movie recommendations.

The rest of the journey passes in silence until Jorge slows the van down and turns into a weed-infested parking lot.

"I think we're here," he says.

I look out the window. A run-down motel sits on the other side of the lot. Red doors and a fifties Art Deco look. I check the sign.

The Sleepy-Time Motel.

Charming.

It's weird to see such a run-down place in these surroundings, hugging the base of the Santa Monica Mountains. The beach is only about ten minutes away, and there are miles of wineries over to the east. Whoever is holding onto this dump must have fended off serious offers from realtors. Which begs the question—in the name of God, why?

I sit in the sweltering heat of our van and check the motel's website on my phone. It says the place has been here since the 1920s. It was built to house the workers who were laying down the Pacific Coast Highway, and after that it was sold off as a motel.

I squint through the bug-splattered windshield. The front face of the motel is just a generic line of rooms, punctuated with rusted ice machines. The parking lot is made up of broken asphalt, slowly melting in the morning heat.

It's weird. No cops. No crime scene tape. No pathology vans.

"You sure this is the place?"

Jorge reluctantly lifts his eyes from his phone. He's chewing gum. Noisily. Bastard doesn't even share. I asked for a piece once, and he said he didn't have any, that he doesn't even like gum. I had stared at him for a full minute before he finally swallowed the piece he was chewing. We didn't break eye contact once.

"Think so."

"What did the work order say?"

Jorge doesn't respond. Just turns back to his phone. I'm about to ask him what the hell he's doing when my phone chimes with a message. From Jorge. Containing the work order.

"Dude, I'm right here," I say.

He doesn't answer. I sigh and open the message, quickly scanning the details. Yup. This is the place. Sleepy-Time Motel. Room fourteen. The preferred stopover for serial killers everywhere.

I climb out of the van, squinting against the bright light. It's invasive. But then, that's Los Angeles in a nutshell, isn't it? Invasive. Unsavory.

Hell, even the sun in LA feels sleazy. A dry, groping heat that crawls into your clothes and sucks sweat from every part of your body, touching and lingering in spaces that are not meant to be touched.

I put my aviators on and cross the parking lot, checking the door numbers. Most of them are missing; all that remains are faded negative images surrounded by sun-bleached wood. I stop before room fourteen. The door might have once been painted red, but it's now a faded salmon pink.

I reach for the door handle, then freeze before my hand touches the metal. Here's the thing. I trained to be a cop once, as soon as I gained my US citizenship. I maybe should've mentioned this before, but I was holding off, you know? Didn't want to overwhelm you with random info. You know how it is: *Oh, hey. My name is Harry Priest, I do this for a living, but I once did that, and these are all the people in my life.* Don't you hate that? I do.

So yeah, I'm from England originally, came out here to seek fortune and glory. And the fact that I decided to do that by trying to become a cop probably says a lot about my level of intelligence. But even though I didn't cut it, the training has stayed with me over the past fifteen years. (Long story. Actually, not long. Pretty short. I failed the final test. And by final test I mean the mandatory—and surprise—drug test. Less said about that the better, really.)

The lack of any kind of police presence is bugging me. If the scene had been discovered last night, the forensics team should have been and gone. There should be evidence of their presence everywhere. You know, empty coffee cups, discarded donut boxes, the faint smell of desperation and loneliness.

But there's none of that here.

I chew my lip thoughtfully. Then I grab the bottom of my vintage *Empire Strikes Back* T-shirt and carefully use it to turn the doorknob.

The door opens with a creak. . . .

And the smell hits me like a half brick wrapped in ten-day-old rancid meat that's been left out on the stack interchange in the summer heat.

I stagger back, slapping a hand over my mouth and nose. I gag, barely managing to keep my breakfast down.

Don't think about the bacon and runny eggs. Seriously. Don't think about it. What are you doing? You're thinking about it! You idiot—

I turn and throw up onto the asphalt. Coughing, spluttering.

I take a few deep breaths, staring down at my half-digested breakfast.

Which causes me to throw up again.

And then one more time, just in case there is anything left. (There's not. Except bile. Lovely. I know. That's me all over, kids. Charming as ever.)

I take a shuddering breath and straighten up. My stomach muscles feel like I've just done a hundred crunches, which is about ninety-seven and a half more than I've ever done in my life.

I glance back at the van. Jorge is approaching, his phone held out before him.

I point a shaking finger at him. "I swear to *Christ*, Jorge. You better not be recording this!"

"'Course not, man!" Jorge grins and lowers the phone. "Would I do that to you?"

Yeah, you little bastard. You would.

Jorge's grin falters as he draws closer. He slows to a stop. "The hell is that smell?"

"Not really sure," I say, turning back to the room. "But my keen detective instincts are telling me there's something unpleasant in there."

"Yeah, no shit, Sherlock."

We approach the door cautiously, each trying to push the other ahead. I squint to let my eyes adjust to the dim interior of the room. Red curtains pulled closed, the sun shining through them with a lurid glow. Motes of light dance and spark. Flies buzz around.

Lots of flies.

"Fuck sake," whispers Jorge.

"Yeah."

The room looks like something has exploded in it. Something organic. That has then been left for weeks to stew.

The ground is moving. I lean forward, peering at the thick brown carpet.

Maggots. The floor is covered with them. The furniture and walls are peppered with shards of bone. The shards have ripped through the couch. Have even shattered the screen of the old box set television bolted to the wall.

"You know what?" I say. "I don't think the cops have been here yet."

Jorge frowns at me. "'Course they have. Why would they call us in to clean up a scene they haven't processed?"

"You see any fingerprint dust? Any evidence markers? I'm telling you. This scene is untouched." I take a step back from the door. "I'm going to find the manager. Don't touch anything!"

"Come on, man. What you take me for? An amateur?"

What I take Jorge for is something I have to keep to myself. Especially if I still want to have a job tomorrow. "Just . . . stay out of the room."

I hurry along the deserted frontage, searching for the manager's office. I find it through a set of unlocked glass doors. Old posters cover the dirty glass, faded in the sun and curling at the edges like dead spiders.

A little bell chimes as I push the door open. A partition with a security grille greets me. An old fan swings jerkily from left to right, pushing the turgid air around.

The office is empty.

"Hello?"

I approach the security grille and peer through. A tatty office chair. An old computer with one of those clunky CRT monitors.

I hit the bell on the counter. "Hello!"

Still no answer. What the hell is going on here?

I make my way back to the room, knocking on doors as I do so. None of the other rooms are occupied. The whole place is deserted.

As I draw closer to room fourteen I realize that Jorge is nowhere in sight. I break into a run. "Jorge?"

He's inside the goddamn room, filming everything with his cell phone.

"What are you doing?" I shout.

"Nothing."

"You're contaminating the crime scene, you idiot!"

Jorge frowns at me. "You might want to tone down the invectives there, homey. Don't want me telling the old man how you treat his favorite son, do you?"

"Just . . . get out of there. Now."

Jorge takes his time, casting his phone one last time around the slaughterhouse before stepping past me.

As he does so, something catches my eye, the glint of something metallic on the floor just inside the entrance. I bend down to study it.

It's a bullet. But it hasn't been flattened, as would happen to a normal bullet if it had hit something. Instead, it's in pristine condition.

It also looks like it's made from silver.

I take my aviators off and prod the bullet with one of the ear hooks. Yup. Definitely looks like it's made from silver.

"What the hell are you doing?" snaps an irritated voice.

I straighten up and turn around to find three figures standing in the parking lot. The one who had spoken is a man in his forties, hair in a buzz cut, face smoothly shaven. Military type.

"I'm trying to do my job," I say.

The man stalks forward and grabs my hands, lifting them up and inspecting them. I yank them away. "Hey. None of that till the second date."

Crew Cut ignores my remark, stepping around me to peer into the motel room. While he does this I study the others. One of them is a woman. Long, red-brown hair—what's the name for that? Not red, not ginger. Auburn? Chestnut? Something like that.

The last one in the line is a guy who looks about twenty years older than me. A bit heavier around the gut, an air of arrogance clinging to him like someone who's used to being in charge.

"Who are you?" demands the man. "I need names. Occupations."

"Harry Priest," I say. "Crime scene cleanup and decontamination."

The man points two fingers at me, like an Elvis impersonator.

"Cool name. You'll go far in the world. I can feel it in my blood. Remind me to take you for a drink sometime and explain about nominative determinism."

"How your name determines your career? Yeah—I'm familiar with it. Doesn't really apply here. If it did my name would have to be . . . Cleaner. Or . . . Coffin. Something like that."

The man blinks at me, surprised.

"Your turn," I say. "Who the hell are you?"

"Havelock Graves. ICD."

I frown. "ICD? Never heard of you."

"Well, shit, that just really bums me out, man," he says, sarcasm dripping from every word. "That you, a crime scene *cleaner*, haven't heard of the *incredibly* important organization I work for. Let me *tell* you the ways that bums me out—"

"Graves." The auburn-haired chick. I notice she has green eyes, pale skin. Freckles. Graves looks at her, and she gives a small shake of her head.

"Yes. You're right. No time. You and your . . ." Graves glances at Jorge leaning up against the wall, texting on his phone. ". . . friend?"

I shake my head.

". . . associate need to clear out. We're taking over."

"We have a work order for crime scene decon," I protest.

"This site hasn't even been worked yet," snarls Crew Cut from behind me. "I swear. If you two amateurs have compromised—"

"Hey—GI Joe," I snap. "Why don't you suck my dick? We know what we're doing, okay?" I turn back to Graves. "We were given the contract to clean this scene. We're not leaving till we speak to someone in charge."

"*We're* in charge," says Crew Cut.

"So you say."

Graves leans closer and whispers, "No, he's right. He's just very unpleasant. Doesn't have much of a bedside manner. His parents divorced when he was young. They both cited him as the reason for the separation. Don't think he ever recovered." He straightens up again. "This crime scene doesn't fall under the jurisdiction of the LAPD. As I said. The ICD is in charge, and we have our own scene cleaners. Dicks."

I blink. "Did you just call us—"

"No, idiot. Keep up. Dicks. DDICS." He spells out the initials. "Disposal Department for Interstitial Crime Scenes. Look, it's a long, complex, *incredibly* interesting explanation, but one I'm not prepared to go into right now. Which leaves you both on the cusp of something world-shattering and amazing, quivering and red-faced but without the happy ending, I'm afraid. But that's life. Leave now and you won't get your license revoked."

I stare at him, then take out my cell phone and dial my contact at the LAPD. "Mills. It's Harry. That crime scene at the motel. You sent it our way last night?"

I listen for a moment, frowning, then hang up. Graves grins at me. It's a really annoying grin.

"All set?" he says. "Groovy."

"Did you seriously just say groovy?" I ask.

"Yes. It's a wonderful word, isn't it?"

I catch Jorge's eye and jerk my head toward the van. I move away from the motel, Jorge following as I climb inside and slam the door shut.

"What gives? That was our scene."

"Mills confirmed. It was handed over to them early this morning. We just never got the call."

"So who the hell are they?"

"I've got no idea."

I start the van and pull out of the parking lot. Onto the highway and back toward LA.

I look in the rearview mirror and see Graves standing in the parking lot, watching us leave.

"Dicks," I mutter.

CHAPTER TWO

I grab a beer from the fridge, open the patio door that leads onto my balcony, and slump into the plastic lawn chair I use while watching the plebs below from my incredibly spacious and palatial balcony. (One foot by three feet.)

The rest of the day was a shitstorm of epic proportions. And I mean that literally. After we left the motel we got a call out to another death scene. A heart attack. And let's just say the victim . . . soiled himself before death. I mean, they usually do, but I think today I just noticed it more.

The scene this morning at the motel has been bugging me all day. Something is going on. Something I feel I'm being purposefully left out of. And I hate that.

Who were those people? What the fuck is the ICD? Because I Googled it and came up blank. They don't exist.

There's a voice mail waiting from Megan on my cell phone. I sigh, wondering how long I can put off listening to it. But there's no point. Might as well just get it over with. I play the message while the sun sets over a toxic horizon. The sunset is tinged with green tonight. Green, purple, and pink. Lovely and apocalyptic.

"Harry? Listen, I was wondering if you can take Susan next weekend instead of this one. I want to go visit my mother. I already talked to Susan, and she said she's fine missing her weekend with you."

Fucking Megan. Master of the passive-aggressive knife to the heart. I check the time. Shit. Nearly missed it.

I end the voice mail and dial home—actually, not home. Not anymore. Still, hard to stop thinking of it that way.

"Hello?"

"Megan." No need for long conversations. Or short ones, really.

"Did you get my message?"

"Yeah."

"Well?"

"Come on, Megs. It's not fair to even ask me. It's the only time I get to spend with her."

"I don't have a choice. I couldn't get time off work. It has to be the weekend."

"How is that my problem? Just leave Susan with me and go see your mother yourself."

"I want Susan there."

"And I want Susan here."

A pause. I can feel this building up into another one of our pointless fights. About nothing. About everything.

"Let me speak to her," I say.

"She's doing her homework."

"Megan, she's six years old and it's seven o' clock at night. She's not doing her fucking homework. Put her on."

I hear a muffled clicking as Megan drops the phone. I sigh, grabbing my beer and heading back inside to slump onto the couch. How the hell could something that was once so . . . perfect turn so bad? We were so good together once. Christ, I would have died for her. Where the hell did it go wrong? I've thought about it, over and over. Apparently, it's one of the things people do after a divorce. (I looked it up.) I traced back the months and years, trying to pinpoint the exact moment when it fell apart. Except there wasn't one. Neither of us cheated. It wasn't anything like that. Twenty years on and we just started to . . . drift apart. And after every fight it became harder to pull it back together again. Until one day it was easier just to end it.

I stare into the distance, feeling the depression cresting, starting to take over my mind like it always does when I think about it.

Then Susan comes on the phone and my whole day just ... gets better. It's as if every shit thing that happened to me is washed away, cleansed by the sound of her voice.

"'Lo, Daddy."

"Hi, honey. How's it going?"

"Horrible. A stupid boy pushed me at school."

"Bastard. What did you do?"

"What you told me. I pushed him and stood on his stomach."

"That's my girl. Did ... you get in trouble?"

"Nope. Nobody told."

I smile. Screw all this New Age parenting bullshit. I taught Susan from the moment she could understand my voice never to take any crap from bullies. Hit them back and hit them hard. They'll never bother you again. Megan doesn't know. At least, I don't think she does. I probably would have heard about it if she did.

"So you ready?" I ask.

"Ready, Daddy."

"Great." I get up, grab the book from the table in my apartment, and sit back down on the couch. "What page were we on again?"

"I don't know!"

"Come on, kid! You should be able to read by now. What page number?"

"Daddy! You're supposed to keep track, not me."

I smile. "Page thirty. You ready?"

"Ready."

It's something I insisted on, being able to read to her every night. Megan can have the house, the car, everything else. But reading was the one special thing I had with Susan. Every night before bed.

Nowadays, it's the one brief moment of happiness in my shitty life.

About half an hour later I hear Megan talking in the background.

"No, Mommy!"

More mumbling. I sigh.

"Time for bed, honey," I say.

"I'm not sleepy."

"Doesn't matter. If mom says it's bedtime, it's bedtime. We'll finish up tomorrow, okay?"

Susan sighs. The sigh of a child denied her way, as if the whole world is against her.

"Fine!"

"G'night, honey. Love you lots like jelly tots. Have nice dreams."

Our exchange of good nights is getting longer and longer. It started out with just good night. But then Susan had a bad dream, so I added in, "Have nice dreams," which stuck. Then Susan decided she liked "love you lots like jelly tots," and I added that too. Even now I'm sure I've forgotten something.

Her silence confirms it.

"Uh . . ." I close my eyes and rack my brain.

"Daddy . . ."

"Yeah, honey . . ." What is it? I've done the jelly tots thing. Done the nice dreams thing. Oh! Bedbugs.

"Don't let the bedbugs bite. If they do, squish a few."

Phew.

"'Night, Daddy. Love you lots like jelly tots. Have nice dreams. Don't let the bedbugs bite. If they do, squish a few."

I open my mouth to say I love her, but as soon as Susan finishes talking, the phone line goes dead. Megan.

I toss the phone on the couch next to me and down my warm beer. I love reading to Susan, but it always depresses me. Thinking about how much I've lost. Where I am now.

I look around the tiny apartment. Boxes of books still stacked up against the walls. My laptop showing a screenplay I haven't worked on in over three weeks.

Move to LA, man. Follow your dreams. You can be anything!

Yeah, right. If by anything you mean a divorced, lonely, minimum-wage worker. (Note I didn't put middle-aged in there. Because I still have some dignity.)

My phone rings. I check the caller ID. Jorge. I frown. The hell is he calling me at this time of night? We don't socialize.

I hesitate, wondering whether to just blow him off. But it might have something to do with work.

"Yeah?"

"Harry! Thank fuck. You gotta get over here."

I sit up straighter. Jorge sounds scared. No—*terrified*.

"You hear me?"

"Yeah . . . yeah, I hear you. What's wrong?"

"That crime scene today . . . I . . . Listen, just get over here. I'll text you my address." His voice lowers to a horrified whisper. "We are so fucked, man. Seriously. We're finished."

The phone goes dead.

I stare at it, puzzled. The crime scene? Had we stepped on more toes than we thought? Shit. Maybe the FBI is involved.

My phone pings with Jorge's address. I stare at it, pondering. Can I actually be bothered with this? I'm tired. Driving around in the heat all day really takes it out of you.

Another ping.

Get over here now!

I sigh and heave myself off the couch, grab another beer from the fridge, and head out of the apartment.

Jorge better remember this when he's the boss and my annual assessment comes around.

§

I sit in my pickup, staring up at Jorge's apartment. No lights. It isn't dark yet, but the sun is gone, swallowed up by the gray-brown haze that coats the city like a chemical cloud.

I dial Jorge's number. No answer.

I get out of the truck and climb the steps to the front door. I pull open the bug screen and knock.

The door swings open at my touch.

Shit.

Shit, shit, shit.

What the hell am I supposed to do in a situation like this again? My academy training was so long ago I can't remember. It's all been wiped away by bad cop shows.

"Jorge?"

See? Right there. Don't call out when you're entering a suspicious property. It just calls attention to yourself. Now the bad guys know I'm here.

So ... what now?

Make them fear you, that's what.

"I ... brought a gun, Jorge. Uh ... like you asked."

I pause and frown at the floor. Was that a smart thing to do, or was it really dumb? I'd *thought* it was smart. Just in case there *are* any bad guys lurking around inside. But now that I think about it, it might have been stupid. If they think I'm armed they're more likely to shoot first.

Jesus, I really would have been a terrible cop. It's just as well I failed the drug test. If I passed I'd probably be dead by now.

I enter the apartment. The door opens directly into a surprisingly neat kitchen. Stainless-steel mixer, fancy coffee machine, a blender that looks like it cost more than my TV.

The kitchen is open plan, the lounge visible beyond the breakfast counter. There's a massive flat screen mounted on the wall. An Xbox *and* a PlayStation sit in the black cabinet below.

If I'd known Jorge lived like this, I'd have tried harder to get to know him. This is a sweet place to hang out. Better than my dump. I bet Jorge doesn't have to deal with someone like the screamer. (A man who, at four o'clock every morning, gets up, steps out onto his balcony, and screams at the top of his voice for a full minute before returning to bed.)

There's a sound off to my left. A soft, scraping noise. I take a hesitant step into the lounge, peer through a partially opened door. I can see black-and-white tiles on the other side. The bathroom.

"Jorge?"

The sound stops.

"You okay?"

The door slowly opens. Like, really slowly. About an inch every second. I glance quickly over my shoulder to make sure no one's sneaking up on me with a knife. (There's not, but yes, I watch a lot of horror movies, okay?) The door carries on opening, to finally reveal—

Jorge. Standing there looking pretty goddamn normal.

I sag with relief. "Jorge? What the hell, man?"

Jorge doesn't say anything. He's really starting to creep me out. His eyes are unfocused, the pupils massive. Is he high?

Then Jorge shudders and blinks, as if waking up from a dream. He focuses his attention on me.

"Harry? That you?"

"Uh . . . sure is, buddy. Listen, you take something? You want me to call an ambulance?"

"I . . . took something. Yes."

I hear a sudden sound behind me. Some kind of animal-like chittering.

I whirl around, scanning the apartment. There's nothing there. Just the closed door to what I assume is Jorge's bedroom.

I turn back . . .

. . . straight into Jorge's arms. He puts his arms around my waist, leaning in as if he's going to nuzzle my ear. I try to pull away, but he has a tight grip.

"Jorge? What the hell? Let go."

"I took something," he whispers.

"Yeah, I'm kinda getting that."

"From the crime scene."

I stop trying to wriggle out of Jorge's grip and look into his eyes. "Today?"

Jorge nods. Tears trickle down his cheeks. "I'm in so much trouble."

"Uh . . . look. I'm sure we can fix it." I hate tears. Especially in adults. I never know how to respond to them.

"Can't fix it. They already found me. I'm dead, man. Dead."

"You're not dead. Trust me." I reach up to awkwardly pat Jorge's shoulder. "There, there," I add. Just in case it helps.

I freeze.

My fingers touch what feels very much like short, bristly hair.

Bristly hair?

Jorge finally lets me go and steps back. I unconsciously wipe my hand on my jeans.

"I . . . think they scooped my brains out."

I'm starting to get seriously freaked out here.

Then Jorge turns around.

I let out a shriek of incredibly unmanly fear and stagger back. I hit the leather couch and tumble over the back, somersaulting onto the hardwood floor. I scramble to my feet and leap behind another couch.

"What the actual *fuck*, Jorge?"

I can't believe my eyes. Clamped to Jorge's back, its legs nestling together and following the exact contours of his body, is some kind of . . . spider. It's *massive*. Huge and hairy, as tall as Jorge is, perfectly molded to his back so you can't see it until he turns around.

I raise a shaking finger. Pointing. Accusing. "Jorge!" I scream. "Why is there a big-as-fuck spider on your back?"

It's a pretty lame response. I'll be the first to admit. But I've found that people tend to state the obvious when confronted with panic.

"Seriously, man. A . . . a *tarantula* or something!"

Except tarantulas don't grow that big.

There's something else. I lean forward, peering closer while trying to shy away at the same time.

The spider's fangs are clearly embedded in Jorge's brain. "It's eating your goddamn brain!"

And then, just when I think I've seen everything, the spider explodes, bursting into thousands upon thousands of smaller spiders. They drop to the floor, onto the couch, skitter up the walls and across the floor, a black wave heading toward me.

I only have a moment to see Jorge's now spider-free back before he drops to the ground. The entire rear half of his body is gone. Like he's been sliced in half from top to bottom. I can see his spine nestled amid pink-and-purple tissue.

I turn and bolt for the last remaining door in the apartment. The bedroom.

A spider lands on my head. I shriek again, flailing at it before yanking the door open, rushing inside and slamming it shut behind me.

My back is up against the door, my breath coming in short, panicked gasps. I'm dreaming. That's it. I got wasted. Drank a six-pack in front of the TV and passed out. Yeah, that's it. That explains everything.

The door thuds behind me. I jerk away, stumbling against Jorge's bed. The door thuds again, rattling on its hinges. I look around for a weapon. Nothing. Just tasteful white linen and clean blinds.

Even in the middle of my panic, I take a moment to appreciate Jorge's taste. I've seriously underestimated the guy.

Another thud. I yank open the bedside drawer. Magazines. Condoms. Lube. A dildo. (A big one. Anemic white with bulging veins running up its fifteen-inch length.)

"Gross."

I check the other drawers. What I need is a gigantic can of bug spray. That would really hit the spot right about now.

Nothing.

Shit, shit, shit.

I reluctantly pick up the dildo, brandishing it like a lightsaber. It flops around a bit, but it's still pretty heavy. Should be good enough to squash a few spiders.

A few thousand spiders.

I hurry to the window. Pull the blinds up. The back of the apartment block has a drop of about three stories down to some dry scrub. Could I jump? I could. If I wanted a broken ankle.

I turn back to the room. One wall is just closet doors, but these kinds of apartments usually have en suite bathrooms, right?

I pull the doors open until I find it. A small bathroom. Beige tiles, a shower, a massive mirror.

And a monkey. Sitting on the toilet.

I blink. The monkey blinks back, seemingly as surprised as I am.

It takes me another second to realize what is odd about this situation. (Besides the monkey on the toilet.)

The monkey has a human face. A human face of a man in his seventies. Wrinkled skin. Bald head, rheumy eyes.

"'Infected be the air whereon they ride!'" the monkey shrieks.

I brandish the dildo in panic. The monkey doesn't seem fazed.

"'And damned all those that trust them!'" it shouts.

Fuck this.

I take a step forward, imagining I look like fencers do when they do that fancy lunge and strike.

Except I'm trying to lunge forward in a tiny bathroom with a white dildo as a weapon.

I hit the monkey across the face.

There's a meaty thud. The monkey shrieks its anger, turning around on the toilet. At first I think it's trying to get away from the dildo, but a moment later it turns back with a huge revolver. A Smith & Wesson if I'm not mistaken.

"'By the pricking of my thumbs, something wicked this way comes!'"

I frown. That sounds . . . oddly familiar. But I don't have time to ponder it any further. Not with a gun pointed at my face. I duck out of the bathroom, pulling the door closed.

An explosion rings out, and a huge hole appears in the door. The bullet flies past my head, missing my cheek by an inch.

A flash of pain. I reach up, feel something warm and wet. My ear! I feel gingerly around. There's a nick taken out of my earlobe!

That goddamn monkey shot me in the ear!

I should have hit the little bastard harder.

There's another bang on the bedroom door. This time higher up. At around arm height.

That gives me pause. How? Who the hell is banging on the door?

I hurry over and put my eye to the keyhole. At first I can't see a thing. Just a vague darkness. Then the darkness shifts back, lightening as it goes.

My eyes widen. The spiders have clumped together again, this time forming a full humanoid shape. With arms and legs and everything. I can make out individual spiders scrambling across the figure, disappearing into the mass then appearing again.

I jerk back, trying to fight down panic. What do I do? Jump out the window, probably breaking my leg in the process, or run past the weird spider-monster in the lounge? Nothing in life has prepared me for this situation.

There's a click behind me. I whirl around to see the bathroom door slowly opening. I catch a glimpse of an old rheumy eye appearing at knee height, peering cautiously out of the bathroom. I lunge forward, colliding with the door. It flies inward, hitting the monkey-pensioner and sending him crashing back against the toilet.

The monkey's still holding the gun. It tries to point it at me, but I grab its tiny wrist, pushing it up toward the ceiling.

"'Bloody thou art; bloody will be thy end,'" snarls the monkey through clenched yellow teeth.

The gun goes off at the exact moment I realize the monkey is talking in Shakespearean quotes. The bullet hits the light. A flash of brightness, then the bathroom is plunged into darkness. Glass showers over my head as I bunch my fist and punch the monkey in the face.

Now, don't get me wrong. I'm not one for cruelty to animals, but demonic monkey-pensioners are different, right? They don't count.

I yank the gun from its hands and close the door. Back to the bedroom door. I peer through the keyhole but can't see the spider-man anywhere.

Now's my best chance.

I pull open the door and sprint out into the lounge. I skid in the blood and gunk leaking from Jorge's sheared back, only just managing to right myself. I leap over the couch, heading toward the front door.

I cast a quick look over my shoulder and instantly wish I hadn't.

The spiders are swarming across the roof toward me, a solid black mass of skittering, pulsating, arachnoid nightmare fuel.

I open the door and run outside, slamming it shut behind me. I stuff the gun into the waistband of my jeans and run down the stairs, heading toward my pickup. I bang up against the truck. Fumble for my keys. A quick glance over my shoulder and I see the spiders erupting through the door, pouring over the balcony like a wave of sand and pooling on the asphalt below. Then they rise up, forming into the shape of a man that starts to run toward me.

I wonder if I'm going mad. Did I inhale some dodgy chemicals today? Ingest some acid? Maybe that's why the crime scene had been shut down. Some kind of secret government testing.

Thing is, I'm not going to wait around to see if the spiders are real or not. They sure as hell look real, and right now that's good enough for me.

I unlock my door and climb in. Start the truck and wheelspin out of the parking lot, almost sideswiping a Humvee. The Humvee swerves to the side, honking, the driver leaning out the window to scream obscenities at me.

I put my foot down on the gas, veering off the small roads and heading back to the south side. I check the rearview mirror. Nothing. Just normal LA rush hour traffic.

What that means is I'm not actually moving very fast. Which is cool because it means no one else can come after me fast either.

I need to figure out what to do. No—I need to figure out what I'm on. I need to get tested. So . . . hospital?

Except . . . I don't really feel high. I did acid once, and it wasn't like this at all. Back then I thought I was an Egyptian solar god and the sun was trying to make out with me. I'd been blind for a week after staring up into the afternoon sky with a huge smile on my face. But it was worth it. The sun was a good kisser.

But right now . . . I feel totally fine. Which I'm not. Obviously. Because . . . if I'm fine it means that what just went down *actually* went down. Which is crazy.

I chuckle to myself, ignoring the creeping sense of dread and horror that is taking up residence in my stomach and spreading throughout my body.

Crazy.

Yeah.

I flick the radio on. Old-school tunes. Kylie Minogue and the Locomotion. There we go. Good old Kylie. She's still hot, even after all this time. She must be older than me, but she's still bangin'. Yeah. There we go. Stop thinking about the massive spiders. And the creepy monkey man. Think about lovely Kylie.

I hear it first, a dull crashing and crumping sound from somewhere behind me. But I refuse to take any notice of it as I sing along desperately to lovely Kylie.

Then comes the screeching of tires. The heavy thud of concrete.

I feel the panic rise up. *Don't look*, I tell myself. *If you don't look, it can't be real.*

The crashing sounds grow louder, accompanied by the blare of car horns.

My eyes swivel upward, drawn to the rearview mirror.

A swathe of slow-moving cars is being parted behind me, plowed aside into the concrete bollards as a huge eighteen-wheeler thunders through them.

BARP! BARP! The air horn of the eighteen-wheeler.

It's impossible, I know that, but I feel like whoever is driving the truck locks eyes with me. Like I'm in a movie or something.

The truck puts on a burst of speed, screeching and juddering through the traffic.

I punch the horn. "Move!" I scream. "Get out of the way!"

I hit the gas, bumping up against the car in front of me. The driver jams on his brakes, yanks the hand brake up, and gets out, swearing and gesturing at me.

Until he sees the truck coming up behind us. He shoots back into his car and tries to get away.

I drive forward, bumping and jostling the cars in front. They move aside as much as they can, trying to get away from the crazy driver, so I'm able to edge slowly forward, scraping past the cars and leaving behind a trail of very angry commuters.

I wind down the window. "Look behind you, morons!" I shout.

They do. That shuts them up. It also starts a panic that spreads through the slow-moving cars like the rumor of a raid at a whorehouse.

Which is fine for me, because I make it to the off-ramp and shoot off the freeway, taking random turns until I find myself on a deserted piece of road huddled beneath a freeway overpass that curls overhead.

I stop the truck and get out, straining to listen. Nothing. No horns. No screeching tires. No screaming motorists. I did it. I got away.

I wipe the sweat from my brow and turn in a slow circle, allowing myself to feel some relief.

But the thing about relief? It's always a lie.

Because at that moment a waterfall of spiders spills over the edge of the overpass and slaps to the ground only twenty feet away, quickly followed by the monkey with the old man's face.

"'Brevity is the soul of wit!'" he screeches, bouncing up and down.

I make for my truck, but the spiders are already moving in a tide toward it. They climb over each other to form into the shape of a man and slam the door shut, turning to me with a gaping smile replete with spider legs and the glint of black eyes.

I pull the gun out and fire. It cuts a hole through the spider monster and hits my pickup.

The monkey jumps onto the roof, screeching at me and jumping up and down.

I shoot it in the head.

It falls off the truck and hits the ground. Then I turn and start to run.

Wait! What the hell am I doing? I skid to a stop and whirl around, my high school English classes coming back to me.

"'Good night, good night! Parting is such sweet sorrow,'" I shout. "Boom! Take that with your weird-ass Shakespearean quotes fetish, you creepy motherfucker."

Then I run.

I don't get far.

The spiders have used the time to surround me. A wall that slowly starts to constrict, rising higher as it comes.

I turn in a slow circle, my gun raised. I don't shoot, though. Waste of bullets.

The spider-wall stops moving. I notice movement behind it and see that there are more bugs coming. Beetles, centipedes, scorpions, more spiders. They stream from cracks in the road, from the weeds along the shoulder, rippling in streams that join up with the wall.

The creatures shiver and rise up, taking on the shape of a man once again. The mouth opens, and a long tongue flops out (a brown centipede). The centipede rises up, making it look like the figure is licking the air.

"Where is-s-s-s i-t-t-t-t . . .?"

I blink, look around. Did that wall of insects just talk to me?

"Where i-s-s i-t-t?"

Yup. It did.

"Uh . . ." I say, feeling incredibly stupid. "Where's what?"

"Give i-t-t-t-t to u-s-s-s."

"No idea what you're talking about," I say nervously. I look around. There are no cars around this little side road. They're all up on the overpass. This is LA, for Christ's sake. Why is there no one about?

Not that anyone would do anything. They'd just record it on their phones, thinking I was filming a movie.

Thinking this, I realize it's a surprise that the cops haven't turned up to check my filming permit. Someone gets shot? Nothing. Suspected of filming without a valid permit? The fucking SWAT team moves in on you.

I hear a tiny *plink* sound behind me, like a vial of glass being snapped in half.

I whirl around and find myself face-to-face with a figure that has a naked skull for a head. A skull with odd runes and drawings etched into the bone.

The figure is holding a huge gun.

I fire the revolver before I can even think about it. The bullet hits the figure in the chest.

Which is pretty unfortunate, because the figure yanks off the skull—which turns out to be a mask—to reveal the pain-filled features of Crew Cut, the dude from the crime scene this morning.

"You . . . dick," he snarls, blood spilling from his mouth.

Crew Cut drops to his knees. The massive gun falls from his grasp, hitting the ground.

"And that's . . . d-i-c-k," he says, painfully spelling it out. "In . . . case you were wondering."

Then he dies.

CHAPTER THREE

"**S**hit. Shit, shit, shit."

I drop to my knees and prod Crew Cut Dude. He doesn't move. I put my fingers to his throat. No pulse.

Definitely dead. I mean, the huge hole in his chest is a pretty good indicator, but still . . . you live in hope. Especially in a situation like this.

So . . . to recap. I, Harry Priest, am a murderer.

I'm going down. Life behind bars.

If I survive long enough, that is.

I get to my feet. The spider-wall is drawing closer. Actually, I can't even call it that anymore. The creepy-crawly wall is more fitting. I'm pretty sure I can even see a couple of snails trying to catch up in the background.

It's only about ten feet away now.

Plink.

That sound again. Like a tiny vial of glass breaking open.

I whirl around and instantly stagger back, tripping over Crew Cut Dude and falling on my ass.

Standing before me is a fifteen-foot-high . . . monster. It's black and shiny, its body covered in some type of armor so that it looks like a beetle. A white, putty-like head has been shoved down into a hole on the top of its body, protected on the sides and back by a collar of glistening cartilage. Its eyes are black and empty, and its arms . . . its arms are long, tipped with lethal-looking talons.

"Give me the coordinates," the creature whispers.

"The . . . ?"

"Coordinates."

"Sorry. Don't have a clue what you're talking about." I peer quickly over my shoulder, but the creepy-crawly wall is hanging back, content to let this creature do the talking.

I fire the last few bullets in the revolver, but they do absolutely nothing to slow the creature down. I look frantically for another weapon and spot the gun that Crew Cut dropped lying about five feet away. It doesn't look like any gun I've ever seen before—bone white, covered in bumps and knots—but at least it's something.

The creature steps forward.

"Give me the—"

"Yeah, the coordinates. Heard you the first time, pal. You know what—fuck this."

I throw the revolver away, then roll to the side and grab the gun.

But as soon as I touch it I almost drop it again. It feels warm to the touch. Clammy. And now that I see it up close, it looks like it's made from bone and sinew. It shifts unpleasantly in my hand. Almost as if it's alive.

No time to be squeamish. I roll onto my back and fire.

The gun makes a grunting, satisfied noise that instantly makes me think of someone orgasming. Nothing solid comes out the gun, but the air convulses, as if a sound wave has hit. Black veins crawl up the creature, and then it explodes wetly, turning into a puddle of black and crimson.

The section of creepy-crawly wall behind the monster also falls apart, the beetles and spiders turning to dust that floats up into the air.

I stare at the gun in amazement. Nice. I climb to my feet and fire again, holding the quivering trigger down. I turn in a slow circle, aiming the muzzle at the insect wall until there is nothing left.

I take my finger off the trigger. The gun shudders once. Twice. Three times. Then gives a satisfied sigh. I toss it away in disgust and wipe my hands on my shirt.

Silence.

I hold my breath, waiting for another attack.

It doesn't come.

My gaze falls on Crew Cut Dude and the mask he'd been wearing.

Why was he wearing it? I mean, the guy is ugly, but not hide-your-face-from-the-world ugly.

I pick it up. It looks like it's carved from real bone, the eye holes filled with dark green glass. I try to follow the spirals and runes etched across the yellowing surface, but they shift and squirm as I look, dancing away from my gaze.

I frown, slowly lifting the mask. As I bring it closer for a better look, I feel it pull inward. I freak out and try to tug it away, but it jerks in my hands, throwing itself against my face.

I cry out, try to yank the mask away. It doesn't budge. Feels like it's glued there. I spin in a circle, struggling to get my fingertips beneath the bone. But I can't. No gap. It's as if the mask has joined seamlessly to my face.

It's at about this moment that the new noises I'm hearing manage to penetrate the bubble of panic and fear. The noises that started up when I put the mask on.

I stop whirling around. Bend over. Stare at the ground. Listening.

Screams. Shouting. Gunfire.

I unlatch my fingers from the mask. Straighten up.

And my entire world changes. (Not that it hadn't changed before. You know, with the freaky monkey and the wall of insects. But . . . all that other stuff, maybe I could have put it down to food poisoning. Or a psychotic break. But this . . .)

I'm looking through the glass eyes of the mask, and they reveal to me a world that wasn't there a moment ago.

The first thing that catches my attention is the massive rip hanging in the air before me, like someone has peeled the wallpaper of reality away to reveal the wood and mortar behind. Except in this case the wood and mortar is a huge area where a pitched battle is currently being fought.

The rip is about twenty feet wide and thirty feet high. I walk slowly forward, my mouth hanging open in amazement.

I see the guy from the crime scene earlier today. Havelock Graves, I think he said his name was. He's whirling and ducking with surprising agility, firing what appears to be a double-barrel shotgun into . . .

. . . well, into creatures straight from the stuff of nightmares. A giant black scorpion, ridden by what looks like an orc from the Lord of the Rings movies, lunges at him. Graves doesn't even flinch. He shoots the scorpion's tail, and it explodes into steaming ichor, the black fluid landing on the orc and instantly burning through its skin. The orc screams and leaps from the back of the scorpion. Graves shoots the orc before it hits the ground, its ugly head exploding in a fine red mist.

There are other creatures—things that look like werewolves leaping through the air and savaging anything in their path. Others, covered in tentacles that writhe in the air. Still others that look like blobs of shapeless slime and even some kind of monstrous birds—crosses between beetles and pterodactyls.

Graves is accompanied by three others. A tall girl wearing eighties clothing, the woman with auburn hair, and what looks very much like a sullen goth chick. The sullen goth chick has two swords in her hands, and she's whirling through the air, the blades invisible as they cut through the creatures trying to break the line the four of them are attempting to hold.

The army of attacking creatures is led by a woman with long gray hair. She stands toward the back of the battle, watching it all unfold with glittering eyes and calling out orders to her troops.

I hesitate; then I scoop up Crew Cut's gun and step into the rip. (In case you haven't noticed, I'm not really one for thinking things through.) It feels like my skin is being sucked off the back of my body, like I'm leaving it behind me as I walk. Or like I'm stepping through an invisible spiderweb. There's heavy resistance as I enter, but I push against it, forcing myself through the opening.

But it's not an instant transition. Not like it looks from outside. I'm in a sort of no-man's-land of psychedelic trippiness. A long tunnel with violet-and-blue lights warping around me. Black shadows tinged with red reach out as I take step after step. I hear distant chittering, and I feel impossibly tiny, a speck of nothingness in a cosmic play. The violet light glints on primeval skin half-glimpsed from the corner of my eye. The skin is dark gray, almost black, and it looks like a shark's. Ancient stars glitter around me, constellations I've never seen before.

I quicken my pace, feeling a primitive panic rising up in me, a desire to run from the night, from the unfathomable depths of the icy ocean. I break into a jog, and the pulling sensation increases slightly before suddenly snapping away.

And I'm through the other end of the tunnel.

The chaos of battle surrounds me. Gunfire, screams, shouts, and commands.

Graves and the others are being pushed back, struggling to hold the line. I can see they're not going to last. And there are too many weird-ass creatures between them and the gray-haired woman calling the shots. They'll never get to her. Not before they're overrun.

I suddenly realize that nobody's even noticed me. The battle is taking place in some massive warehouse, and I've arrived against the rear wall.

Behind enemy lines, so to speak.

Like, all the way behind enemy lines.

Look, I'll be the first to admit I'm not the most intelligent person out there. And I might not always be aware of the nuances of life in all its many guises. But the ugly, creepy monsters here *kinda* look to me like they're the bad guys. And yeah, I know I shouldn't judge by appearances and all that, but come on. Creepy thin woman with gray hair? Orc-looking army riding scorpion creatures? Werewolves? Tentacled beasties? And again, sure, Graves and his crew are human, so I might be a bit biased toward them, but I'm going to make a leap of logic and assume they're the good guys in this scenario. Hey, I might be wrong, and if I am I'll hold my hands up before I die and say, "My bad." But you have to make a snap judgment in a situation like this, you know?

I raise the gun to shoulder level, aiming it at the woman. I have a clear line of sight. The gun shudders, leans in toward me so that it's actually sticking to my skin. It's warm and moist.

I try to ignore it as I recall my firearms training. Deep breath. Squeeze the trigger, don't pull it—

The gun licks me.

I cry out in horror, and my finger convulses on the trigger. The woman whirls around and spots me. The bullet—or whatever it is that the gun fires—misses her entirely.

She shouts a warning.

Instantly, the battle stops.

Silence falls. I take a nervous breath and turn slowly.

Every creature and person in the warehouse is staring at me.

Graves and the three women are exchanging confused glances, but everyone else just looks like they want to kill me.

I raise my hand in the air and give a small wave, trying not to gaze into the yellow, red, and demonic eyes glaring into my very soul.

Then I turn and run.

Back through the massive rip in the air. Along the weird tunnel. I look over my shoulder, see Graves and the other three coming after me, now wearing those weird skull masks. And behind them, the first of the weird creatures, one that looks like it's made from oil that shifts and reforms into different figures.

I put everything I have into running. I can see LA up ahead, as if through an irregularly shaped window. The fading light as night draws in (God, but this has been a long day), the concrete overpass. Safety. Normalcy.

I leap through, land heavily on the asphalt, and roll over, coming to my feet as Graves and the others burst through with me. They all whip off their masks, turn expectantly to me.

I stare behind them, at the oil-thing coming through the tunnel. "Close that!" I shout.

Graves sighs with exasperation, steps forward, and touches something on my chin. I feel the sucking of released pressure, and the mask falls away from my face.

The rip in the air instantly winks out of existence.

I sag with relief. Then everything that's happened to me tonight catches up in one huge tidal wave of adrenaline. I run to the side of the street and throw up in the scrub.

Twice in one day. Nice.

Once I'm done I turn back to see them all staring at the body of Crew Cut Dude. I hesitate, wondering if I should just make a run for it.

Graves looks at me. "What happened?"

Should I lie? Say the beetle-armor monster took him out? But shit, why should I? It wasn't my fault. The guy appeared from nowhere. With a gun. How was I supposed to know?

"I . . . kinda shot him. A bit."

Graves raises an eyebrow. "You shot him?"

"Yes."

"A bit?"

"Well . . . a lot. He . . . materialized in thin air. Right in front of me. The goddamn spider wall was closing in. I'd just shot a talking monkey with an old man's face. I was on edge."

"You were on edge?" repeats Graves. "That's the excuse you give for murdering one of my top operatives? You were *on edge*?"

"Come on, man. I've had a rough day. Look, I'm sure I'll feel terrible about it tomorrow. I'll probably have to go for counseling. I'll drink myself to sleep every night to try and forget the look on his face when he died. And you know what? That's something I have to deal with. That's my burden for what I've done. For the life I've taken. So I don't need you on my back as well."

Graves studies me curiously. "You really mean all that?"

"No," I say. "The guy was an asshole. I'm sorry I killed him, but he shoulda known goddamn better than to sneak up on someone with a gun. Especially wearing that creepy-ass mask."

Graves sighs. He looks around at the deserted road, squints at the puddle on the ground. "And that?"

"Some kind of monster. Black armor. Like a beetle."

Graves looks at the woman with auburn hair. "What do you think?"

She turns to me. "White head? Like a tick?"

I nod.

"A Dimensional Shambler."

"A what?"

"A Dimensional Shambler," says Graves. "One of Lovecraft's, I think."

I think about this. "Lovecraft? As in, H. P. Lovecraft?"

"The very same."

"The novelist? The guy who made things up for a living?"

"No. The guy who subconsciously tapped into an entire multiverse and channeled that into his writing. Now," says Graves, glancing briefly up at the evening sky. "What did you take?"

"Huh?"

"From the crime scene. This morning. These creatures wouldn't have been after you unless you took something. What was it?"

"I didn't take a thing," I protest. "I'm not a thief."

"No. Just a murderer," says the goth girl.

"Look, you must have taken something," presses Graves. "You might not even know it was important. I'd be very surprised if you did, actually."

"Why? Because I'm just a stupid crime scene cleaner?"

"Pretty much."

"Bite me, you piece of—" I freeze. Back at the apartment. When Jorge hugged me. What was it he said? That he'd taken something? Then I'd felt his hand brush my side when he hugged me, but the whole spider-on-the-back thing had distracted me.

Jorge had put something in my pocket.

"The bastard!"

I feel through my jeans pockets until I find an unfamiliar object, small and round. Hard. Like a marble.

I fish it out. "The bastard was trying to get them to come after me! I can't believe him! What a shit. What a . . ."

I'm aware that the other four are staring at me with wide eyes and very serious looks on their faces.

"What?"

"That," says Graves, pointing. "That is what they were after."

"Why?" I study the little ball. I can see colors swirling around inside. Purples and greens. And . . . are those numbers? I squint at them, but the numbers fade away, replaced by the swirling gases, like a nebula. "Just looks like a marble."

"Yes, well, I seriously doubt that's what it is. Please. Hand it over."

I shrug. "Take it," I say, and toss the marble to Graves.

Even as I do so I realize it's a bad move. I see Graves's eyes widen as he lunges forward to catch the tiny glass ball. I watch him trip over the gun I'd dropped. Watch him fall flat on his face.

Watch the ball hit the ground and shatter into dust.

We all stare at the ground. I swallow nervously.

"Uh . . . you got a spare?"

They all shift their gazes to me.

"No? Well . . . at least the bad guys won't get their hands on it now?"

Graves pushes himself to his feet. I get the feeling he's trying very hard to calm himself down. Very hard indeed.

He smiles. That's even worse, to be honest. It's like when I was a kid and my old man would speak in a really soft voice. That's when you knew you were in deep shit.

"You have just done something potentially very, very stupid. Lots of people were willing to break a lot of very important laws to get the item you just destroyed."

"Hey, it's not my fault. You should have caught it!"

"Of course. You're right. Not your fault. I mean, how were you to know?"

"Well . . . yeah. How *was* I to know?"

"Exactly. So no matter what happens next, if you wake up one morning in your sweat-stained bedsheets, surrounded by empty beer bottles, and see reality unraveling around you . . . If you step out of your tiny, disgusting apartment and witness an invasion of gods know what rising up from the depth of the oceans . . . If some kind of tentacled monsters arrive here from the many-angled worlds and start plucking you stupid people up into the sky and sucking your insides out, just know, in those split seconds before you are turned inside out and devoured, that you *weren't to know*. Okay then? Good."

Graves stares at me a moment longer, then leans over Crew Cut and places the mask on his face. He nods at the others, and they reattach their own masks, all subtly different from one another, and they wink out of existence.

CHAPTER FOUR

It's kind of hard to just go back to your normal life after you've seen what I've seen.

Everything—the slightest echo at night, the glimpse of a spider in the bathroom, a weird sound when I'm out driving—reminds me that there's a hidden world out there I know nothing about. A dangerous world out to hurt me. Out to hurt those I love.

Basically, in the weeks since that . . . *eventful* day, I've become a bit of a mess. Looking over my shoulder all the time. Staring at people, wondering if they're really human or puppets controlled by arachnids hidden beneath their clothes. Peering out behind the curtains at my apartment, wondering where all the monsters are hiding. And I'm telling you now, I'm not just being paranoid. I'm *sure* someone's following me. There's an old Cadillac driven by a young woman with purple hair, and I'm *convinced* I've seen her a few times over the past couple of weeks. So far, she hasn't transformed into a wall of beetles or anything like that, but I'm sure it's only a matter of time.

I lost my job. Not just me. The whole business closed down. Jorge's old man went to pieces when he found out his son had died. I was cleared of any wrongdoing, which was something at least. I was at Jorge's apartment. No arguing with that. Too many people saw me. But I came up with a story about Jorge calling me in a panic, saying someone was trying to kill him. I'd shot over to my buddy's house to help out, found him lying there cut in half, saw someone run, and gave chase.

It got pretty unpleasant in the interview room, but call records to my phone and the timing of my arrival all bore the story out, so the cops had to let me go. Much to their collective disgust.

So that was that. I'd caught a glimpse behind the curtain of life, was held in custody for three days, lost my job, and developed some kind of low-level PTSD thing where I'm paranoid and terrified and angry and depressed all at once.

"So yeah," I say, waving my beer at the drunk guy sitting next to me. "That's been my life the last few weeks. How about you?"

A cockroach scuttles across the bar top. I squeal in fright, then slam my hand down so hard the bug's guts squirt out the sides.

"Can't be too careful," I say to my new best friend as I wipe my hand on a napkin. "Could be part of the creepy-crawly wall. You know, the one I told you about?"

The drunk carefully takes his beer and slides off the stool, moving along the bar to sit with a sixty-year-old hooker wearing fishnets and a push-up bra.

"Suit yourself," I mutter.

Because that's the thing. I can't talk to a shrink about this, can I? Who would believe me? *I* sometimes don't believe me, and I was there.

I mean, what if it *didn't* happen? What if it *was* some kind of psychotic break?

Nah. It happened. I don't have that kind of imagination. Not to make up stuff like that.

"Hey. How's it hanging?"

Ooh. A new friend. Someone else for me to bore with my stories of a reality gone bad.

I turn in my chair . . .

. . . and find myself face-to-face with Havelock Graves.

I stare at him. He's smiling smugly at me.

I punch him.

He falls back off the stool with a shout of surprise. Hits the floor hard. I leap onto him like a bad wrestler, pin him down, and roughly prod his face.

"You bastard! Do you have any idea what I've been through the past few weeks?"

I pull his hair a bit, then release it. I should be punching him or something; that's how pissed off I am. (I was never much of a fighter.) I bunch my fist, but before I can hit him he gets a shot in first, striking the side of my head.

We both cry out in pain. He shoves me off, and we roll over. I clamber to my feet, holding my skull. "What the hell? Why'd you punch me in the head?"

Graves is cradling his hand. "I miscalculated. I meant to break your nose."

"Oh, that's *very* nice, that is. First you mess with my whole perception of reality, then you want to break my nose? Your social skills leave a lot to be desired, asshole."

"You hit me first!"

I glare at him, then stagger over to a booth and slide in. The three other people present (my new best friend, the geriatric hooker, and the bartender, a young guy called Todd who's in a rock band or something) studiously ignore us. It's the kind of bar where this kind of thing happens many times before lunch.

Graves sits down opposite me. I stare at him, shake my head.

"You ruined my life, you know that?"

"That had nothing to do with me. You turned up at the wrong crime scene, and your partner stole something that didn't belong to him."

"Yeah, well he's dead, so I'm blaming you instead."

"Whatever makes you feel better."

I lean forward. "You don't understand." I glance surreptitiously around. "Everything's changed. I can't sleep. I'm convinced I'm going to turn around and see these . . . things coming after me. I sit outside my ex-wife's house all night."

"Hey, now. You can't pin your stalking on me."

"I'm not *stalking*. I'm *watching*. Protecting my kid. In case any of those . . . things turn up."

"It doesn't work like that."

"Then how does it work?" I shout. "Because I don't know!"

"Do you want to know?" he says softly.

I blink.

"I mean, *really* want to know? Because . . . that's actually why I'm here. To offer you a job."

"A . . . job?"

"At the Company. Well, the ICD."

"Which is?"

"The Interstitial Crime Department."

"You're speaking words, but I have no idea what you're saying."

"It's very hard to explain. It's like . . . explaining the concept of time travel to an ant."

"You can time travel?"

"What? No. I . . ." Graves sighs. "The ICD is like your FBI, right? We look into crimes, but on a cosmic scale."

I shake my head. "Not following."

Graves sighs in frustration. "Are you familiar with the multiverse theory? That there are an infinite number of universes out there, some with only minor differences. Some with major differences. Like, there could be a dimension identical to this one, except all humans have nine fingers and toes. Or . . . or where dogs can speak. Or where the Nazis won the war. Or where humankind all has telepathy. Or a world *totally* different, where magic works and orcs and ogres exist. Where you can live out your Lord of the Rings fantasy. Or another universe where you can travel the stars in solar-powered sail barges, coasting solar gases through the infinite voids of space."

"Poetic. Still don't know what you're talking about."

"I think you're being willfully stupid."

"Nothing willful about it."

"You said it, moron. But you get the idea. An infinite number of worlds means someone has to watch over them. Hence, the Company.

And an infinite number of worlds means an infinite number of crimes. Which is where the Interstitial Crime Department comes in. See . . . a lot of people know about these shifting realities, and you know what people do when they see an opportunity like this?"

"Somehow use it for sex?"

"That's another department," says Graves crisply. "No, they use it for crime. Say . . . a crime lord somehow gains access to multiverse-jumping technology—which is pretty hard, I'll tell you—there are only a finite amount of masks, and we're always trying to track them down."

"Masks?"

"The masks we wear? They're actually parts of skulls. Of the Elder Gods. Long dead now, but they were able to step between realities." Graves sighs and rubs his face. "There's too much to explain. You know Cthulhu? The Old Ones? The tentacled beasties? The Shadow over Innsmouth? H. P. Lovecraft? All that?"

"I'm familiar with them."

"They're all real. The Old Ones, Cthulhu and his brothers and sisters. They were put in a prison a few million years ago by the Elder Gods. A place called the Dreamlands. And in every single multiverse the Cthulhu mythos exists. The Old Ones and their stories are the one thing that is consistent between all the alternate realities we've visited."

"Why's that?"

"No idea. But the Elder Gods, they were here first, right? They created the Old Ones. They could travel between these realities. And their skulls retain this power. You following?"

"Barely."

"The ICD has most of the masks, but there are more out there, scattered across the multiverse. Hell, some say there are still Elder Gods out there, hibernating. Waiting for the time they're most needed."

"Like King Arthur?"

"No. Nothing like King Arthur. Wherever the Elder Gods died on their travels, that's where their bodies stayed. We try to track them all down, but it's difficult. Lots of people would love to get their hands on them. Think about it. A reality where Leonardo da Vinci isn't famous. So someone could get their hands on his paintings and sketches for next to nothing, step between realities, and sell them for millions. Or . . . a mob boss loses his wife. So he searches through realities until he finds one where he exists and so does his wife. But she's still alive. So he knocks her out. Kidnaps her, brings her to his reality, and boom, problem solved."

"Does she know?"

"Know what?"

"That she's been taken to another . . . reality?"

"Doesn't matter. Not the point. The point is what he's done is illegal, so we have to track him down and arrest him."

"How do you know he's done something illegal?"

"The ICD headquarters. We call it Wonderland. Or the Maze. Or the Rabbit Hole. Or Hell. Depends on how bad a day you've had. We have people there who can sense intrusions into realities. If they're not officially sanctioned, we get sent in to sort it out."

Graves gets up and orders two beers. He brings them back and downs one of the beers in a long gulp, then takes a hefty gulp from the second.

I blink, decide to say nothing, and raise my hand at Todd the barkeep to bring me my own beer.

"So . . . you're a cop? A . . . cosmic agent?"

"Something like that."

"Interesting. And you really have no idea why these Cthulhu monsters are in every reality?"

"None. We have a specialized department for Cthulhu-based crime. The CBC. Pretty much the highest you can go in the ICD. They deal with the offspring of the Old Ones. Their minions, the secret societies that spring up, all that stuff."

I sense a bit of bitterness in his words there, but decide not to ask about it. My head is still reeling from what he's said.

"So," says Graves. "You up for it?"

I wait, expecting something more. But he just stares at me expectantly. I shake my head, confused. "Up for what?"

"Joining the team!"

"Wait—you're *really* offering me a *job*?"

"Yes, idiot. What do you say? The pay's shit, but it's never boring."

I stare at him in amazement. "*No!*"

"No?"

"No! Shit no! *Hell* no!"

"I don't understand. You're saying you don't want the job?"

"No! I want to forget! Can you do that? Can you make me forget everything I saw?"

"Why would you want to forget?"

"Because I can't sleep! I'm terrified that something is going to leap out of the shadows and steal my kid! I spent six years telling her there aren't any monsters under the bed—"

"Why would you do that?" Graves asks. "That's incredibly irresponsible parenting. In fact, there's a reality where the monsters under the bed have eaten all of humankind—"

"I don't want to know! I treasured my ignorance, thank you very much! You took it from me, and I want it back."

Graves stares at me for a while. "You really want to forget?"

"Yes!"

"Because I can do that. I have this magical device thing. Blanks peoples' memories. For when they see things they shouldn't. But . . . I just don't get it. You've seen behind the curtain! You should want to come with me. Adventure! Dead bodies. Travel. More dead bodies."

"Sounds charming. But I just want to go back to my normal life."

"You think that's the best thing for your daughter?"

I frown at him. "What do you mean?"

"You say you're terrified of these things hurting her. Yet you want to wipe your memory clean? Wouldn't it be better to learn everything you can instead? Gain as much knowledge as you can and use *that* to protect her? You honestly think hiding your head in the sand is a feasible survival strategy?"

I look away. He has a point. How can I protect her if I don't know what I'm protecting her from?

"And it's not as if we're helpless. We do make a difference. Join up and you'll have access to whatever you want. Grimoires, reality coordinates, maps, the differences between your earth and the others. The truth behind the conspiracies, the secret government cabals, the cover-ups, everything."

"You really have access to all that information?" I have to admit, my curiosity is piqued. I've always been interested in that kind of stuff.

"Plus," says Graves, speaking slowly. Laying his winning hand on the table. "Family of ICD employees are entitled to intra-dimensional protection."

"What does that mean?"

"It means we know that ICD employees are vulnerable to . . . coercion, so we ensure their families are looked after."

"How do you do that?"

"Surveillance. Hexes."

"Hexes? Like . . . magic and stuff?"

"Yes. Magic and stuff. It works. Any of our hexes get broken and that triggers an alarm at the ICD head office. A rapid response team would be dispatched to nullify the threat."

I sit back in the booth, staring at Graves. Twenty-four seven protection from the monsters under the bed, or wipe my memory and go back to my boring life? Unemployed. Depressed. Lonely. . . .

"Plus, there's no commute," says Graves.

I look at him sharply. "I don't believe you."

"It's true. You own your own mask. We set up a Slip—that's what we call the doors between realities—direct to your home. You wake up, put on the mask, step into the Slip, and you're at work."

That really clinches it. I reach across the table, holding out my hand. "You got a deal."

CHAPTER FIVE

I wake up the next morning wondering if it was all a dream.

I roll over and see the mask lying on my bedside table, green glass eyes glinting in the dim light.

Not a dream, then.

I check the time. Seven thirty. Graves told me to get ready for an eight a.m. start. Plenty of time to get ready.

I jump out of bed, light on my feet for the first time in months. Actually excited to face the day. It's an odd feeling, and I pause halfway across my room to properly experience it. No worry. No fear. No regret. Just . . . anticipation. Nice.

I shower then stand in the middle of my room, deciding what to wear. Graves didn't say anything about a dress code, so I just pull on jeans and a T-shirt. If anyone complains I'll dress up a bit tomorrow, but best to begin as I hope to carry on.

I finish my second cup of coffee and check the time. Seven fifty-five. I return to my room and pick up the mask.

I take a deep breath and start to lift it slowly to my face, remembering the way the mask attached itself to my skin last time. It wasn't a pleasant feeling.

Still, I don't have much of a choice. Not if I want to keep my kid safe. Not if I want this job.

I close my eyes and raise the mask the rest of the way. It sucks gently against my skin. It feels cool and comfortable. Not like I remember it. But last time I *was* whirling around in a panic, trying to rip the thing off.

I open my eyes. Everything looks the same. The green glass in the eye sockets doesn't even tint my view. It's as if there's nothing over my eyes at all.

Just to check, I probe around under my chin until I find the catch that releases the mask. It comes away smoothly and painlessly.

I put the mask back on and check the time. Seven fifty-nine. Wonder if Graves is the type to be punctual or—

A bright, blue-white light suddenly flares to life in my bedroom. I stagger back as a rectangle of light unfurls in the air before me, the size and shape of a door.

A silhouette appears, a dark shadow moving against the glare. A hand extends out through the door.

"Come with me if you want to live."

I frown.

"Sorry," says Graves, stepping into my bedroom. He's wearing his mask, but I can hear the grin behind his words. "Always wanted to say that."

I point at the door. "How come that . . . Slip looks different? To the one in the street that time?"

"Because that Slip wasn't a Slip. It was more of a tear, what we call a Rip. Unsanctioned. Shoddy workmanship. This," he says, stepping to the side and gesturing to the door like a magician's assistant, "is an officially sanctioned intra-reality dimension Slip. And if you'd care to follow me through, we can get started with the workday."

He steps back through the door and disappears. I approach it slowly, my stomach fluttering with fear and excitement. This is it. This is really it. I'm going behind the curtain, and there's no turning back once I've done it. Well, there *is*. Technically. I could just ask Graves to mind-wipe me. But I won't. Not now. This is the beginning of a new life. One where Susan can be proud of me. One where I can protect her from the things that go bump in the night.

I step through the door, and suddenly remember all those movies I've seen, where someone is dying and their loved ones shout at them to stay away from the light.

Oh, shit. Maybe this is a huge mista—

Too late.

The door winks out behind me, and I'm plunged into a terrifying darkness. Not just darkness, but the complete absence of light. What I imagine the universe was like before the big bang.

A blinking green cursor appears in my lower vision. I squint and try to focus on it.

Two words appear. *Please wait . . .*

Then, *Syncing device with new bio-print.*

Analyzing . . .

Analysis complete.

Body in advanced state of tissue degradation. Cholesterol . . . through the roof. Blood pressure . . . dangerously high. Estimated age of subject based on analysis . . . sixty-four.

"Fuck off!" I exclaim.

Please proceed through the tunnel. If you can make it without dropping dead.

What the hell? Is this thing modeled on Graves's personality or something? I start walking. The darkness lightens after a few steps, and I see I am indeed in a tunnel. Similar to the one I'd passed through three weeks ago. I don't hesitate this time, but walk quickly through the darkness, not looking left or right.

After a few moments a rectangle of light appears up ahead: another door. I hurry toward it and step through, stumbling down three steps onto a tiled floor.

I straighten up and look around.

I'm in a massive room. Like, football field massive. Behind me is the blue-white door, but it's not the only one. Receding away to either side are hundreds more, some of them flaring to life, others winking out of existence. People come and go through the openings, chatting to each other as they go about their business.

"This going to take long?"

I turn and find Graves seated on the edge of a cluttered desk, one of many that take up the far side of the huge room. Behind the desks are computers and employees, typing away and talking into headsets. In charge of the Slips?

Graves isn't wearing his mask anymore, so I reach up and thumb the catch beneath my chin. The mask falls away into my hands. I hold it up accusingly. "This . . . thing has an attitude problem."

"Ah. That's the operating system. It runs our internal systems, ferries comms to agents in the field, that kind of thing. It's a database of all the realities. When you go to a new alternate, the mask should have the background info ready for the operative. That way you don't go making a fool of yourself by doing something stupid." He hops off the desk. "Come on, we're already late."

He turns and walks away. I start to follow, but then stumble to a stop, distracted by the view out the floor-to-ceiling windows.

I walk forward, my hand coming to rest against the glass. Outside . . . outside is the night sky, but like nothing I've ever seen. It's shown in such detail it's like seeing something in super high definition after watching old, crappy Betamax tapes for your entire life. The stars and nebula are crystal clear, strewn across the night sky like bright fairy lights hanging above the table at a hipster dinner party.

Then my attention is drawn downward. The building I'm standing in is obviously huge. Like, bigger than the Empire State Building huge. And it . . . I peer down through the glass—yup, the building has been placed smack dab in the middle of a maze. An honest to God labyrinth.

If my perspective is right, the maze is easily the size of a city, receding into the distance on all sides of the building. There are lights in the maze, enabling me to see the twists and turns. Some of the lights are moving. People are walking through the maze. Every once in a while I see a flare of blue-white light, like the one I experienced when the door appeared in my room.

"Welcome to Wonderland," says Graves, appearing at my shoulder.

"What is this place?"

"A pocket dimension. Owned by the ICD."

"You can own a dimension?"

"*We* can."

I gesture at the maze. "And that?"

"The Elder Gods built it." He nods at the flashing lights. "Those are the doorways we use to get to various realities. The ones the Elder Gods used before they died out. All programmable from the ICD offices."

"So . . . you're saying you guys have to find your way through a maze to actually respond to an emergency call? Not very efficient."

"It's not like that. We're guided through the labyrinth by the masks."

"Still seems a very roundabout way to do your job."

"I'm not disagreeing. Like I said, not our idea. The system was in place when we got here. Come on, sport. You need to clock in."

I drag my eyes away from the view below and follow Graves as he heads directly for a bank of elevators. We move around the ranks of desks, most of them occupied by men and women looking as bored as any other office worker on the planet.

There's another bright flash behind me, and I glance over my shoulder to see a woman step through one of the doorways. She's dressed in a pants suit and sipping from a coffee cup, ready for a day's work.

"Top floor is where all the employees arrive and depart from," says Graves as he hits the call button. A door slides open three elevators over, and we step inside. Graves punches a number, and we start to descend. The elevators are attached to the outside of the building, soaring down the glass exterior.

"What floor is the ICD on?"

Graves winces, turns, and leans up against the side of the elevator. "Yeah. About that."

"What?" I say, with a sinking feeling in my stomach.

"You know how I said I wanted to recruit you into the ICD?"

"Yeah," I say.

"I may have bent the truth there. A little bit."

"How little?"

"Actually, a lot. A whole lot. You know that whole thing with that globe you broke?"

"You mean the one you dropped?"

"The one you broke, yes," says Graves. "Well, the thing is, turns out that was kind of an important case. And when the globe was shattered, some people who had it in for me used it as an opportunity to . . . put me out of the picture."

"Wait—you're saying there are people here who don't like you? I'm shocked."

"Funny guy. But the thing is, I . . . we . . . the team got demoted."

"To where? Desk job?"

"Even worse. Department Zero."

"What's that?"

"DDICS."

I try to remember what that stands for. He'd told me. Back at the crime scene. "Disposal . . . Department for . . ."

"Interstitial Crime Scenes."

"Which is?"

"Basically? We clean up intra-dimensional and supernatural crime scenes."

I stare at him for a moment then burst out laughing. "Seriously?"

"I'm glad you think it's funny."

"You've been demoted to crime scene cleanup?"

"Pretty much."

"Wait, you said *supernatural* crime scenes?"

Graves shrugs. "An infinite number of universes, remember? There are worlds out there, just like yours, but where vampires are real. Or wizards roam the streets of New York. Where witches rule England

and the Nazis mastered black magic to win the war. If there's crime, we put in the time."

"Nice tagline."

"I like it."

"So . . ." I say, trying to decide how pissed off I'm about to get. "All that stuff about learning about the monsters under the bed?"

"Still applies. We have access to the ICD files down in the Dee-Zee."

"The . . . ?"

"Dee-Zee. Department Zero."

"Oh. Right. But . . . no investigating? No actual police work?"

"Not . . . as such."

I should have known it was too good to be true. I'd screwed my chance to be a cop once before. No one ever gets second chances in this life. Just the way it is.

"But we'll get back into the investigative branch. One day. You think I'm going to live out my life in a bunker surrounded by weirdoes and losers?"

"Nice way to talk about your coworkers."

"You haven't seen them yet. Department Zero is where all the . . . undesirables get sent. You know the ones. They piss off the wrong people. Don't know when to shut up."

"Kinda like yourself, then."

"No, idiot. I'm nothing like them. Thirty years I've been an ICD investigator. I don't deserve this shit. Because of one screwup? I don't even know why the higher-ups took it so badly in the first place. It was just a standard intra-dimensional art theft. I've covered a thousand of them in my time."

"So . . . I don't get it. Why do you want me, then? You must have enough freaks and geeks on your team already."

Graves looks away, stares at the rapidly descending numbers on the digital readout. "I . . . liked what I saw. You handled yourself well. Jumped into the fight." He glances over his shoulder at me. "I want people on my team who won't cut and run. Loyalty is very important to me."

"How noble of you."

"Which isn't to say you have any of these characteristics. You're on probation. We'll see how you do."

"I'm on probation? To clean up body parts?"

Graves smiles at me, and I really don't like that smile. Not at all. "Oh it's a lot more than that, my friend. A lot more."

Then we're plunged into darkness as the elevator drops below ground level, soaring down into a metal shaft that cuts into the earth.

A couple of minutes later and we're still dropping.

"Um . . . how far down is Department Zero?"

"Picture the deepest hole you can dig. Then when you hit the bottom dig a second hole next to it. Just as deep. Then dig down some more. That will get you about halfway to us."

"Shit, man. They really don't like you, do they?"

"That is an understatement. Department Zero is an embarrassment to the ICD. We put up with them because we must, because no one else will do the job they do."

"You're talking like you're on the outside looking in. But from where I'm standing you're one of them."

"How dare you! Take that back!"

"Um . . . no. I don't think so."

"I'm going to get out of the Dee-Zee. Believe me. I don't belong there. None of my people do."

He folds his arms and turns his back on me. He doesn't say another thing until the elevator eventually bumps to a stop and the door slides open into a chaotic, open-plan office. Desks laid out in uneven grids, covered with files and ancient computers. Workers drinking coffee, smoking cigarettes, chatting about last night's television shows. And . . . yes, a few people swigging whisky. It looks like an office from the eighties. Before health and safety was actually a priority.

"I hope you have a fetish for paperwork," says Graves. "Like, a deep, ongoing love affair for it. If you don't, my advice is to pretend you do."

He steps out of the elevator and makes his way through the alleys between the desks. No one greets him. People look up at him, but they quickly turn away as soon as they see who it is.

Havelock Graves is not well liked.

I follow Graves to the farthest corner of the room, where four desks have been pushed into a square to make a private office, with the desks forming the walls and a small, empty space in the center.

The desks are occupied by two of the people I saw fighting in the Rip three weeks ago.

"This is Ash," says Graves, waving at the woman with the auburn hair. He turns to the young woman. "And this is . . . What name are you going by this week?"

"Asmothep, destroyer of worlds," she says. She's wearing a *Knight Rider* T-shirt, lace gloves that go up to her elbows, dark eye makeup, and a tutu.

"Right. And this is Harry Priest," says Graves. "I'm sure you'll all get along wonderfully."

He gestures at an empty desk. "That's yours."

Introduction done, Graves flops into a chair behind a desk covered with files and paperbacks and drops his head onto the desk with a loud *thunk*.

Ash nods at me in greeting. "You know those little desk signs people used to think were funny? 'You Don't Have to Be Mad to Work Here, But It Helps?'"

I nod.

"Those signs were invented here. *For* here. And they weren't a joke."

"Seriously?"

"Seriously. We have certified insane people working here. On the twentieth floor."

"Why? Do you go and stare at them? Does it help office morale?"

"What? No. That's sick. Why would anyone do that? Is that what you would do?"

"No! It was a— Forget it. Why do you have mad people working here?"

"Dangers of the job. Sometimes you step into a reality that's so different to the human mind that it—" she clicks her fingers, "—breaks you. Just like that."

"Just like that?"

"Just like that." She smiles. "Welcome to Department Zero."

Behind me, Graves groans loudly. "Don't say that! It sounds so final. We're not going to be here long. I told you that."

Ash raises her eyebrows at me and tosses a file onto Graves's desk. "Hope you've had your coffee, boss. First job of the day."

"Let me acclimatize, woman! I've only just got here!"

"It's half past eight. We should be in the field by now."

Graves sighs and sits up. "Fine! What is it?"

"Illegal alien. A retrophile."

"Perfect." He looks at me. "Your first job is the most boring type of crime we have to deal with. Lucky you."

He heaves himself out of the desk chair. "Come on then."

Ash and I follow after Graves as he trudges back to the elevator.

§

We take the elevator up to ground level and step out into an echoing foyer covered with glossy black tiles. We cross the floor space, passing other (I assume) ICD operatives. And they're not just human. I see giants trudging along, joking with small gnome-type creatures perched on their shoulders. Plus I see a group of what appears to be walking trees, chatting away as they move slowly across the tiles. Lots of humans, but lots of weird beings too.

Ash sees me staring. "An endless amount of realities, an endless amount of possibilities."

"Yeah, but . . . *literally*? Are you saying there are an infinite number of these realities?"

"We don't know. We've only catalogued the tiniest fraction. The Company has an explorer division for that."

"So you've got an explorer division, a Cthulhu crimes division, and the ICD. How many others?"

"Hundreds."

"And Department Zero is the afterbirth," says Graves without turning around. "The juice that collects at the bottom of the Company's garbage cans."

The front entrance to the building is a long line of revolving doors, at least fifty, and all of them in use. We pass through and head down a wide set of stairs. The light of the stars is bright enough to illuminate our surroundings. The maze towers above us, a dark line against the night sky.

"Suit up," says Graves, attaching his mask. His is slightly different to mine. Wider, broader around the cheeks. And his eyes are made from red glass. But it's still covered with etchings and runes.

Ash's mask is narrower, and has the look of a fox to it. Her eyes are golden. Ash and Graves are both staring. It's pretty unnerving having those blank-eyed skulls just standing there looking at me.

"What?"

"Your mask, idiot," says Graves.

"Oh. Yeah. Right." I'm still holding my mask. Haven't put it down since stepping out of the tunnel on the top floor. I lift it to my face and let it suck against my skin. Immediately, a heads-up display flashes into existence, floating in front of my eyes. The HUD displays a flashing orange arrow leading ahead.

Graves and Ash start walking. I follow, heading toward the maze. The walls rise high as we approach. This isn't some little hedge maze you get in eighteenth-century France. This maze is twenty feet high and made from stone.

The flashing arrow leads into the labyrinth. I hang back a few paces and let the other two get ahead. Just . . . taking a moment. Trying to take everything in. I look back and see the huge building silhouetted against the cosmic backdrop, employees coming and going as if it's the most normal thing in the world.

"Hustle up, idiot!" calls Graves.

I sigh and step into the maze. The path is about ten feet wide, easily enough space for large groups of people. We pass plenty of Company workers. Some nod at Graves; all of them nod at Ash. No one gives me a second look.

We make our way along the twists and turns, following the orange markers on our HUDs. We must pass at least a hundred Company operatives using the blue-white doors that appear and disappear in the maze walls.

"I still don't get why you do it this way," I say. "Doors in a maze? Seems a bit showy. Pointless."

"Every single Company operative will agree with you," says Ash. "We don't know why it was set up this way."

"And what do you do if you're called to emergencies? You never said."

"There are doors in the various departments," says Graves. "We used to have some. In the Penthouse."

I look inquiringly at Ash.

"The Penthouse. The ICD murder room. Where we used to work," she adds in a low voice.

"This is us," says Graves, stopping before a blank piece of wall.

I check the arrow in my HUD. It has turned blue and pulses gently right ahead of us.

Graves glances over his shoulder. "Ready?"

I shrug. "As I'll ever be."

The door flares to life and we step in.

CHAPTER SIX

We step out of the tunnel and onto a sand dune.

The skies are gray, heavy clouds scudding across the horizon. A cold wind buffets me, sand whipped into stinging whirlwinds.

I look around and shiver. The air feels different. Sharper. Colder. Well, it would, wouldn't it? I'm in a goddamn new reality. A new dimension.

I turn in a slow circle. Kind of a letdown, if I'm honest with you. I mean, it feels a bit different, sure, but not another *reality* different. More like I'm in England and not LA different.

"Hey, do we get to go to a Conan reality?"

"A what?" asks Graves.

"You know . . . magic, the mad cults, snake priests. Barbarians and long-lost civilizations. You ever been to a place like that?"

"No. We haven't. And thank the gods. Sounds horrendous."

"Bummer." I think about it. "But they exist, right? They must."

"I suppose," replies Graves.

"Can you seek them out? When I was a kid I used to love the books. I'd spend hours imagining I was in those worlds."

"How incredibly sad for you," says Graves. "Now shush, the grown-ups are working."

I follow his gaze and see there is a group of five people standing on the beach about fifty feet away. Graves frowns at them for a moment before striding off down the dunes, swearing and cursing as he goes.

"What's with him?" I ask as we follow behind.

Ash gestures at the group on the beach. One of them, a huge guy nearly seven feet tall, draws my attention. Bald, grizzled, a long trench coat hanging off his massive frame.

"That guy there. He's called the Inspectre."

"He's an inspector?"

"No. He's the Inspectre. It's a title. A rank in the ICD."

"Okay. And?"

"And Graves was up for the promotion same time as Jarvis over there. Then the . . . well . . . then *you* happened."

"His name's Jarvis? That's cute."

"Don't call him that. He'll hit you so hard you won't remember your mother's name."

"I'm adopted."

"Really?"

"Nah. But point taken. Thanks for the heads-up."

"Asshole. And no problem."

As we draw closer I see there's a body lying in the wet sand. He's wearing a neon T-shirt, Ray Bans, cargo pants, and Pumas. He also has a big hole in his chest.

"What did you say this case was? A retro what?"

"Retrophile," says Ash, nervously watching Graves as he stands behind the Inspectre, who seems to be enjoying ignoring Graves's presence. "It means he's a man out of time. You ever see those old photographs that do the rounds every once in a while? A guy in modern clothes standing in a black-and-white picture from the thirties? Or a street scene from the twenties that has a woman talking on a cell phone?"

"Sure. People post those on the Net all the time."

"They're fugitives. They've crossed through an illegal Slip into another reality to escape whatever it is they've done in their own."

I nod at the guy lying on the beach. "And that's what this guy is? How do you know?"

"Check your readout. Upper right-hand corner."

I unfocus my eyes from the scene before me and look at the writing scrolling past my vision. It's going too fast for me to read. "Slow down."

The text slows to a *Star Wars* crawl. *Apologies, sir. I wasn't aware you had difficulty reading.*

I check the readout. It's information on the reality we're currently standing in. The code of this alternate is 5583/Beta 584-H96. Catchy. The text scrolls up, telling me I'm in England on the southeast coast, it's autumn, and . . .

"Ah," I say. The text says the date here is 1911. I look at the guy on the beach in his DayGlo clothing. Now I see.

"Does this happen a lot?" I ask Ash.

"Yup. Criminals thinking it will be easier to hide in an alternate reality. People wishing for a simpler life. Sometimes they don't even know they're not in the same time period when they arrive. Black market Slips are unpredictable. They can't hold them open for long because as soon as they start searching for alternates, we pick them up at ICD and the chase is on." She nods at the body. "But this case is different. Retrophiles are trickier."

"Why's that?"

"Because they're actively seeking out different time zones between alternates. They try and introduce advanced technology a hundred years before its time. Or they use science to set themselves up as a powerful ruler. Or a god. We get a few of those. Big egos, retrophiles. Very annoying. Like to declaim their plan when they get caught. Love the sound of their own voices."

Graves has obviously had enough of standing around because he whips his mask off and strides forward, shoving his way between a couple of the ICD operatives standing around the body.

"You lot finished staring?"

"Hey, check it out," says the Inspectre. "It's the dicks."

Graves ignores him and squats down to inspect the body. He takes out a pencil and uses it to push the corpse's jacket open.

"What the hell do you think you're doing?" snaps the Inspectre. "You're tampering with evidence. You're not ICD anymore, remember?"

Graves frowns and straightens up again. "Then get your pet monkeys to finish up here so we can do our job. You think we have time to wait around for you?"

"You do if I say you do," says the Inspectre pleasantly.

Graves frowns, clenching and unclenching his jaw. "Fine," he suddenly says, and claps the surprised Inspectre on the shoulder. "We'll be over there, relaxing. Call us when you've finished processing your scene."

He strides away from the dead body, splashing along the shoreline. Then he stops, gets down to his knees, and starts scooping sand into big piles.

Ash and I approach him, both of us detaching our own masks. "What you doing, boss?" she asks cautiously.

He squints up at her. "My dear girl, I'd have thought that was abundantly clear. I'm making sand castles. Come. Join me."

I glance over my shoulder. The five ICD guys are watching Graves with their mouths hanging open in amazement. The Inspectre barks something, and they jump back to work, taking photographs of the body and the surroundings.

"So who killed the stiff?" I ask.

"Probably him," says Graves, scowling back at the Inspectre.

"Is that the punishment for sneaking between alternates? Death?"

"Depends what the perp has done. Or if he tries to attack the ICD operatives."

I nod. "And . . . what happens if one of these guys materializes in a crowded city? Or in someone's house? What do you do about the witnesses?"

"We have ways of making them forget," says Graves.

"Like what you were going to do to me? If I didn't agree to take the job?"

"No. If you didn't take the job I was going to shoot you. What?" he says in response to my astonished look. "You'd seen too much. I don't think a memory wipe would have held."

"So you were just going to kill me?" I shout, enraged. "Who the hell do you think you are? You can't just walk around killing people because they happen to witness—"

I stop when I see Ash's smirk. Oh. Nice.

"You're joking," I say.

"Of course I am, idiot."

"Graves!"

We turn and see that the Inspectre and his crew are walking away from the body, attaching their masks and heading to a rectangle of blue light that stands in the water a few feet from them.

"It's all yours," he shouts. "Have fun cleaning up!"

"Asshole," mutters Graves, pushing himself to his feet and heading back toward the body.

By the time we get there the Inspectre and his crew have gone, the blue door winking out of existence. We stare down at the corpse.

"So . . . what do we do with him?" I ask.

"What did you used to do?" says Graves.

"Body like this, it would have been taken away by the coroner." I look around. "Truth is, there wouldn't be much call for us here. Not much of a crime scene to clean up once he's gone. We'd move any sand that has his blood on it, but that's about it."

"We work a bit differently," says Graves. He takes out a small contraption that looks like it's made from bone and metal. It's covered in runes, similar in style to the masks. He squats down and attaches it to the corpse.

"What's that?"

"A DTD."

"Which is . . . ?"

"A Deviance Transference Device," says Ash. "Ships the corpse back to home base. We have a morgue and recycling plant there."

I frown. "Recycling plant? Recycle into what?"

"Got to make the office plants grow somehow," says Graves, straightening up again. "Stand back please."

I follow them out of range, and about twenty seconds later there's a bright flash of light and the corpse vanishes.

"Ash," says Graves. "Site recon."

Ash nods and gestures for me to follow her.

"What are we doing?"

"Making sure there's no evidence left behind. Nothing that some random kid is going to find and stash in a locked box only to be unearthed in twenty years' time and make everyone wonder how the hell such advanced tech ended up locked away for so long."

"Ah."

We scour the beach but find nothing. Twenty minutes later Graves calls us back and tells us to mask up. He triggers the Slip, and we venture back through the tunnel and reemerge into the starlit twilight world of Wonderland. Or the Maze. Or the Rabbit Hole, or whatever the hell they call it.

I check my watch. We've been away for two hours. I reach up to take off the mask, but Graves holds a hand up.

"Not so fast, flyboy. We're still on the clock."

As he finishes talking, an arrow flashes to life in the HUD.

"And off we go for round two."

We follow the arrows to a door closer to the entrance of the maze. We step through the Slip and emerge into a long, low warehouse. Electric lights illuminate row upon row of cages.

I step forward and peer inside the closest. Empty. I look to the next. Same.

"There's nothing here!" I call out to Graves. "What's the crime supposed to be?"

"Category A," says Ash. "The introduction of magic-based lifeforms into a science-based society with the aim of destabilization and illicit gains."

"Magic-based life-forms?"

Ash nods. "This alternate is a Class One space-faring society. Colonies on the moon and Mars. No mythological species allowed."

"That's what I'm not getting," I say. "What mythological species? All I'm seeing are empty cages."

"The criminals planned on starting a circus and freak show peopled with fairies and creatures of folklore," says Graves.

I blink. "Fairies and . . . ?"

"Folklore," says Graves. "Are you deaf?"

I peer into another cage. Empty—

No. I look closer. There's a tiny form lying at the back of the cage. I open the door and gently pull it toward me. It weighs nothing. Like a feather.

I take it out of the cage and move to stand beneath a light. It's a fairy. Like from the story books. Tiny, lying dead in the palm of my hand. The creature's thin, wood-colored face is gaunt and drawn. Black sightless eyes stare into nothing. The creature is wearing earthen colors, dull and muted. It has four wings attached to its back, wings that have been broken and crushed.

I feel a wave of anger surge through me. "So . . . what? They were just crammed in these cages? How many?"

An image flashes up in my HUD. Crime scene photographs from before the creatures were taken away. The fairies were crammed into the cages like battery hens.

"Those bastards!" I turn to Graves. "Have you caught them?"

"We have them in custody, yes."

"What will happen to them?" I hold up the tiny creature. "This is murder, yes?"

"Of course it's murder," says Graves. "Don't worry about the criminals. They'll be taken care of."

I take a deep breath, filled with fury and anger and . . . helplessness. Wanting to lash out at something. Anything. Another reason I'd probably have been a shitty cop—I can't stand injustice. It really gets to me. Who knows how long I'd have lasted in the force if I was confronted with a crime scene and had the criminals in hand?

"Check the cages for any bodies," says Graves. "We need to round them all up. No evidence left behind."

I lay the tiny fairy down on a piece of sacking in the center of the warehouse. Then Ash and I move slowly from cage to cage while Graves scours the perimeter for any other traces.

When Ash and I finish, we have a pile of thirty-four fairies of various types. Some no larger than my pinkie, some as long as my forearm. All of them crushed or suffocated.

"You know, back in my . . . world. Reality. Whatever. We only clear up what's left behind after the bodies are taken."

"Things are different here," says Graves. "Unless the body needs to be taken away for inspection as part of an ongoing investigation. Then Department Ten does that. That's the medical and morgue department, before you ask."

We gather around the pathetic line of bodies. "What will you do with them?" I ask.

"We know which alternate they're from," says Ash gently. "We'll try and track down their clans and families. That's Department Twenty's job. I worked there for a while. Before being promoted. And then demoted," she adds, with a thoughtful glance in my direction.

I open my mouth to protest, but what's the point? They think what they think. I can say none of it was my fault till I'm blue in the face, but they all lost their jobs regardless.

"How do we get them back?" I ask, deciding the better path is to just change the subject altogether.

Graves looks around. "Bring that crate over here."

I look around. There's a long crate stuck in the corner, filled with old sacking. Ash and I drag it across the floor, and we carefully lift the bodies and lay them gently on the bottom.

Graves activates a Slip. The door flares to life, and we pick up the crate and carry it through. We emerge into the Maze and track it back to the ICD building.

"I can't help but think this is a bit . . . low tech? Can't you just magic them into the building?"

"I left magic behind when I was recruited into this job."

"Okay," I say, filing that little nugget away for the future. "But what about some kind of portal or something? Like you did before with the retrophile."

"Too many of them," says Ash. "We don't have enough DTDs. I'm afraid it's low tech or nothing."

When we exit the maze, Graves hands the crate over to people he seems to know.

"Take them to Twenty. Have them processed and sent back to their home alternate." He turns back to us. "Ready?"

"For what?"

"Lunch. Then back to work."

§

The afternoon shift takes us through to a modern-looking boardroom. We arrive just as the Inspectre is making his arrest. He has a skinny guy bent over the mirrored boardroom table and is cuffing him while reading him his rights.

"You have the right to legal counsel, blah-blah-blah."

He hauls the guy up and shoves him at one of his colleagues.

"Nice to see you keeping the standards high," says Graves.

The Inspectre glares in our direction. "You guys aren't supposed to turn up till after we give the all clear. Do your job properly, Graves. Otherwise . . . no— Wait. I was going to say you'll get demoted, but there's nowhere to demote you to."

Graves doesn't react.

"Because you're already at the bottom," adds the Inspectre.

"Yeah, I got it, idiot. And we were told you'd have the arrest cleared after lunch. Not my fault if your lunches are taking a bit longer nowadays." Graves casts a pointed look at the Inspectre's waistcoat. The buttons are straining slightly around a protruding stomach.

The Inspectre flushes slightly and tries to suck his stomach in. "Asshole," he mutters, and activates a Slip for his men to take the perp through. He follows, and the Slip slowly sinks downward and vanishes into the floor.

"Right," says Graves, clapping his hands together. "Our first case this afternoon is an illegal profit-sharing coterie."

"A what?" I ask.

"The man who was just arrested is from another alternate. Or he's been contacted by someone from another alternate. But this other alternate is almost identical to this one in every way, except it runs three days in advance. So the perps in the other alternate are passing info to our criminal, getting him to play the markets, make bets for them, that kind of thing. Very stupid, because any odd payouts always triggers the alarms at ICD."

I look around the office. "So what are we supposed to clear? There's no body. No blood."

Graves pats me on the shoulder. "Poor guy. You're like an abused dog, aren't you? Not all our crime scene cleanups are like that. We're looking for any links to the alternate. Anything linking our perp to his coconspirators. I mean, we could just torch the place, but I find that kind of thing a bit extreme. Softly, softly, catchy monkey, I always say."

"Do you?" I say, nodding wisely. "Do you really?"

"Yes," says Graves, staring hard at me. "I do. Along with groovy. You got a problem with that?"

I raise my hands in the air. "No problems here, amigo. Whatever floats your boat."

I take a backseat on this job, watching more than I participate.

Ash goes through the computers and smartphones, checking the perp's accounts, e-mails, etc. She saves anything pertinent to a flash drive, then uses a local EMP device to fry the electronics.

Graves looks through the file cabinets and desk drawers, searching for any hard copies, instructions, or means of contacting the alternate reality.

He soon finds what he's searching for. A tiny, handheld radio made from the same kind of weird bone and gristle as the gun Crew Cut Dude had dropped.

"Got it," he says, standing up. "Ash? We good?"

"We good."

"Splendid. On to the next job then."

§

It's the end of the day, and I'm exhausted. Utterly empty. We're standing in the huge empty floor at the top of the building, Slips flashing and winking out of existence as the shifts change over.

"So. You survived your first day," says Graves.

I can't help noticing he sounds oddly disappointed.

"Still, there's always tomorrow," he says. "Off you go. Get a good night's sleep."

I hesitate. I wanted to talk to Ash about everything that happened today. I have questions, so many questions. But Graves doesn't look as if he's going anywhere, so I shove my hands in my pockets and nod. "'Night then."

"'Night," says Ash.

I approach one of the workers sitting behind a desk.

"Uh . . . hi. I need to go home. How do I do that?"

"The mask will be linked to your home address. Just approach the doors and a Slip will take you back."

I nod and head toward one of the hundreds of door pedestals.

Some are empty, just three short stairs leading up to nothing. Others have blue-white rectangles waiting for the workers to use. I put my mask on and climb the steps of the closest pedestal. The door flares to life, and I step inside, finding myself in the long tunnel. I don't hesitate this time, but walk quickly through the darkness, not looking left or right, not listening to the slithering from the shadows, trying not to acknowledge the half-glimpsed creatures, the writhing tentacles, the cosmic emptiness of it all.

I reach the end of the tunnel and enter my bedroom.

I pause and look around. The Slip makes the room look like something out of an alien abduction movie. Harsh, brilliant light cuts into the corners and reveals the mess of my life.

Then the Slip closes and grungy orange light filters through the window. I stand where I am, looking around at the utter mundanity of my apartment. After everything I've seen today this, the real world, seems somehow out of place. Unreal.

I take a deep breath, going over the day in my head. But I can't. I shy away from everything. It's like it doesn't compute. My brain can't handle everything in one go.

I take a shower, then grab a beer from the fridge and check the time. Seven. Not too late.

I slump into the couch and dial home. Ex-home.

Susan answers, and it's like the whole day didn't happen. I feel a smile tugging at my lips as I hear her voice. "Hey, kiddo. You ready?"

"Yeah!"

"Cool. It's your turn to read to me, right?"

"D-a-a-d!"

I smile and start to read. And everything else just falls away.

CHAPTER SEVEN

A new day and a new crime scene.

We step out of a Slip into a devastated city speared with early-morning sunlight. Smoke billows into the winter blue sky, wavering stalks reaching high and spreading out to form a haze. Every building in sight has been destroyed. It looks like a war has been fought here.

"Shit, Graves," says Ash, her voice small and quiet.

That makes me feel better. Because I'm freaking out a bit looking at this shell of a city, and I was really worried that this might be considered normal.

"What's the crime scene here?" I ask. "The whole city?"

Graves has his back to us. He doesn't answer at first.

"Graves?"

"Not the whole city," he says softly. "The whole world."

I blink, not understanding. "The whole world?" I look around again. "The whole world is like this?"

"Some psycho from an alternate with real Superiors came through here and . . ." He gestures around us. ". . . did this."

"Superiors?"

"What you'd call a superhero," says Ash. "Or a super villain."

"You're saying Superman did this?"

"No. This is what would have happened if Superman wasn't there to stop General Zod."

I look around again. And that's when I realize the whole city—the whole planet—by the sounds of it is utterly silent. No birds, no people, no life.

"Is . . . is everything dead?"

"Everything," says Graves.

"But aren't you guys supposed to stop this kind of thing? The ICD? Isn't that your job?"

"We must have missed this. Somehow . . ."

"You missed it?" I say incredulously. "Well, that's just dandy! I bet that makes the billions of people who lived here feel a whole lot better! That you somehow missed it! I mean, fuck it, yeah? You're only human. Not your fault, right?"

"Harry . . ." Ash throws me a warning look.

"What? Oh, am I hurting Mr. Graves's feelings? I'm sorry. I'm sorry you're so shit at your job! Seriously, what's the point of you people if you can't stop . . ." I wave at the horror around me. ". . . this kind of thing from happening? Who are you accountable to?"

Graves turns and runs at me. I stare in shock, then stumble back, tripping over a fallen column. Graves is on me before I hit the ground, pulling me back up by my shirt.

"Who are we accountable to?" he shouts. "We're accountable to ourselves! You think I'm happy with this? You ever think maybe we missed this because I got demoted? Because of the shit you caused? Ever think of that?"

I yank free of him. "You're blaming me for this?"

"Are you blaming me?" he snaps back.

I hesitate, then look away. I don't want to do this. Not here. Not now.

"Come on, Graves," says Ash gently. "We have a job to do."

"Yeah." Graves carries on staring at me for a few seconds longer. "Another time, then."

"Sure," I say. "I'll be waiting."

Graves turns and walks away through the rubble-strewn streets. Ash and I follow, moving past hollowed-out buildings, scarred and pitted, stained black with smoke.

I really don't like it here. There's a feeling . . . a heaviness . . . that weighs me down.

Then I see the bodies.

I blink, look away. Scrunch my eyes shut. Because I can't look at the hundreds—no, thousands—of dead bodies piled neatly on the broken tarmac.

I hear Ash's indrawn breath, force myself to open my eyes.

It's like some kind of twisted, interlocking jigsaw puzzle, each body laid head to toe, one on top of the other, to form neat rows. The bodies themselves are mangled and torn, ripped apart, limbs and torsos used to fill gaps in the lines.

We stare at the bodies for a long moment.

"Tell me we're not responsible for cleaning this up," I say, and immediately regret it. "Sorry. Bad joke."

We move past the bodies, heading deeper into the broken city.

"Where's the team at?" asks Ash.

"The town square," says Graves. "Should be just up ahead."

The team is indeed in the town square. And over it. And round the edges. And . . . pretty much everywhere, really.

The ICD team sent here to nullify the Superior are all dead. Their bodies are strung up between two half-broken statues, intestines hanging in the air like bunting. Their eyes have been plucked from their heads, left to dangle against their cheeks.

I look around in confusion. "Did the Superior do this? I thought we were here to clean up the scene after these guys fixed it."

"We were." Graves turns in a slow circle, studying the perimeter of the square.

"So what—"

"Hsst." Graves holds up a hand to stop me talking. Then he points. "There."

Ash and I both look. There's a figure hanging from the doors of what looks like the town hall. He's blond, seven feet tall. Wearing blue spandex with a red logo on the chest. I can't see what the logo is. An M, perhaps? It's hard to make out.

But that's not really important. What is important is the fact that the Superior is dead as well, his throat ripped out so his head hangs from a piece of skin.

"Yeah, hate to be the guy asking the stunningly obvious question here, but if this guy is dead, then who took out your team?"

Graves turns to stare at me. There's something behind his eyes. Triumph? Elation? No. I must be wrong. Those emotions don't make sense here.

But then Graves smiles. "I thought so," he says.

I turn to Ash, but she looks as confused as me.

"Graves?" she says. "What have you done?"

"Nothing. I haven't done a thing."

And then I hear it.

Plink.

Plink.

Plink.

Like tiny glass vials snapping apart.

Graves yanks his backpack around and pulls out the bone guns. He throws one to Ash, then grabs the one that belonged to Crew Cut Dude and tosses it to me. He grabs his own shotgun and racks the chamber.

"Graves, what's going on?" demands Ash.

Graves doesn't answer, but he doesn't have to, because approaching us across the square are three amorphous . . . blobs. They're about ten feet tall, bulbous, and misshapen. Like a kid's Play-Doh figurine. Their skin is translucent and wet. I can see black blood coursing through their veins.

"Shoggoths!" shouts Graves.

I glance at Ash. "Another one of Lovecraft's, right?"

She nods. I watch the creatures coming, wondering how they found us.

And that's when I realize the truth.

The look of disappointment on Graves's face after we'd finished work yesterday. I couldn't figure it out at the time. Now I know. He was bummed out we hadn't been attacked.

I ignore the approaching blobs. Lower my gun and turn to face Graves. "You set me up!"

Graves doesn't even look at me. His hands clench and unclench around the bone handle of his shotgun as he scans the square.

"I've no idea what you're talking about," he says.

"Yes! You do! That's why you offered me a place on your team, right? I'm bait! You're using me to get your old job back." I turn to a wide-eyed Ash. "Did you know about this?"

"No! I swear." Her eyes shift to Graves. "Graves? It's not true. Right?"

"Of course not!"

"Why else would you seek me out? You have hundreds of people at ICD to fill your team. Why me?" I glance at Ash. "Didn't that seem weird to you?"

"Kind of."

"And? What did he say?"

"That he . . . felt bad leaving you behind. Wanted to bring you behind the curtain."

"Bullshit. He wants to solve the case that started this off. Wants to get out of Department Zero. Right?"

"Oh, God's sake!" shouts Graves. "Fine! Yes! So what? I figured this lot would be after you. Decided to dangle the carrot in front of their faces. What does it matter? We get out of the basement, wonder boy here gets to experience life outside of his hitherto shattered and pathetic existence, we bag the bad guys, and the Inspectre gets egg on his face. Everybody wins!"

"Everybody wins?" I shout. "Are you kidding me? You lied!"

Graves finally turns in my direction. "I lied? What are you, twelve? So what if I lied? It was for the greater good."

"That's not cool, Graves," says Ash softly.

"Look, can we debate the ethics of this later?" He gestures at the approaching shoggoths. "After we deal with these guys?"

He raises his gun. "Just don't kill them. We need to find out who sent them."

The lead shoggoth pauses. Two red eyes emerge from inside the pulsating mass. A long, misshapen arm rises up and points at me. "Give...us...the...coordinates," it says in a wet, gurgling voice.

Graves and Ash look at me. I shrug. "The other one asked me the same thing. The Dimensional Shambler? I have no idea what it means."

I hear a ripping sound off to my left, like flesh being torn in half. I turn and see a crack of blue-white light hanging in the air. The crack jerks and shudders, ripping wider and wider. Light spills out, bathing the shattered stone in a pallid, hospital glow.

"Is that a Slip?"

"No," says Graves. "I keep telling you. That's a Rip. Ours are officially sanctioned. Planned out. That there is a rip in reality. Barreling through God knows how many alternates and forcing its way here."

A shadow appears behind the crack, fluttering against the light.

"Uh..."

"Stand firm," snaps Graves. "Wait for it to come through. Ash? Cover the others."

"I am."

"What are they doing?"

"Um...smiling."

Graves and I both turn. Sure enough the three shoggoths are standing on the edge of the city square, watching the rip open up with satisfied smiles on their bulbous faces.

A horrific shriek echoes through the square. We whirl around and see a huge creature pulling itself through the Rip. It's a bird of some type, easily the size of an elephant. A black-beaked head lunges and snarls, teeth snapping at the air. Huge, bat-like wings erupt outward, flapping as it tries to drag itself through the Rip.

It's like I'm witnessing some nightmare creature giving birth.

Then the creature bursts through and falls to the stone. It lays there for a while, panting.

"What is that?" I whisper.

"A shantak."

"A . . . ?"

"A shantak."

"Another—"

"Will you please stop asking if every single creature we come across is one of Lovecraft's? So far, that is indeed the case, yes. Which says more about you or that globe you shattered. If a creature *isn't* from the mythos, I'll let you know, how does that sound?"

The shantak scrambles to its feet and starts to pull the Rip wider apart.

That's when we all realize we should be firing our guns.

Graves shoots first. The shantak launches itself into the air, flapping its wings to gain height.

I track and fire. The weapon convulses and shudders, invisible strands sending shock waves through the air. But the shantak is fast. It dodges and spins, veering effortlessly through the sky.

"Behind us!" shouts Ash.

I turn and see two more of the creatures pulling themselves through.

I run toward them, not even realizing what a colossally stupid thing this is to do. I fire. Again.

"*Harry!*"

I turn as soon as I hear Ash's warning. The first shantak is diving for me, claws outstretched.

I throw myself to the side, and the creature soars through the air where I was standing. I roll onto my back, finger pressing down on the quivering trigger. But it's hard to aim when you can't actually see the bullets. I sweep the gun back and forth, but the shantak dodges, screaming at me as it darts and weaves against the gray clouds.

The other two shantak pull through the Rip and rush toward me. I shift my aim, pointing the gun at them. I hit one of the creatures in the leg, and the limb bursts into a puddle of ichor. The shantak screams and stumbles, hitting the ground as black blood pumps out of its stump.

The other shantak keeps coming. I shift my aim again, but the creature barrels into me, knocking the gun flying. I fall back, the creature on my chest. It snaps at me, trying to rip away my face.

Then it bursts like a water balloon. If said water balloon was filled with vile, foul-smelling, hot blood.

The liquid falls directly on me. Into my mouth, up my nose. I roll over, vomiting and coughing. It's disgusting. Like oil and blood mixed together. I stagger to my feet. I can't get the stuff off. I try to pull it away with my fingers, but it just stretches like gunky string.

"Down!" shouts Ash.

I drop to the ground again and feel the whoosh of wind above me as another shantak flies past. I wipe the crud out of my eyes and look for my gun. There. About thirty feet away.

I scramble to my feet and make a run for it. There's a screech of triumph behind me. I glance over my shoulder and see two shantak flying toward me. I try to coax some extra speed from my rubbery legs. Twenty feet. Ten. Another look. The shantak are close. I can see their eyes, black against yellow.

Five feet. A shriek of pain. A quick look and I see one of the shantak is now a cloud of black ichor pattering onto the stone. I turn back, reach out for the gun—

And then I'm yanked backward. My breath explodes from my body, and I fold up with a gasp of pain. The gun recedes below me as I'm lifted into the air. I try to pry the shantak's claws from around my ribs. Then I realize how stupid that is, considering how high up I am.

Down below, the three shoggoth freaks have chosen that moment to attack Ash and Graves. The shantak banks in the air and drops lower. I think it's about to join the fight, but it changes direction and heads back toward the Rip.

I realize what's happening and quickly fumble at my belt for my mask, jamming it hard onto my face just as the shantak flies straight into the Rip.

Blue-white light surrounds me, slices through me. I scream in pain, and then everything goes black.

CHAPTER EIGHT

I wake up in darkness with a headache that makes me think I must have had a goddamn amazing time last night. Usually when my day starts this way I do a quick mental run-through of events, trying to figure out if I need to be embarrassed or happy.

When I do the run-through this time, however, I sit bolt upright in fear.

Or try to. I can't, because I'm strapped to some kind of stone altar. Legs, arms, chest. Everything.

I remember the attack back in the town square. Being grabbed. Pulled through the Rip.

Crap.

I can still move my head. I look left and right, trying to get an idea of where I am. I see old stone pillars, a low, vaulted ceiling, and wine racks up against the far wall. The air is damp and cold. Old-fashioned bulbs hang from the ceiling, giving off a flickering orange glow. Some kind of cellar. A big one, by the look of it. And it has wine.

Which is annoying as hell, because I could really do with some of that wine right about now. A couple of bottles, if I'm honest.

A door creaks open from somewhere behind and above me. I wait, straining my ears, my whole body on edge. Then I hear footsteps. Lots of them. Soft feet shuffling along the stone.

A few seconds later a dark-robed figure appears in my peripheral vision and slowly walks around the altar. The figure is followed by another, then another, and another, until I'm surrounded by a ring of sinister figures wearing black robes, cowls pulled up to hide their faces.

They just stand there, not making a sound.

"Uh . . . hey," I say, trying to keep it light. Overwhelm them with charm. "You should give your stylist a raise. Black, you know? Very slimming. And the cowl thing? Perfect. Intimidating *and* mysterious. Two for one."

The clamps are around my forearms, so I manage to raise both my thumbs in the air.

No response.

I stare at them, waiting to see what is going to happen next. Minutes pass. No movement.

"Yeah, kind of getting a bit awkward now, guys," I say. "Any idea when things are going to kick into gear?"

Nothing.

Another few minutes pass, and just when I think I'm about to explode with built-up tension, the robed figures all step back, revealing a new arrival. A man.

He's robed, but doesn't have a cowl over his face. He looks . . . Egyptian, I think. Or Middle Eastern.

I tilt my hand up and give a small wave. "Hi." I squint at him. "Are you wearing eyeliner? Or are your eyes really like that? It looks good. Suits you. Makes them pop."

The figure steps forward. My heart thumps erratically in my chest. I check his hands to see if he's holding a sacrificial dagger, but they're empty. That's something, at least.

He reaches out and puts his fingers on my head. His touch is cool and dry.

"Come on. You haven't even bought me dinner yet."

His fingers press into my skin. It gets painful pretty quickly. I try to move my head, but his fingers pin me to the altar.

"Hey . . ." I start to say, but then I freeze as I feel his fingers sink *into* my head.

I scream. I can feel his fingers in my mind. In my brain, rooting around, playing with my thoughts. He's rifling through my memories like an office worker rifling through a file cabinet, searching for something.

My cry trails off. My thoughts drift into nothingness, my mind fogged and fuzzy. I no longer know what I'm doing here. No longer care. I just lie there, mouth half-open, drooling, while this freaky-deaky dude plays with my brain.

Then he finds something. A memory that I see before me. That day on the freeway. Me, taking the small glass globe out of my pocket, staring at it in surprise before I toss it to Graves. The brief flash of awareness when I see those numbers hidden in the depths of the globe, so quickly I barely registered them at the time.

The memory freezes there, the Blu-Ray of my life on pause. The numbers leap into sharp focus. There are two separate strings: 58384-689fh-63al/7 and 583030-65839h-64ak/4.

The numbers imprint themselves on my mind. I screw my eyes tight against them, but they just hang there, hovering against my eyelids.

I open my eyes again. The robed figure steps back, extracting his fingers from my mind. He turns to the others and claps his hands together.

"All right. There we go, people. All done and dusted. Wonderful. Super. I like what I'm feeling here. It's positive; it's warming. You know? I feel the love. Praise Azathoth."

All the cultists respond, "Praise the Great Old Ones!"

"Yeah. The Great Old Ones. Those super cosmic gods. Praise to those hoopy dudes. Come on. Let's go have some canapés and soda."

They turn and file slowly through the basement, leaving me lying there feeling violated and used.

"Hey," I say weakly. "You guys gonna let me up?" No answer. "At least put a bottle of wine in my hand!" I shout, mustering all my energy.

The door creaks shut again. I close my eyes, exhausted. The numbers are still there, clear as day. What the hell are they? Why are they so important?

More to the point, how the hell am I going to get out of this?

I strain against my bindings with everything I have. Nothing. The straps are old leather and metal buckles, the kind used to lock down crazy patients in old movies. No way am I getting out of this.

"Graves," I mutter. "I curse you and your bloodline from now to eternity. I hope you contract an embarrassing sexually transmitted disease."

I stay like that for the next hour. My arms and legs turn numb. I'm so bored I doze off for a bit.

Something startles me awake. You know how it is. You wake up, heart racing, but have no idea why. You lie there, every one of your senses straining to detect the murderer you know is coming for you.

"You look comfortable," says Havelock Graves.

I peer through the gap between my feet. He's standing there, smug as ever, looking around the cellar with interest. I see he's holding a dusty bottle of wine in his hands. He inspects the label.

"Good year," he says.

"Wonderful," I snap. "But could you put the wine down and get these things off?" I shake my hands and feet.

Graves stares at me for a moment. "You're not going to do anything silly if I do?"

"Like what?"

"Like blame me for all this."

"Who else should I blame?"

"Well . . . me. Sure. But you're not going to attack me or anything like that?"

"No, I'm not going to attack you. We're not in high school."

Graves stares at me a bit longer, then puts the wine down next to my leg and unbuckles the straps. I sit up, rubbing life back into my wrists and ankles while Graves hunts around the cellar.

"No corkscrew," he complains. "How the hell am I supposed to open this?"

I hold my hand out. "Give it here."

He hands it over, and I give the top of the bottle a quick tap against the altar. The neck of the bottle breaks and falls to the stone floor. I check the break. Clean. No splinters. I hold the bottle above my mouth and pour the wine in. I manage to get half the bottle down me before I hold it out for Graves.

When he reaches for it I hit him. Right in the cheek.

Graves dances back, holding his face. "You said you wouldn't hit me!"

"So I lied. Asshole."

We stare warily at each other.

"You done now?" he asks.

I think about it, then nod.

"Good. And just so you know, I always had a plan. I knew they might come for you. I tracked you through your mask."

"Oh. It was still a shitty thing to do. Where's Ash?"

"Back in the office. She's not talking to me."

"Good." I hop off the plinth. "Just so you know, they were after some numbers in my head."

"Numbers?"

"Yeah." The numbers come instantly to my memory. They're imprinted there. "They're 58384-689fh-63al/7, and 583030-65839h -64ak/4."

Graves stares at me. "Those are coordinates."

"For?"

"Alternates. That's why they were after that globe. It was like . . . a map."

"To what?"

"I have no idea."

I look at Graves expectantly. "Well? We know what they wanted. Open up the Slip. Let's get out of here."

"The Slip's not here. Besides, we're not leaving yet."

"Why the hell not?"

"Because we need to find out what's actually going on. That's what all this has been about. Or did you miss that?"

"No, I didn't miss that. I just thought you could do it without me. I've undergone a traumatic workplace experience. I could probably sue the Company for worker's compensation. Hey . . . I might never have to work again."

Graves snorts. "Good luck with that."

"Why?" I ask suspiciously.

"Because the Company makes sure it's absolved of all responsibility for that kind of stuff. I'm not saying they wouldn't . . . you know . . . lend a hand if you went crazy. Or give you a few free sessions with the in-house shrink. But compensation? Not a chance." He sets off toward the stairs.

I wait a few seconds, then kick the altar and follow. What choice do I have?

§

The cellar stairs take us up to a door that opens into a long corridor. A faded carpet travels the length of the passage, and oil paintings hang on the walls. I stare at the closest one. It's some kind of monster. A massive creature with tentacles hanging from its face and bat wings on its back. The next one is a painting of space, but hanging between the stars is a glass tetrahedron, inside of which is a huge eye staring balefully at the viewer.

"Was I kidnapped by a Dungeons & Dragons cult?" I whisper.

"What is Dungeons & Dragons?"

"It's a game."

"Then no, you have not been kidnapped by a Dungeons & Dragons cult. The people we're dealing with are very dangerous."

"Which is why we should leave," I say, checking over my shoulder as we make our way along the corridor.

"These people are responsible for me losing my job!" says Graves. "And now I know where they are you want me to run away?"

"Not run. More . . . strategically withdraw. You know, so you can come back with reinforcements."

"Reinforcements? Led by the Inspectre? So he can take all the credit? No thanks."

He stalks along the corridor, and I follow close behind. I'm not sure if the place is a manor house or a small castle. Either way, I'm not very impressed. All I see is a cold stone building with too many corridors. Don't know why anyone would want to hole up in one. Heating bills must cost a fortune.

Two times we almost run into robed cultists, and both times we just manage to dart through a door to avoid being discovered. We finally stop before a massive iron door. Graves puts his ear to it and listens, then nods at me.

"They're in there," he whispers.

Graves ducks down into a crouch and opens the door a crack. The mutter and grumble of conversation drifts out from the room beyond. Graves waits a few seconds, then slips through the door.

I follow. We're on a wide balcony high above a wide room. The balcony is dark, but a fierce orange light flickers up the walls of the room below. I can hear the spit and crackle of a fire.

"A new age is upon us, people," calls a voice from below.

Grave glances at me, eyebrows raised. Then we both inch forward toward the balcony railings.

"The new moon approaches. It's like . . . new . . . and . . . big. You know? Cosmic. No—eldritch! Yeah, that's the word. Eldritch. And the time of the Unbinding draws close, you know?"

The space below slowly inches into view as we creep forward. It's a huge sitting room, the kind you get in Victorian ghost stories. Leather suites surrounding mahogany tables. Books lining the walls, a huge hearth with a fire roaring in the grate.

All the cultists are there, their attention turned toward the Egyptian-looking dude who stuck his fingers into my brain. Next to him is the woman I saw fighting Graves back in the Rip a few weeks ago. She's wearing a robe as well, but hers is trimmed with gold.

"Who's he?" I ask.

"I don't know."

"The stars are all lined up in this super-cosmic alignment, right? All ripe and juicy for the mighty Cthulhu's release from R'lyeh. I'm loving the energy here, by the way. You're all super committed to the cause, and I love that about you. Really. Super cool."

I sense Graves stiffen at these words, but I'm too busy watching the Egyptian guy to ask what's wrong.

"We'll usher Cthulhu into the world, yeah? Begin a new age where the Old Ones won't, like, bow down to earthly powers? Where they won't be imprisoned by these horrible human beings. You know what I'm talking about, right? They're just awful. Present company excluded. You guys are super awesome." The guy gives the cultists two thumbs-up. Then he points at one of the cultists. "You. My man. Come forward. It's okay. Come on."

The cloaked figure lowers his hood and approaches. "My Lord Nyarlathotep. How may I serve?"

"You may serve . . . by *dying*!"

An inrush of panicked breath from the cultists, then Nyarlathotep cracks up laughing. He puts a hand on the terrified cultist's shoulder. "No, no. I'm just messing around with you. It's cool. It's all good."

Nyarlathotep then shifts his hand and lightly touches the man's face.

I can feel the power resonating from Nyarlathotep even from where we're hiding. It's like a silent thunderclap, a wave of pressure, oily, cloying. It flies outward in a shock wave of heated air, carrying the sweet stench of gangrene and burning hair, the copper taste of blood. It tingles over my teeth, setting them on edge as if I'd bitten on metal.

The priest standing before Nyarlathotep folds in on himself, as if he's collapsing from within. His face ripples and flows into his mouth and pulls, the skin bursting and reversing itself with a wet sucking sound. And instead of running away in fear and terror, the other cultists rush forward to be touched by Nyarlathotep.

Every one of the cultists shakes and comes apart before my eyes. Bones splinter, flesh tears. Their ribs split open, spilling organs onto the floor. Skin and muscle slough off their limbs, their arms and legs turning backward at the elbow and knee with sharp cracks. The cultists' necks and spines stretch, drawing them up taller—seven, eight feet in height. Barbed spines burst through the skin. Their faces are stretched and frozen in tormented expressions of pain, their eyes filled with blood, their mouths Os of eternal horror. Tentacles erupt from their faces, writhing in the air like the tentacles of an octopus.

Their limbs are too long for their bodies. Their fingers are spindly twigs, and on the back of their wrists they have a single black claw. They stumble and lurch around like newborn foals getting used to their legs, and where these claws connect with the other cultists, the flesh tears open like melted butter and drips steaming to the floor.

Soon there are only two humans left standing. Nyarlathotep and the woman, the latter staring around with a twisted grin on her face. The nightmarish creatures stalk around them, tasting the air with purple tongues, their tentacles writhing and probing.

"The Hounds of Tindalos," says Nyarlathotep, looking around with paternal pride. "You guys are beautiful. Seriously. I love you guys. Yeah? And now it's time for you to scour the multiverse and wipe out the unbelievers, okay? Right? You'll all help me break the Old Ones from their eternal prisons, won't you? I'd really love that. It would be super, and I bet once it's all finished we'll be rewarded. Like an endless pool party. With cocktails and no hangovers. Does that sound good to you?"

The hounds begin to howl. The sound is earsplittingly loud.

"Listen to them," shouts Nyarlathotep, "the children of the night.

What music they make! Love the enthusiasm, guys, just lower the tone, yeah?"

The hounds fall silent and stare expectantly at him. He smiles brightly.

"Thanks! *Loving* the obedience. Now, I want you to follow my loyal priestess here—she's awesome, yeah? her name is Dana by the way—to the alternate that holds the spear. Can you bring it back to me? I'd really like that. It would be like the *best* early Christmas present *ever*."

He then turns around so his back is to us. I lean forward and see he's fiddling with something on a low altar. Messing around with switches.

A blinding crack of light opens up in the air against the far wall of the room. It rips through reality, a jagged blue-white tear.

"Go, my hounds. Go forth and, like, conquer and stuff. But have fun! You have to have fun in your job because, like, what's the point otherwise?" He points at Dana. "You know what I'm talking about, right? 'Course you do."

Half of the hounds bound through the Rip, howling and hissing as they do. Nyarlathotep turns to the woman and takes her hand.

"And you, my super-sexy love. Find the Spear of Destiny, yes? Get the Jesus-poker for me, and I'll search for the Jewel of Ini-taya. Then we'll get together and have brunch and compare notes about how amazing I am."

"I will, Exalted One."

"Hey now, no need for such cumbersome titles." He smiles. "My lord will suffice."

She bows her head. "As you will, my lord."

"Off you pop, then."

She runs toward the crack and leaps through it. It flares once, then winks out of existence.

There are still about ten or so hounds waiting in the room. Nyarla-thotep looks upon them. "Are you ready?"

The hounds howl in response.

I turn to Graves. His face is pale, troubled. He gestures for us to back up.

Before we move, an eerie silence drops across the room. Graves and I are still staring at each other, but we slowly turn our heads, looking back at the scene below us.

Nyarlathotep and his hounds are staring directly at us.

Graves and I scramble to our feet and start running around the balcony, heading for a door on the opposite side of the room. The hounds howl and shriek, lashing out, tearing at each other in their rush to get to us.

"Why don't we go back the way we came in?" I shout.

"Because my Slip is in the kitchen. Now shut up and run!"

One of the hounds uses its comrades as leverage and leaps up to grab the balcony to my left. Graves turns and fires his gun. The hound's arms explode into black goo, and it drops onto the others with a shriek of hatred.

Graves yanks the door open. We bolt through, and he yanks the door closed behind us.

"Can we lock it?" I ask.

"Do you have a key?"

"What? No!"

"Then no, we can't lock it."

He runs down a set of stairs. I follow, slipping and stumbling in my haste. He leads us deeper into the bowels of the house while behind us the hounds howl and screech as they give chase.

Our surroundings change slightly, the walls becoming bare, plastered stone. No one else is around. I notice that Graves is slowing down, looking a bit confused.

"Do you know where we're going?"

"Of course I do!"

We reach an intersection. Graves runs left, then stops and turns right. He grimaces apologetically as he passes me. "All under control."

Wonderful. That makes me feel so much better. I pause briefly to listen for pursuit. It's still there, but distant now. We seem to be pulling ahead, losing the hounds in the twisting corridors.

Graves leads us down another flight of stairs, along another corridor, and then we find ourselves in the kitchen. It's a huge room, easily double the size of my ex-home. Huge tables and industrial-sized ovens dominate the space.

Graves slows to a walk and grins over his shoulder at me. "There. Told you I'd find it. No problem. No problem at all."

Yeah. That's why he looks so relieved.

We hurry across the kitchen, and Graves pulls open the back door. Blue light spills inside. I peer around him and see the rectangular Slip standing in a messy courtyard.

"Masks!"

We put our masks on and leap through the Slip as the howls of the Hounds of Tindalos grow louder.

CHAPTER NINE

I follow Graves as he strides through the DDICS office toward his little huddle of cubicle heaven. Ash is sitting at her desk, reading through files and checking something on her screen.

She looks up as we approach, her face pinched with guilt.

Graves slumps into his desk and starts typing away on his keyboard. Ash stands up as I pull my own chair out and sit. I spread my hands over the surface of the desk, take a few deep, calming breaths. They don't work.

"I didn't know."

I look up at Ash. She's playing with an elastic band, nervously twisting it between her fingers.

"About . . . what he did." She throws a glare in Graves's direction.

"I believe you."

"Really?"

"Really. Only a sociopath like Graves would do something like that."

"Nyarlathotep," says Graves loudly.

Ash frowns at him. "What?"

Graves twists his monitor around. On it are various images of different people and monsters. I recognize Nyarlathotep immediately, but there are others. A huge creature with lethal claws on the end of its arms and a long tentacle for a head, a winged birdlike creature with a single red eye, a grotesquely fat woman covered in small tentacles, her mouth hanging open so wide it's bigger than her actual head, etc.

"Who are they?" I ask.

"Nyarlathotep. Some of his nine hundred and ninety-nine forms. That's who we're dealing with," he says to Ash.

"Graves, are you sure?"

"Oh, yes. I saw him."

"Then we need to take this upstairs. Now!"

"No!" snaps Graves.

"We have to! We've been after this guy for years."

"Exactly. And if I take this upstairs, we lose the case. And our chance to get our old jobs back."

"I don't get it," I say. "Who is this guy? Why's he so important?"

"Nyarlathotep is . . . he's the messenger of the Old Ones. He carries out their will in the multiverse, while they're all locked away in their prisons in the Dreamlands. His only goal is to set them free, to cause as much chaos and destruction as he can. He has cults all over the multiverse, all over the worlds. He uses his followers to further his aims."

"He's one of the CBC's most wanted," says Ash.

"And we've never had a lead on him. Until now."

"Okay." I think about this. "And he wants the Spear of Destiny why?"

Graves turns the monitor back and types into his computer. "The Spear of Destiny," he says. "Otherwise known as the Holy Lance, or the Lance of Longinus. It's the spear that was apparently used to pierce the side of Jesus Christ when he hung on the cross."

"It's just a legend, though," I say.

"No such thing," says Graves. "Not in our line of work. The stories connect the spear to several rulers over the centuries. All of them thought the spear gave them special powers."

"Like?" I ask.

"Charlemagne. Apparently he carried it with him into forty-seven battles. Won every single one of them."

"Because of the spear?" asks Ash.

"That's what he believed. They say as soon as he dropped the spear he lost the next battle and died. Similar story with the Holy Roman Emperor Frederick I Barbarossa. And Alaric, the king of the Visigoths. Napoleon was after it too."

"And they all believed this spear gave them power?"

"Not just power. They believed it gave them the power to control the destiny of the world. But they all died as soon as the spear left their possession."

"And these legends are the same across all realities?" I ask.

"No. There are variations. But all realities that are similar to yours—Class C, we call them—have the same legends. For instance, in your reality, it's said that Hitler had a raging hard-on for the lance. Some say he actually started the war just to get his hands on it. General Patton and his men retrieved the spear from Hitler himself in 1945, and Hitler committed suicide soon after. After Patton handed it over, he died in a car accident at his army camp."

"And this is what Nyarlathotep is after?"

"You were there," says Graves. "You heard him."

"Yeah. But . . ."

"But?"

"It's crazy talk."

"Listen, idiot, if you can't accept this kind of thing as real from now on, you're going to have a hard time settling in. This spear exists somewhere, and in some alternates it will have the powers listed here. If Nyarlathotep and his hounds have the location of the alternate where it *has* this power and they get their hands on it . . . well . . . that's not good for anyone."

"But what does that have to do with the Old Ones?"

"I don't know," says Graves uneasily.

"If this is so important, maybe Ash is right. Maybe you should tell that Inspectre guy?"

"Wash your mouth out!" snaps Graves. "We can handle this. It was my case to begin with."

"Yeah, but—"

"No buts. If we crack this case I get my job back. Which means Ash gets her job back. Which means you don't have to clean up brains and blood anymore. Unless you *like* cleaning up brains and blood? Is that it?"

"No."

"Then shut up and listen to the plan."

I look at him expectantly. So does Ash.

"Which we have to come up with first," adds Graves.

"Well . . . first thing is to stop them getting the spear," says Ash.

Graves points at her. "Good thinking. We figure out why they want it afterwards."

"So that means we need to travel to this alternate. The one in my head?" I ask.

"Do you remember the coordinates?"

I think back. "The first one was 58384-689fh-63al/7."

Ash types them into her computer and starts reading. Then she flops back into her chair with a groan. "It's an Apologue alternate."

"Son of a bitch!" snarls Graves.

"A what?" I ask. Graves doesn't answer, so I turn my attention to Ash. "What's an Apologue alternate?"

"It's . . . a reality influenced or drawn from a literary wellspring."

"I don't get it."

"It's an alternate based on a piece of fiction."

"Based on? How is that possible?"

"We don't bloody know!" snaps Graves. "It just is."

"Take this alternate," says Ash, nodding at the computer screen. "The coordinates he drew from your head. You know *The War of the Worlds*?"

"The H. G. Wells book?"

"In this reality, it's not a book. It really happened. About . . ." She reads something on her screen again. ". . . forty years ago. In this alternate, the British government reverse engineered the Martian technology and has put it to use in everyday life. Using Martian life-forms spliced with man-made technology. And now the British Empire is totally reliant on this new technology. Also . . ." She frowns. ". . . Queen Victoria has been alive for over a hundred years."

"How is that possible?" I ask.

"Martian tech. Her scientists perfected cloning, and they rehouse her soul into a younger body every ten years. They call it the Day of Ascension."

"Anything else?" groans Graves.

"It's 1899 in the British Empire. Has been for the past few decades."

"And everywhere else?"

"Everywhere else it's 1938."

"So we're talking a repressed society, then?" says Graves. "Backwards. Tainted by advanced technology that the Crown tries to control."

I look to Ash. She's reading the screen as Graves talks, nodding. "That's what our man in the alternate says."

"Wonderful. How embedded is this Martian technology?"

"Very. They use it for everything. Ground zero for the war was the area around St. Paul's Cathedral. Lots of downed tripods that the scientists used to figure out all the tech. The area is off-limits now. Apparently it's contaminated with Martian germs and stuff."

Graves leans back in his chair and stares up at the ceiling. "Right," he says, slapping his hands on his thighs. "I suppose we should get going then."

"Tonight?" I say. I glance at my watch. It's after six.

"You got a hot date?" asks Graves.

"No. But . . ." I take out my phone. "Will this . . . work here? To phone my kid?"

Graves slides the phone on his desk over to me. "No. Use that. Dial six-six-six for an outside line."

"You're kidding, right?"

"Of course he is," says Ash. "Dial zero."

I pick up the phone and dial the number to my old home. Ash and

Graves don't seem in a hurry to give me any privacy. I turn my back on them as the phone is picked up and Susan's voice comes through the lines, traveling between universes.

"Hello?"

"Hiya, sweetie. How's it going?"

"Daddy!"

"Just called to say good night. No time for a story tonight."

"Aw, Dad!"

"Sorry, sport. Dad's busy. Got a new job."

"Doing what?"

I smile. "Fighting inter-dimensional crime."

"Cool!"

"'Night then. Love you lots like jelly tots. Have lovely dreams. Have a nice night. Don't let the bedbugs bite. If they do, squish a few."

I ignore Graves's snort from behind me.

"'Night, Dad. Love you lots like jelly tots. Have lovely dreams. Have a nice night. Don't let the bedbugs bite. If they do, squish a few."

"Love you, kiddo."

"Love you too."

She hangs up. I replace the handset and try to suppress the heavy feeling that always hits after I say good night.

"You done?" asks Graves.

I nod.

"Let's go see some Martians."

CHAPTER TEN

We step through the doorway into a cluttered room lit by the harsh blue glare of the Slip.

I blink and look around. There's an old wooden desk in one corner. It's covered with loose paper and old leather binders. A large globe of the world sits on top. Wooden filing cabinets take up one wall, while another is covered with a floor-to-ceiling bookcase.

The Slip winks out of existence, plunging the room into shadow. The only light filters beneath a door off to our right.

"What is this place?" I ask.

"A safe house. We have them on all the catalogued worlds. Manned by ICD agents."

"They live here?"

Graves nods. "We rotate them once a year so they don't turn native. It's actually quite a sought-after position. Unless you get one of the crappy worlds. Those are usually reserved for punishments."

Graves heads to the door and pauses to listen. Apparently satisfied, he pulls it open. Orange light spills into the cluttered office.

"We'll find clothes here. The local currency. Latest gossip, that kind of thing," he says, stepping through the door.

I follow after him and find myself in a sparsely furnished apartment. Everything is muted browns and grays. A simple wooden table takes up the center of the room, a functional couch sits beneath the window, and against the far wall a huge wooden box that turns out to be a radio.

But that's not what draws my attention. No, what draws my attention are the numerous worm-type creatures attached to various pieces of equipment around the room. I inspect the closest. The worm is beige-white, anemic. Blue veins are visible beneath the surface, and it's covered with a coating of mucous. I glance at the others. They're all half-fused to items, the upper half of their bodies merged seamlessly with wood or Bakelite.

"Uh . . . what's with the worm things?"

Graves is standing in the center of the room, hands on his hips, staring around with a frown of concentration. "Reverse engineering," he says.

I nod wisely. "Okay." Then, when that doesn't make anything clearer, I add, "What's that got to do with worms?"

"Weren't you listening to Ash? The government reverse engineered the Martian technology from the war and put it to use in everyday life. Those . . . things—" he gestures at the worms, "—are Martian organisms. Biotechnology interface. It's how the Martians controlled their tripods, apparently. They use them for everything now. Recording messages. Phone calls. Weapons. You name it."

I lean over the worm and gingerly prod it. It lets out a high-pitched screech. I snatch my hand back and stare in shock as it starts to speak.

"*Good day to you. This is Jeremiah Slant.*"

I peer at the worm in amazement.

"*I am currently not in attendance, but if you leave a message the transcriber will record your details and I will endeavor to get back to you as soon as possible.*"

The worm falls flat onto its stomach once it finishes talking. I point at it with a trembling finger, then turn to Graves, eyes wide.

"If a talking worm gets you hard," says Graves, "then the definition of 'happy ending' is going to have to be seriously rethought when you see some of the other worlds out there."

"But . . . it talked."

"Yes. But it's not self-aware. It just . . . absorbs audio waves as imprints and sort of spits them out again."

I open my mouth to ask more questions, but Graves holds his hand up to stop me. "Enough. Find us some clothes. There should be false identity papers around too. And money. Don't forget the cash."

I briefly consider arguing, just for appearances, but decide against it. Instead, I open the closest door and find a small, functional bedroom. A metal-framed bed, a tall wooden wardrobe, and a nightstand with a Charles Dickens novel on it. *Drood*, the spine says.

I step inside and pull open the wardrobe, finding sets of clothes in various sizes, all stinking of mothballs. I search through them and pull out the first that looks like it will fit Graves. A tweed suit with herringbone pattern, a silk cravat, and a walking stick. I smile. That'll do.

I'm a bit pickier with my own clothes, eventually settling on a nicely cut suit with a large tweed trench coat and a scarf. Ooh! And a fedora! I've always wanted one of those. It's a proper one too, not those stupid trilby things that hipsters *think* are fedoras.

I change my clothes and perch the hat on my head at a rakish angle. I check myself out in the mirror mounted on the closet door. Looking damn good, even if I do say so myself.

I take another walk around the room. There's a painting on the wall that shows a scene from what I assume is the Martian invasion. Weird, tentacled creatures crawling out of metal tripods and attacking people. The Martians actually look a lot like those Cthulhu paintings I saw back in the manor house. They even have tentacles on their faces. I wonder if the Martians are this alternate's versions of the Old Ones.

But that isn't what draws my attention to the painting. It's the fact that it's protruding from the wall by a few inches.

I touch the frame, and it moves outward on a pair of hinges, revealing a hidden hole in the wall.

There are papers inside and old-fashioned booklets. Plus some huge money bills, folded together. I grab everything, shoving it all into my trench coat pocket. I head back into the sitting room, tossing Graves's clothes onto the chair.

"There you go."

Graves starts stripping off his clothes right in front of me.

I turn around while he gets dressed. "What's our first move?" I ask.

"I'll ask around. Check out the local library, try and get hold of our man in the city. I know where he works. We'll see how the spear sits in this world. Is it hidden? Has it been found? Do they think it's a true magical weapon? That kind of thing. You can turn around now."

I turn to face him. He's standing there looking proud of himself in his tweed suit and boots. He even has a gold chain and a timepiece.

"What do you think?"

"It's an improvement."

"Impossible. You can't improve on perfection."

I follow him out into the corridor and down a set of dark stairs. Graves pulls open the door to the outside world, letting in a blast of muggy air and the loud roar and babble of city life.

Graves disappears outside. I follow him, but I stumble to a stop as soon as I hit the street, staring around in awe.

Low, dark clouds mask the afternoon sky, black smoke spewing up from hundreds of chimneys. I cough, my lungs filling with smog and smoke as some kind of bus passes me by. But instead of wheels, it has legs, four on each side: scorpion-like, segmented, and tipped with claws. It skitters along the street, stepping over the tops of smaller vehicles.

Old-fashioned cabs are pulled by gray-white monsters, crosses between horses and spiders. I stare at one as it passes. Hundreds of tiny black eyes dotting the grotesque horse's head roll in my direction. One-man helicopters buzz through the air with people strapped inside, legs dangling as they bob and weave between soot-covered buildings, narrowly avoiding crashing into each other.

The folks on the sidewalks are just as strange. Some are taking huge beetles for walks, holding leashes to stop the insects from running away. Others have what appear to be cockroaches the size of cats mounted on their shoulders. The cockroaches wave their feelers in the air, reaching out to briefly touch each other if the people pass close enough. Other pedestrians talk into large, writhing worms, using them just like we use cell phones back home.

Buildings tower high into the smog, the majority of them easily as tall as the Empire State Building. A zeppelin breaks through the clouds, its sides covered with moving advertisements. It banks slowly and heads toward a tower, slowing down as it approaches in preparation for docking.

"You going to stand there with your mouth hanging open all day, or are we going to get some work done?" asks Graves.

§

An hour later I'm sitting at a corner table at a local pub, surrounded by thick clouds of pipe smoke and locals shouting for beer and whisky.

Judging by the clothes of those around me, I'd probably be classed as well-to-do, or at least middle class. I'm getting a few looks from the rougher patrons, but I ignore them. I have a cover story, after all. According to the papers I took from the safe house, my name is Atticus Pope, and I'm a consulting detective, which is the coolest thing I've ever been, *ever*.

And I'm quite liking the new look. The hat really suits me. I wonder if I can pull it off in LA. Probably not. I'd get beaten up by a group of anti-hipsters. Or mistaken for an aging barista.

Graves finally appears and sits down opposite me. He looks tired and grumpy.

"I'm a consulting detective," I say proudly.

"You're a cretin."

"What do your papers say you do for a living?"

"Doesn't matter."

"Come on. Tell me."

"Factory worker, if you must know."

I stifle a laugh. "One of the working class? Nice."

He leans over and takes my coffee, draining it in one go. He doesn't even wince, and it's bitter as all hell.

"Come on," he says, getting to his feet again. "We have work to do."

We leave the pub and head back out into the heaving throngs of people. "You found out where the spear is?"

He slaps a newspaper against my chest. I unfold it and read.

"Biblical Artefacts Collection to Debut at British Museum," I read. I skim through the first few paragraphs of the article, then stop when a familiar phrase catches my eye. "The controversial Vienna Lance, thought by some to be the mythical Spear of Destiny, is part of the collection and is on loan from the Weltliches Schatzkammer Museum in Vienna, Austria. The collection opens tonight with an exclusive showing unveiled by Her Majesty, the queen."

I fold the newspaper up again. "Well . . . that was easy."

"You think?"

"Sure. An hour of research and you have the location."

"But we don't have the spear. And if we know where it is, then so does Nyarlathotep and his little band of merry cultists. Never trust easy, Priest. It's a trick designed by life to give you hope before you fall on your ass."

§

A couple of hours later we're standing on the plaza outside the British Museum. A huge brass statue dominates the plaza: a British soldier on horseback shoving a lance through a Martian invader. Hidden spotlights illuminate the tall pillars that front the museum. Tuxedoed and bejeweled guests make their way to the entrance, making sure they're seen by any journalist watching from the sidelines.

"How do we get in?" I ask, nodding at the heavyset men guarding the door and checking tickets.

"We could shoot them," says Graves.

"Really? That's your first response? We can't just shoot innocent people."

"*God*, you're so boring. Fine. Wait here."

Graves disappears into the crowd, leaving me to idly watch all the transports arriving, some undulating along the sidewalk like caterpillars, others that kneel down with long legs so those inside the cabs can disembark.

Graves appears five minutes later and hands me a ticket.

"How did you get them?"

"Fastest fingers in the ICD."

We hand over our tickets to the security guards, studiously ignoring the man in the expensive suit frantically searching for the missing tickets that he insists were just right here in his pocket, he swears, while guards escort him and his partner away.

We climb the stairs and head through the wooden door into the museum itself. There are bright lights everywhere. A young guy in a tuxedo plays a violin off to our left, and a woman in an evening dress plays a harp to our right. The two instruments merge and complement each other perfectly, a finely tuned performance. I look at Graves, and he has his eyes closed, a small smile on his face as he listens.

He opens his eyes to find me staring. "I used to play," he says. "On my own world."

"Your own world?"

"You would have liked it. What was it you said you wanted? Mad cults and magic?"

"Something like that."

"That was my world. Floating cities, magical creatures. Wonderful place. Lots of annoying people, though. Kings and queens and the like. I hate royalty. Very annoying. I should tell you my theory that royalty are actually aliens come to the various alternates to—"

"So do we split up?" I say quickly. I really don't want to hear his theory on lizard people or whatever the hell it is.

"Yes. Probably wise. We can cover more ground that way."

So saying, he wanders away, grabbing a glass of champagne from a passing tray.

I make my own way through the crowds, listening to the gossip as I search for the spear.

". . . I say we should bring all our soldiers back from Mars. Bomb it from orbit. Only way to be sure . . ."

". . . Crossbreeding Martians and humans in a lab! That's what the journalist said. Of course, he was arrested for treason. Executed, I think."

I shake my head in bemusement. A few days ago I was worrying about finding a new job and getting kicked out of my dump of an apartment. Now I'm listening to high-society gossip on another world and trying to stop some sort of H. P. Lovecraft cult from getting its hands on the Spear of Destiny.

Life is weird.

"Welcome, ladies and gentlemen."

I turn to see an old guy wearing inch-thick glasses squinting at us from a raised dais at the opposite end of the hall.

"I would like to thank you all for coming to the opening of our Biblical Artefacts collection. We must give thanks to our comrades at the Vienna Museum for including us in their touring schedule. Champagne and nibbles are available. But please, do not over imbibe and fall over into our glass cases, no? Very bad form, that. It happened at our last launch. The prime minister was very apologetic, but that's a priceless Ming vase the world won't be seeing again."

Muted laughter from the crowd. The old man frowns.

"That was not a joke."

He waits while the laughter fades away into an uncomfortable silence. He surveys the crowd severely, then nods in satisfaction. "Good. And now, to officially open our exhibition, I give you Her Graciousness, Queen Victoria."

He steps aside, and the crowd applauds loudly as a huge brass-and-wood wheelchair trundles onto the stage. The chair is a monstrosity of design, gears and cogs in full view, whirring and spinning as the chair moves front and center.

But the woman in the chair itself . . . The queen of England? Gross. She looks . . . drained. Empty. A bag of wrinkles that has been poured into the chair. I assume it's nearly time for her rehousing, or whatever they call it. The one where her soul is moved into another body. But still . . . this is what she looks like after ten years? That's some serious wear and tear. Unless she goes on a year-long drug bender before the rehousing. No consequences if she has a new body, right? That's what I'd do.

It looks like she's fast asleep. One of the queen's handlers shakes her gently. She doesn't respond, so he has a quick, whispered conversation with another aide, then reluctantly pokes her in the ribs. Still nothing. The handler leans down, putting his ear next to her chest, then straightens up and gives her a hard slap.

The crowd gasps in horror as the queen starts awake, looking around in confusion. "Alfred?" She peers ahead, taking note of the crowd. "Alfred, we're not doing the swinger's ball till I've been rehoused, I told you that."

One of the handlers leans down again to whisper in her ear.

"What? Oh . . . Yes. Of course. I now declare this . . ." The handler leans down and whispers again. ". . . exhibition open. Jolly good."

She slumps back and closes her eyes. The chair reverses slowly along the stage and disappears into the wings again.

"Great speech," I say to a guy in a top hat standing next to me. "Very moving. Inspiring." I wipe my eye. "I told myself I wouldn't cry, but—"

Top Hat gives me a dirty look and moves away. I grin and head through the closest door, to the first room of the exhibition.

I move toward the glass display cases. The first contains two pieces of gray rock with Egyptian hieroglyphs on them. The little card pinned to the case says it's *The Autobiography of Weni*.

"Only two pieces of rock?" I mutter. "Couldn't have been very famous." Maybe he was the member of a boy band, the one who left before they hit it big.

I lean closer and read the rest of the description. Apparently it's the record of the earliest-known Egyptian military campaign. Boring. I move on to the next case. This one contains something called the Lachish Letters. *A series of letters written in Ancient Hebrew on clay ostraca*, says the card. I stare at the pieces of clay, then look to my right. There are another . . . sixteen cases of similar tablets.

There are no more cases in this room, so I move through the door into the next. This room is much larger. There's a huge skylight in the roof covered with a white dusting of snow.

I walk across the tiles, moving past a group of men and women huddled in a circle. One of them mutters as I pass.

"*Wir bewegen jetzt,*" he says. The guy looks really familiar to me. Slicked-back hair, small, round glasses. Why do I know that face?

"*Nein, wir sollen erst später auf heute Abend warten,*" replies a blonde woman.

I frown, trying to remember my high school German as I stop before the first case.

My eyes widen in shock. It's the spear. The Vienna Lance.

It's a bit of an anticlimax. It's not even really a spear. More of a spearhead. It's long and thin, about the length of my forearm, and has gold strips wrapped around the middle.

The Holy Lance, says the card. *Also known as the Holy Spear, the Spear of Destiny, and the Lance of Longinus. It is said that the Lance was used to pierce the side of Jesus as he hung on the cross.*

Wir bewegen jetzt. What the hell does that mean? We . . . go soon? No. That's not it. We go now? No. We *move* now. That's it.

And what had the woman said back?

Nein, wir sollen erst später auf heute Abend warten?

I close my eyes and concentrate.

We should wait till later tonight.

Hmm.

I turn slowly around.

The group is now staring at me. No—not me.

At the Holy Lance.

And that's when I realize why the guy looks familiar. I've only ever seen him in black-and-white photos or on the History Channel, but it's definitely him. Heinrich Himmler, head of the SS and Hitler's right-hand psycho.

I open my mouth to shout for Graves. I don't get the chance, because at that moment Himmler pulls a gun out and fires it into the air.

"Jeder cool, das ist ein Raubüberfall!" he shouts.

I concentrate. *Everybody be cool, this is a robbery.*

The guests scream and run for the exits. But there are so many doors, it quickly descends into a chaotic riot of people tripping over each other in their rush to escape.

I turn back to the case. No need for subtlety now. I pull out my gun and hit the case. The glass shatters, alarm bells erupting around me.

I grab the spear. The Germans are coming toward me, shoving guests out of the way. There are two doors leading out of the room. Both are blocked. Shit. Haven't really thought this through.

A terrific cracking sound echoes above the screams and the ringing of the alarm. Everyone looks up just as the glass in the skylight gives way, huge shards of glass and snow dropping to the tiles.

As well as some people, which is a bit odd.

They slow down as they descend, and I see they're attached to ropes. They're also wearing balaclavas and holding guns.

The Germans fire at them, the shots echoing loudly in the huge room. Some of the new arrivals flop loosely on their ropes then slam hard into the floor. Those that avoid the bullets land lightly and run straight toward me.

I run in the opposite direction, clutching the spear tightly. The Germans see me making off with their prize and come after me too, both sides moving at an angle, ferrying me into a corner of the room.

I try to zigzag toward the closest door, but a bullet hitting the tiles at my feet sends me scurrying back. I reach the wall. I whirl around, fire my gun at the closest attacker. He erupts into dust, and one of the others skids to a stop as he stumbles through the cloud that used to be his comrade. I shoot him before he can recover, but by this time one of the newer arrivals has reached me. He knocks my gun aside and then fumbles at my belt.

I look down in confusion. "What—"

I don't get a chance to finish, because at that moment the rope he clipped to my belt goes taut and I'm yanked forward off my feet.

I hit the floor and am pulled across the tiles, knocking assailants' legs out from under them, sending them tumbling like bowling balls. I scramble around at my belt, trying to unclip the rope, but it's too tight, and I'm still trying to hold onto the spear with my other hand. Graves runs toward me, firing at the Germans as he comes, but before he can get to me, I'm yanked up toward the broken skylight.

I don't make it. There is a flash of darkness, like smoke moving fast past my vision. A wet, guttural snarl and suddenly I'm falling, the rope severed by something razor-sharp.

I hit the floor. Chaos all around me. Screams. Panicked shouting. Gunshots. I wince and roll over, squinting through the running legs.

The Hounds of Tindalos.

They're galloping through the crowd, tearing people in half as they go, sweeping left and right with those talons on the back of their paws. Anything the claws touch liquefies. Skin, clothes, whatever. One lightly scratches a woman's face. She screams in horror as her skin melts like hot wax, dripping off her skull to pool in liquefied fat and blood at her feet.

Jesus. I search frantically for Graves. He's up against the far wall, firing randomly. (Hell, with all the different groups attacking us, he's bound to hit someone on the other side.)

I'm still gripping the spear tight against my chest. I loosen my grip, fumbling at my belt to try and unhook the rope. The screams and shouts are getting louder. I can smell blood and fear, the stench of bitter vomit and bile as the hounds slice open stomachs. Got to get out of here.

I look around. Graves has vanished. The only people remaining in the room are those fighting for the spear. Luckily they're distracted enough with each other that—

The spear is yanked off my chest. I look up in surprise and see one of the second group holding it in his arms, eyes shining, a huge grin on his face. He looks at me, then turns and runs directly for one of the windows.

I scramble to my feet. I finally manage to unhook the rope, then sprint after the thief. He's already used the spear to smash a window and has disappeared outside.

I follow, into the freezing winter night. I land on icy flagstones and slip onto my back. My breath explodes from me, and I find myself staring up into a bright, white light. I raise a hand, squinting against the glare, and see a huge zeppelin floating in the sky, black ropes snaking down from inside.

A noise to my right. I roll over and see the thief sprinting onto the main road. I push myself to my feet and follow.

No way that bastard is getting away with the spear.

CHAPTER ELEVEN

So here's the thing. When I set off after the guy who stole the spear, I really didn't expect to end the night chained to an altar in the ruins of St. Paul's Cathedral while my blood is about to be sucked from my body by a group of insane (and unfit) cultists frantically working foot pumps in an attempt to bring the rotting corpse of a Martian invader back to life.

But them's the breaks, honey.

And to be honest, it's actually a step up from some of the stuff that's been going down lately.

But let's backtrack a bit. After struggling to my feet outside the museum, I set off after the thief. The way through the streets is lit by gas lamps along the sidewalk and the spotlights of floating blimps displaying advertisements for child-friendly gin and cigarettes (that apparently cure ailments ranging from the common cold to a chest cough).

The thief leads me into a more run-down area of town. One moment I'm moving past swanky hotels and well-lit streets, and the next I'm in an alley leading into an abandoned street with not a single person to be seen.

Not even my target.

I stop moving, instincts warning that I might be about to get jumped. I wait, listen.

Nothing happens.

I move cautiously to the end of the alley and peer into the ruined street beyond. Some of the buildings are half-destroyed. Rubble and bricks strewn everywhere. It looks like a war has been fought here.

I frown at the sudden change in the city. I backtrack a bit and peer around the corner. Life and lights, people laughing and shouting. And behind me, darkness and ruin.

I head back to the end of the alley and see a flash of movement in the distance. My prey, about thirty feet ahead of me. I hurry across the pitted street, moving past the abandoned shops and shattered windows. I follow after him as he turns into a narrow street. I glance up at the sign.

Wawrick Lane.

I move through the darkness, eventually sensing a huge building to my left. I look up and realize it's St. Paul's Cathedral. Didn't Ash say this was ground zero for the Martian war?

Wait. Didn't she say something else? That this part of the city is supposed to be deserted because of the Martian germs and stuff? Crap. Am I going to get poisoned?

I pause and sniff the air. Seems normal to me. And I don't see anything floating around. Probably pointless worrying about it now. If there *is* anything in the air, I've already inhaled it.

I continue pursuing the guy as he moves along the west side of St Paul's, then turns left into the huge square in front of the cathedral. I hang back behind a stone fountain, watching as he jogs across the deserted concourse. He climbs the wide set of stairs, moving beneath the huge columned portico before disappearing inside the cathedral itself.

A blimp floats across the sky, throwing a huge spotlight down onto the dome. The place resembles an overgrown tumor, the church now almost hidden beneath carpets of red-and-black fungus.

I sigh. Graves isn't going to miraculously appear in the street and save the day. Suppose I might as well get this over with.

I sprint across the square, my trench coat flapping behind me in a manner I *know* looks incredibly cool. I move up the stairs and creep to the side of the open door. I peer inside.

Nothing.

I listen for a few seconds then get down onto my knees and slowly crawl into the cathedral. (Dignity? What's that?) The tiles are cold beneath my hands. My fingers push through fresh mud: the thief's footprints.

I wait for my eyes to adjust. The dim light from outside creeps in through the door. There are pews to either side, the path between them leading to a large central space beneath the dome.

The sound of footsteps echoes back to me. A match flares to life, and I see the thief standing before an altar on the far side of the central space. The golden light slowly increases as he lights a row of candles.

I crawl along behind one of the benches to the far wall. I pause when I reach a doorway off to the side of the main church. A set of stairs leads up.

I climb the stairs until I reach a wide gallery that circles the empty space beneath the dome. I get down on my knees and inch forward, staring down between the railings. The church is still dark, but the candlelight is expanding outward, touching the benches in front of the transept.

And . . .

And the thirty or so people sitting there watching the thief.

I swear under my breath. I hadn't noticed them from where I was crawling around on the floor. The people sitting in the benches wear dark robes, their faces rapt and attentive. They creep me out. None of them are talking. Just staring straight ahead.

Goddamn it. More cultists? Well, I suppose I did ask for them, didn't I? What's the saying? Be careful what you wish for?

"My fellow Dusters!" says the thief.

Dusters? What the hell are Dusters?

"We are close to bringing back our rightful rulers! We stand on the cusp of achieving our aims! Of resurrecting the Martian overlords. With this spear we can finally accomplish our task!"

So . . . what the hell do I do now? I thought I was taking on one thief, but now it's over thirty. This is a bit above my pay grade.

The thief has put the spear down on the altar while he talks to the other fanatics. Perhaps I can sneak around behind and take it? The other side of the altar is still wreathed in shadows. They won't be able to see me.

I start to shuffle backward. At the same moment, the thief leans around the altar and touches a candle to something on the floor.

The area behind the altar explodes into golden fire as oil poured into tracks hewn out of the tiles catches alight. The fire traces a path along the walls, illuminating the high ceiling, the nave . . .

. . . and the twenty-foot-tall body of a dead Martian strung up on a wooden cross.

I stop moving. That's not something you see every day.

It also blows my plan to hell. I shuffle forward again.

The Martian's corpse looks like a cross between an octopus and one of the Old Ones. Its skin is the same waxy beige color as those worms back at the safe house, but mottled with patches of black and green. Still, for something that must have been dead for nearly forty years, the corpse looks pretty damn well preserved.

"Are you ready, my fellow Dusters?" shouts the thief.

A sibilant sound issues from the Dusters sitting in the pews. I peer down at them and realize they're actually hissing.

"May earth return to the paradise it once was, the sibling of the great Mars. May humanity return to serve the true masters, the many-limbed ones."

"The many-limbed ones!" comes the chorus of replies.

The thief presses his hands together and bows slightly. "And now we must bring in the Blessed."

From somewhere off to the side a Duster appears and moves slowly toward the thief. She has something slung over her shoulder, and it takes me a moment to realize it's a thick chain, trailing back into the darkness.

I trace the links back until the first person emerges into the light, the chain attached to a collar around his neck. The Duster moves slowly forward, and I count ten men and women following behind. Their eyes are vacant, their heads lolling to the side as they drag their feet across the tiles. Drugged.

The thief gestures impatiently for the Duster to hand the chain over. He takes it from her and attaches it to a metal cog, threading the links carefully over the teeth before locking it down with a hasp and catch.

"Children of the revolution . . ."

I almost groan out loud. Where the hell is this guy getting his material? *The Mammoth Book of Clichés and Cults*?

". . . now is the time. Now is the time we bring back our true masters, and we bow down in subjugation and lick the horrible black stuff from between their toes. Will we shy away in disgust? No. We will lick it and enjoy it, because we are worms. Worms in the eyes of the true gods!"

The thief pulls on a lever, and the cog judders and spins into motion. The chain is pulled tight, the prisoners attached to it yanked high into the air so that they form a semicircle above the dead Martian.

Interesting. I wonder what's next. The orgy? That's what people like this usually do, isn't it?

But nope. I'm wrong.

The thief catches something trailing down from the prisoners. Some form of transparent tubing. I trace the tubing back and see it's attached to needles taped to the prisoners' arms.

The thief then attaches the end he is holding to a second, thicker tube that has been inserted into the dead Martian.

He isn't. Is he?

No.

Is he?

Is he . . . actually trying to give a forty-years-dead Martian a *blood* transfusion? With *human* blood?

The thief pulls out something from beneath the altar and puts his foot on it. The Dusters all do the same thing, and a second later they all start to furiously pump their feet up and down.

Foot pumps. Like the ones you get for pumping air into bike tires.

They're pumping the blood from their prisoners into a dead Martian using foot pumps.

I stand up and take out my gun. "All right!" I shout. "Everybody be cool and don't freak out or anything." The Dusters all stop pumping and look up at me. I point at the thief. "You, my man, have a lot of explaining to do."

"Who are you?" shouts the thief.

"My name is . . . Atticus Pope. And I'm here to put a stop to your freaky-deaky shit."

"No, you're not!" shouts one of the Dusters.

"I am!"

"You're not!"

"I am— Look, this isn't a goddamn pantomime. Just put your hands up, okay?"

And it's at around this time that a cold metal bar joins together (at rapid speed) with my soft, fleshy head.

And here we are. Me, groggily coming awake, hanging thirty feet off the ground, ten feet above an overripe Martian corpse, while a congregation of sweating and puffing Dusters tries to suck blood from my body.

"Pump!" shouts the thief. "Pump with all your might, my unfit children. We will bring our master back to life with our sweat and burning lungs. We will raise our Lord from the dead with our rapidly cramping leg muscles."

"You realize it was the bacteria you carry in your blood that killed them in the first place, right?" I shout down.

"Do not listen to the unbeliever. His blood will be the catalyst. His essence will spark the fire of life—"

"I mean, not *literally* your blood. But . . . you know . . . the bacteria here on earth. So, I guess the same bacteria is in our blood? I was never big on biology at school. I sat next to this amazing redhead. Sarah was her name. Very distracting."

"Silence!" screams the thief. "The donors do not speak."

"*They* might not, but I do. Guess you forgot to drug me, huh?"

The thief throws an accusing look at the woman who led the procession of prisoners into the church.

"Apologies, Most High Venerated One. I forgot."

"Don't take it out on her, HVO. Look, let's be serious here. You're not going to resuscitate this creature here. It was on the turn forty years ago."

"We've kept it on ice."

"Yeah, sure. For forty years? Come on. Bits of it must be dripping by now."

"Silence!"

This is getting stupid. How the hell am I supposed to get out of this? There's no blood in the tube dangling from my arm yet. But some of the other donors aren't so lucky. About half the tubes are dark red.

"Wouldn't this kind of thing be better if the blood came from the devout?" I call out.

"Uh . . . no," replies the High Venerated One. "Better if it's from an outsider."

"Why's that?"

"Um . . ." The HVO's leg moves up and down as he operates the pump. "It just is. It's the rules."

"Whose rules?"

"His!" He gestures at the Martian corpse.

"Right. Talks to you, does it?"

"Yes! He communicates with only me! And I pass his wishes on to the congregation."

"Of course you do. I—"

The doors at the far end of the church fly open, slamming hard against the walls. Leaves and old newspapers fly inside, slapping up against the pews.

Nothing else happens. The HVO frowns, stops pumping, then moves into the central aisle. He leans forward, peering toward the door.

The HVO turns to his second-in-command. "Doris, close the—"

Which is as far as he gets. Machine gun fire erupts outside the door, cutting the HVO to pieces. He screams and jerks, blood spurting from his body.

The acolytes scream and scatter from their pews. The muzzle flash comes closer as the gunmen enter the church, firing. They're all wearing long gray trench coats, with huge goggles covering their eyes. They fire at the fleeing acolytes, mowing them down as they try to escape.

I struggle against my chains, but it's hopeless. The attackers stop firing the machine guns, and I decide holding perfectly still might be the best thing to do right now.

The men in gray trench coats move through the pews, heading straight for the altar. The leader lifts his goggles, and I recognize him. Himmler again. He grabs the spear, shouts something at the others about . . . *Wewelsburg Castle*? I think that's what he says. And then they retrace their steps back out the church, pulling the doors shut behind them. Considerate. Bit of a chilly night, after all.

The silence after the gunfire seems like the loudest sound in the world. I stare around the church, at the dead bodies littering the pews, the blood dripping down the walls. I hear a slow, gurgling breath, then nothing.

Wonderful.

The doors slam open again. A shadowy figure appears in the entrance. Have they come back to finish the job?

"Is this going to become a habit?" calls out Graves.

I fight down the traitorous feeling of gratitude that wells up in me when I hear his voice.

"What?" I call back. "Being kidnapped by cultists while trying to clean up your mess? I really hope not."

"No. Me having to rescue you from your own stupid mistakes."

"Get me down and I'll show you a stupid mistake."

"What does that even mean?"

"It means I'm going to punch you again."

"Then why would I let you down?"

Crap.

"Ignore that. I was hit on the head. I didn't mean it."

"I don't believe you."

"It's true. Scout's honor."

"Were you a scout?"

"No." *Crap.* "Yes! Yes, I was!" I sigh, my head hanging against my chest. "Just get me down, Graves. It's been a long day."

CHAPTER TWELVE

Four hours later, Graves and I are flying above the German country-side in a passenger zeppelin, sipping dark coffee in our shared cabin while Ash gives us a lecture through our masks on what to expect in our near future.

(We didn't just abandon those poor bastards back at St. Paul's, though. Graves called the local police to come and pick them up, and we took them down from the chains, making them as comfortable as possible before getting the hell out of there.)

"Heinrich Himmler signed a hundred-year lease for the seventeenth-century Wewelsburg Castle in 1933," says Ash. Her voice sounds crackly and distant. *"Apparently Himmler originally wanted to turn the castle into a training facility for the SS."*

"Wanted to?" I ask.

"Yeah. He decided to aim a bit higher. See, most of the Nazi leaders believe in myths and legends. They think these magical tales dictate their future. Hitler is obsessed with magic, and Himmler decided to turn the castle into a training facility focused on the occult. He called the place the Grail Castle."

"Why?" I ask. "Is the Grail there?"

"No. But the Grail Order is another name for the SS. The castle is where Himmler plans on bringing all the mythical treasures they find. He believes that when the Nazis rule the world, these artifacts will give off a magical power that would help them rule. Himmler named many of the rooms after King Arthur and his knights. There's even a round table with twelve chairs around it."

"And the Spear of Destiny is one of these artifacts?" asks Graves.

"Yeah. Looks like they've been after the spear for years. Ever since Hitler saw it in a museum when he was younger. Some say that's why he invaded Vienna in the first place. To get the spear."

"So it's just a coincidence they came after it at the same time as us and Nyarlathotep?" I ask.

"Looks like it. The display at the museum was the perfect opportunity for all parties."

"Well I think it's just ludicrous," complains Graves. "How is a man meant to do his job when all these cults and secret societies constantly get in the way? It's inconsiderate, is what it is."

"Listen, I'm going to sign out," says Ash. *"I've already exceeded the contact time frame."*

"Thank you, my dear," says Graves. "We'll see you soon."

"Bye."

We take our masks off and stash them in our satchels.

"Any idea what Himmler is going to do with the spear?" I ask.

"Well . . . it's what? 1938? Almost time for the war. I imagine they're planning something they hope will destroy their enemies. Most likely some infernal rite will take place. Human sacrifice will no doubt figure largely. Lots of blood. Probably at midnight. And if there's a storm on the go then so much the better. Adds drama." Graves settles back in his seat and folds his hands over his large stomach. "Now be silent for a while. I want to get some sleep."

I let him sleep. After another hour or so of travel, the zeppelin docks at a place called Büren and we catch a train to the village of Wewelsburg.

Nothing much happens on the train, but I *will* say that traveling with Graves is just as bad as I thought it would be. He complains about *everything*. About the quality of the seating, the tea, the coffee, the food, the light that enters through the window, the constant rattling noise of the train going over the tracks. Everything.

Imagine every family trip you've ever taken with bored kids, then multiply that by a hundred. And I'm not talking family trips nowadays, with iPads and handheld games and portable DVD players. I'm talking an eighties trip. When all we had were books, comics, and your old man's cassette collection. The one that consisted only of Talking Heads, Dire Straits, Kate Bush, and Queen. *That's* what it's like traveling with Havelock Graves.

I've already spotted our destination as the train leaves the station in Wewelsburg. The castle sits atop a small, tree-covered hill in the center of the village, a triangular structure that looks more like an old hospital than a castle. I mean, it has the rounded towers capping off each of the three points. They even have crenellations. But it doesn't scream "Nazi castle" to me. It's the kind of place that would probably serve as a bed-and-breakfast back home.

Speaking of home . . .

"What time is it?"

Graves pulls out the ornate pocket watch from his waistcoat. "After three in the morning."

"What time is that in LA?"

"I have no idea."

"I need to say good night to my kid. I don't know when I'm going to get a chance to talk to her again."

"Out of the question."

"Come on. We just chatted to Ash. Can't the masks . . . forward my call or something?"

Graves frowns, then shakes his head. "No. I *do* have a phone, but it's for emergencies only."

"This *is* an emergency."

"Saying good night to your accidental offspring is *not* what I'd consider an emergency."

"Come on, Graves," I say. "Saying good night is about the only time I get to talk to her."

"Then you should have thought of that before you . . ." He waves a hand in the air. ". . . cheated on your spouse."

"I didn't."

"Became an alcoholic."

"I'm not."

"Developed a gambling problem."

"Again . . . no."

"My God, man! I don't care *why* you divorced. But I am sure it's because of something you did, so now you must deal with the consequences."

I spot a bench outside the station and head toward it.

"What are you doing?" demands Graves. "We have work to do."

I ignore him and sit down.

"Oh, so that's how it is?" snaps Graves. "What are we? Ten years old? Fine. You want to sit there all night, be my guest." He shivers and pulls his coat tighter. "Bit chilly though. Going to be a long wait."

I ignore him and stare at the building opposite us. He makes an exasperated sound and stalks off along the cobbled streets, muttering under his breath.

I wait. To give him his credit, he holds out for twenty minutes before stomping back and dropping a phone in my lap.

"Be quick," he snaps. "If anyone sees you with something like that around here we'll be investigated for retrophile offences."

"Thank you," I say quietly. I dial zero, then punch in the number for home.

Susan answers. "Hello?"

"Hiya, Suse. It's dad."

"Dad!"

"Just phoning to say good night."

"Mom's already read my story. She said you weren't going to call."

"Would I do that?"

"That's what I said!"

"It's fine. You can fill me in on what happened next time. You head off to bed now, you hear?"

"'Kay. Love you lots like jelly tots. Have lovely dreams. Have a nice night. Don't let the bedbugs bite. If they do, squish a few."

"Love you lots like jelly tots. Have lovely dreams. Have a nice night. Don't let the bedbugs bite. If they do, squish a few."

"Love you, Dad."

"Love you too, kiddo," I whisper, trying to disguise the lump in my throat.

She hangs up. I wordlessly hand the phone back to Graves, who—to his credit—doesn't say anything as he stashes it in his satchel.

"Can we go now?" he asks.

I get to my feet. "We can go now."

Graves strides away. "Consider that your tea break!" he calls over this shoulder. "You're on the clock till we finish the job. Understand?"

We make our way through the deserted village, catching sight of the castle between gaps in the buildings.

"I have to say," declares Graves as he takes long strides up the hill, "it's a bit of a letdown, no? The center of Nazi occult learning and this is the best they can come up with? You think the SS is being hit with budget cuts in this alternate? The place looks like a hotel, for God's sake. Incredibly disappointing."

We eventually leave the village behind and follow the cobbled street until we're about three hundred feet from the castle. We hide in a clump of pine trees to get a good look at the structure. The road carries on to a bridge that leads directly to the front door, a deep, arched entrance that cuts through the thick walls. Two guards stand by the doors. They're wearing thick gray overcoats, rifles held against their shoulders.

"What's the plan?" I ask.

"Well," says Graves, leaning casually against a tree trunk, "I thought we could sneak up, knock those two chaps—" he points at the guards, "—over the head, hopefully eliciting a comical reaction from at least one of them, then—"

"*Please* don't let the next words out of your mouth be along the lines of 'we steal their uniforms and sneak into the castle.'"

"Why not?"

"Because that kind of thing only works in movies. Incredibly bad movies."

"Nonsense. It's a solid plan."

"It's not! They'll see us coming and shoot us."

"They're not monsters!"

"They're the SS! Look up 'monster' in the dictionary and you'll see a *picture* of them."

"Oh, now you're just overreacting."

I look at him in amazement. "Do you know what Hitler did? How many people died?"

Graves waves a hand in dismissal. "Thousands, I'm sure."

"Thousands?"

"Keep your voice down," snaps Graves. "Or they might add two more to their count."

I snap my mouth shut and rub my temples. How many hours to go on this shift? All I want right now is my bed and a good night's sleep.

"Ooh!" says Graves. "What about waiting for the laundry service to come? Perhaps we could—I don't know, I'm just spitballing here—dress up as washer ladies and sneak in the service entrance?"

"Perfect."

Graves straightens up. "Really?" he says. "Because I've always wanted to dress up as a washer woman. I'll have to hide my masculine good looks, of course, but—"

"No."

"No?"

"No."

"But you said—"

"I just meant we should look for the service entrance. Try and sneak in around the back."

"You want us to skulk?"

"If it keeps us alive."

"Havelock Graves does not skulk! I refuse."

"Fine. I'll skulk; you can do . . . whatever it is you do. Let's just look for the service entrance first, okay?"

Graves stares at me for a moment, then turns and strides back along the road, keeping out of sight of the guards. I catch up as he hits the bend in the road and hurries across to the other side.

I join him at a low wall. There's a sheer drop on the other side down to the walls of the castle itself. No chance we can get down there. We'll slip and break our necks.

"I don't have time for this," says Graves. "If we don't get back soon I'm going to miss my soap operas. Wait here."

Without waiting for me to answer, he moves along the wall at a low crouch, heading toward the small bridge and the guards. He gets about twenty feet from them before the guards spot him. They call out, and Graves simply straightens up with his gun and shoots both of them, turning them into clouds of greasy ash.

I jog along the road to join him.

"See?" he says. "Easy."

He pushes the doors open, and we walk through the short tunnel into the inner courtyard. It's a lot smaller than you'd think from outside, a claustrophobic, cobbled triangle filled with old benches and wooden chairs. We try the first door we come to. Locked. Same with the second.

The third, however, gives us entry into the castle. We step inside, finding ourselves in a corridor lit by old-fashioned bulbs with glowing orange elements hanging from wires nailed into the mortar.

"So . . . where do we find these guys?" I ask. "We can't just wander around the castle."

"Interesting you should ask," says Graves. "I actually have a concrete plan about that."

"You do?" I ask, surprised.

"Yes. We find the kitchens."

"The kitchens?"

"The kitchens."

"Why?"

"Because culting is hungry work. These psychos get themselves worked up into a right mess, what with all the human sacrificing, blood pacts, demon summoning, and so on. They always like a good meal afterwards. Some red wine to wash down the blood."

I stare at him. "I never know when you're kidding around."

"I never kid around," Graves declares, striding along the passage. "Kidding around is for children and middle-aged, balding office workers with comical wigs and clown noses."

In the end we don't bother with the kitchens. Instead, we stumble upon a cultist wearing a black robe hurrying through the corridors. We follow after him, and he leads us through the passages and up some stairs into what I assume is one of the towers of the castle.

"Softly," whispers Graves as we climb.

I hear chanting as we climb, a soft, monotonous drone. The stairs end at an arched entrance leading into a circular room. Twelve columns circle an empty floor space covered with gray-and-white marble. Inlaid in the marble is a green, stylized sun.

Resting on the sun is the Spear of Destiny.

Behind the columns are twelve alcoves with windows looking out into the night. And standing in these alcoves are twelve figures robed in black. They're swaying back and forth, like trees in an autumn wind, chanting in a language I've never heard, filled with guttural consonants and not many vowels.

"What's going on?" I whisper.

"A summoning," says Graves in surprise. "It looks like they're trying to use the spear as an amplifier. Or perhaps a beacon."

"Can it do that?"

"I'm not sure," says Graves uncertainly. "I have to say I'm really not happy about this. I think this spear is a lot more powerful than we thought it was."

"Praise to thee," says a suddenly loud voice.

Graves and I both turn our attention back to the ceremony. One of the cultists has stepped forward, his arms raised into the air. He lowers his hood to reveal the face of Heinrich Himmler. Seems like ceremonies dedicated to the Old Ones are done in English.

"Ever Their praises," he calls out. "And abundance to the Black Goat of the Woods. Iä! Shub-Niggurath!"

"Iä! Shub-Niggurath!" repeat the other robed figures.

"What is Shub-Niggurath?" I whisper.

"One of the Old Ones," says Graves. "You know, like Cthulhu." He sounds puzzled.

"And they're trying to summon it?"

"They can't. There's no way they have the power. She's locked away in another dimension. Has been for millions of years. The Elder Gods made sure of that."

"Come to us, Shub-Niggurath," calls out Himmler. "Depart the Crimson Desert. Travel through the City of Pillars and the Diamond Fields of the Forgotten Constellation. I, Guardian of the Temple of the Goat with a Thousand Young, call upon you to help us wipe this world of unbelievers."

"What if they actually succeed?" I ask nervously.

"There's no way."

"Humor me. Can they control it?"

"Do you think an amoeba has the power to control you?"

"No."

"There's your answer."

"Come to us, Shub-Niggurath!" shouts Himmler. "Depart your home in the Absolute Elsewhere and heed my call."

"What's the Absolute Elsewhere?"

Graves clicks his tongue in irritation at me. "It's the name of the dimension where they are imprisoned. The Dreamlands."

The cultists start their chanting again. My attention is drawn to the spear. It . . . it's vibrating. And a purplish, black mist is forming around the head of the weapon, tendrils probing outward.

"Um . . ."

There's a silent explosion, as if all the air has been sucked instantly away and then thrust back in. My ears pop. The cultists cry out, stumbling back deeper into their alcoves.

A fierce wind springs up, pummeling against us all. I stagger back against the doorway, grabbing hold before I'm thrown back down the stairs. Graves is standing, legs spread apart, braced against the gusts. I squint, shield my eyes, peering into the center of the room.

The spear is spinning in the air, round and round, over and over. It moves faster and faster until it blurs, then faster again until it looks like a solid sphere of purple-and-black light.

The wind howls and shrieks through the room. The cultists are shouting in fear. And there's something else, a high-pitched whine just on the edge of hearing.

"What's going on?" I shout.

"I . . . don't know!" shouts Graves. "But I don't think it's good."

The sphere of light explodes into black mist, purple lightning flickering around it. The mist grows thicker, and I see tendrils of cloud reaching out, solidifying into oily, black tentacles.

One of the tentacles wraps around a cultist. He screams in horror as the tentacle yanks him up into the air, holding him above the black mist.

Then the mist changes. Snapping jaws appear, ten, twenty of them, serrated teeth biting at the air. Black slime drips to the marble, sizzling and smoking.

The mist parts even more, and a starscape appears behind it. Deathly black skies and glittering, unfamiliar stars, icy and terrifying.

The SS officer is yanked through the . . . portal . . . gateway . . . whatever it is. As soon as he is pulled through, his body convulses. His eyes bulge out, then explode. Blood and viscera freeze instantly, flying back through the gate to pepper the stone walls of the castle like bullets.

I push against the wind to where Graves is standing. He's leaning into the storm, staring at the spear that now hovers in midair below the tentacles and mist.

"This is bad!" he shouts. "Very bad."

"You think?" I shout back.

"That spear shouldn't have been able to do this. It's literally ripping open doors between our dimensions. Don't you understand how much power is needed for that?"

Obviously I don't, and he realizes it as soon as he utters the words.

"This kind of thing can only be done by the Elder Gods. Which means that spear was made by them."

"Kind of explains why everyone wants to get their hands on it then."

"We need to get the spear away from here. If Shub-Niggurath comes through, it will wipe out this entire world in a matter of days."

"You sure they won't be able to control it? Even with the spear?"

"Don't be absurd. It's a creature of the ice plains. Of the Forgotten universe. It's older than the sun and stronger than anything you or I could ever imagine. That creature has floated in endless night while millions of years pass it by, waiting for this very opportunity."

"So that's a no then."

In response, Graves pulls out his gun and aims it. He fires, narrowly missing the spear and hitting a cultist in the background, who screams and disintegrates into a pile of ash. Graves swears and aims again, but Himmler has spotted us and is running around the circle in an attempt to stop him.

"*Nein! Nein!*" he shouts as he draws closer.

Before he can get to Graves I step forward and punch him in the stomach. He doubles over, and I knee him in the face. His glasses go flying, and he staggers back—

A tentacle whips around his chest, and he's yanked back through the gateway into the dimension beyond. But before he can explode, the tentacle whips away from around his chest, sending him into a whirling spin that ends when huge, disembodied teeth clamp down onto his torso and bite him in half. His legs and pelvis fly into the air, only to be snapped up by another mouth. Yet another snaps at his feet, pulling and tugging like two dogs fighting over a bone.

"Hey. Hey, Graves."

Graves ignores me.

"Graves!"

He still ignores me.

"*Graves!*"

"*What?*" he shouts.

"I just killed Heinrich Himmler!"

"Congratulations. Now be silent!"

He aims his gun again and fires. The bullet hits the spear, but it doesn't disintegrate like the guy did. Instead, the spear starts spinning off-kilter, its orbit now cutting into the mist above it.

Shub-Niggurath senses something is wrong, and tentacles flick out of the gateway, wrapping around the twelve pillars. Graves shoots the spear again. Its orbit gets crazier and crazier. The high-pitched whine gets louder. Then another scream, coming from the gate. Shub-Niggurath moves forward, trying to pull itself into the room. Some of it succeeds, the mist solidifying into a pustule-covered bag with snapping mouths. I peer closer and see the pustules are actually little sacs, and there are smaller creatures shifting inside, floating in blood-tinged amniotic fluid.

Graves fires again, and this time the spear flies out of its orbit and rams itself straight into the wall only a few feet from me. The high-pitched screaming rises in volume. I reach out and grab the spear.

A jolt surges through my system, like an electric shock. I look at the spearhead, and it's like I'm looking through a window into the night sky.

Stars glitter in space. A vast figure trapped in a crystal prison blocks out the stars, a huge creature that sleeps, shifting slightly as if having a bad dream.

I hear a scream. I blink, shake my head, and the image is gone. I turn and see that a tentacle has wrapped around Graves's leg. He hits the floor and starts to slide backward, pulled toward the gate.

I let go of the spear and run to him. At the same moment a bright blue light flares to life in the room. I look around in shock and see a ragged tear appear in the wall just a few feet from the spear.

Graves is almost at the gate now, sliding across the marble tiles. I leap forward and grab his arm.

"Let go!" he shouts.

"What?"

"The spear! Get the spear!"

I look up. A figure steps out of the Rip. It's Dana. The woman who was with Nyarlathotep back at the house when he created the Hounds of Tindalos. She pauses to take the scenes of chaos in, calmly watching us fight against the tentacles of Shub-Niggurath.

She turns to the right and spots the spear embedded in the wall only a foot from her head.

"Let me go!" shouts Graves.

"I can't! You'll die!"

"I don't care, you buffoon. The spear is more important!"

Graves tries to pull his hand away. I hesitate, looking between him and the woman. No. I'm not going to let Graves be sucked into God knows where, no matter how annoying he is.

I pull my gun out and fire it at the woman. She ducks, then yanks the spear from the wall.

I fire the gun again, but she avoids it, turns to me with a huge smile and gives me a thumbs-up. Then she steps into the Rip, the tear slowly sealing itself behind her and winking out of existence.

Shub-Niggurath howls in fury, and the circular gate abruptly contracts and vanishes.

The tension disappears, and Graves scrambles to his feet, pulling the severed tentacle off his leg.

"You fool!" he shouts, rounding on me. "You bloody idiot! Do you realize what you've done?"

"Saved your life?"

"Doomed the multiverse to horror beyond all imagining."

"Well . . . maybe. But I still saved your life."

A clicking sound comes from the other side of the room. Graves and I turn to find the surviving cultists aiming machine guns at us.

"Mask," says Graves, unclipping his own mask and placing it over his face.

I scramble to follow just as he opens up a Slip and the machine gun fire starts. I dive through the door, the stone where I had just been standing now peppered with automatic gunfire.

CHAPTER THIRTEEN

It feels like days since we were last in the Department Zero offices, even though it's been under twenty-four hours. I'm utterly exhausted, stressed, confused, and annoyed. I pour a mug of tepid black coffee with shaking hands and down it in one go, filling the mug a second time and taking it back to my desk.

Graves is deep in conversation with Ash.

"Shub-Niggurath?" asks Ash.

Graves nods.

"*The* Shub-Niggurath?"

Graves nods again.

"No. It couldn't be."

"I know what I saw."

"But . . . it's not possible. The Old Ones are in prison. Put there by the Elder Gods. And you're saying some . . . sub-standard Nazi cult was almost able to free one of them?"

"That's exactly what I'm saying."

"But . . . the kind of power needed to do that is . . ."

"Incalculable?"

"Unheard of. I mean, we're talking Elder Gods here." Ash raps her knuckles on my mask, which sits atop a pile of dog-eared files. "The same as these."

"I know."

"How? What is the spear? Some kind of key?"

"I don't know."

"And the second item Nyarlathotep mentioned? The Jewel of Ini-taya?"

"No idea." Graves groans and stares at the ceiling. "I'm going to have to take this upstairs. Goddammit."

"They might know what to do."

"No they won't! They're all imbeciles. They're going to run around in a panic and blame me." He slams his hands onto his desk. "I just want my job back! This was supposed to get us back upstairs."

"If it was just an average cult trying to summon the Old Ones' minions to fight a war for them, then sure, stopping them might get us back in the ICD. But, Graves, this is bigger than us. This cult nearly succeeded in bringing a Level One entity into the multiverse. That's what this whole place—" she gestures around us, "—is set up to *prevent*. I mean, if Shub-Niggurath actually somehow . . . came through, the Company would have had to nullify that entire alternate. That's not the kind of thing you can keep to yourself."

"What do you mean, nullify?" I ask.

"Wipe out," says Graves. "Eradicate. Destroy."

I stare at him. Then at Ash. "Are you saying you would destroy an entire *universe*, worlds and worlds, if that thing made it through?"

"We wouldn't have a choice," replies Graves. "If even one of the Old Ones makes it through into three-dimensional space, they can then hop between alternates as easy as we can step through a door. Universes would fall like dominoes. One after the other, devoured by the Old Ones until nothing was left."

"But still . . . destroying an entire alternate? You're talking billions of lives."

"Trillions," says Graves. "But if you have a better method of dealing with ancient alien beings like the Old Ones, please let us know. I'm sure we'd all love to hear it."

He stares at me, but I don't have anything to say.

Graves sighs and gets to his feet. "Right. I'm off to make my report. You two, go home, get some sleep. Hopefully tomorrow we all still have jobs."

§

The blue light winks out behind me, and I'm standing in my bedroom once again. I take the mask off and drop it on the chest of drawers. I wince and roll my neck, then stretch, hearing vertebrae clicking all down my spine. If every day is like today, I'm going to rack up some serious therapeutic massage bills.

I grab a beer from the fridge and slump into the plastic chair on the balcony, staring out over LA. It feels weird to be looking out over normal houses, the traffic powered by combustion engines and not walking around on alien/clockwork hybrid legs.

An old Cadillac drives slowly along the street. I frown and lean forward. Is that . . . is that the same goddamn Cadillac? The one that's been following me? The car passes by, and I relax. It's not the purple-haired chick. It's some guy who looks like a salesman from the fifties.

I sit back and shake my head in bemusement. Definitely paranoid. I sip my beer. Three days. Three days I've been at the job. I sometimes wonder if it's even real. If I haven't gone mad. Locked up in some loony bin hallucinating all of this while I bang my head against a padded wall.

I stare out over the twinkling lights. It's after midnight. A long day. I should get to bed. But I stay where I am, and my eyes grow heavy.

§

I open my eyes to find myself standing on muddy shores, cold stars twinkling and glittering above me.

I look around. The dark sea froths and surges, the waves moving in and out in an unsettling manner. It takes me a moment to realize the waves and the sounds are moving in reverse, like movie footage played backward.

I turn back. A vast city towers above me, a city of hard angles and stone structures. I walk slowly forward, my feet sucking and squelching in the mud, as if it's trying to pull me down into its slimy depths.

The structures of the city are alien and unsettling. Not buildings as such, but structures that twist and turn in geometric angles, none of which make sense. My brain hurts when I look at them. They're covered with alien hieroglyphs and carved bas-reliefs, the images showing nightmarish creatures doing things I can't make sense of.

A huge tower dominates the city. A black slab of glassy rock that soars up into the sky, so high it seems to be piercing the underside of the stars.

I feel sick as I look at it, my insides trembling, my brain switching over to fight or flight. I don't understand the reaction, just that my body is responding in a primitive, animalistic way that I can't control.

I don't know what to do. I look around, wondering how to escape this place.

Then I hear the slithering, sucking sound of something approaching. Lots of somethings. They emit a strange whistling sound, and even though I have no idea what they are, I know I have to get away.

I turn and run back to the beach. My feet sink into the mud, down to my shins. I struggle, but I can't get them out. The slithering sound gets closer, the whistling louder. I use my hands to try and pull my feet out, but it's hopeless.

I turn to face my pursuers—

§

I awake with a start, looking wildly around. I relax when I see my familiar balcony, and hear the nighttime sounds of LA traffic.

Just a dream. I must have dozed off. I stand up and stretch. Time for bed, I think.

I freeze.

There's a blue light coming from inside my apartment. The same light that accompanies a Slip through to Wonderland.

Graves, maybe? Coming to talk about the case?

I almost stride into the apartment, demanding to know what the hell he thinks he's playing at, but I stop myself. My old training is kicking in again, making me uneasy. Graves wouldn't do this. He'd just wait till morning.

I press myself up against the wall and peer slowly past the sliding doors. It's dark in the lounge. The glow is coming from my bedroom, the anchor point. I chew my bottom lip nervously. What do I do?

Then I see the tactical team entering the lounge and fanning out around the furniture. Dressed in black, faces covered, holding the ICD freaky-ass versions of tactical assault weapons against their shoulders as they check for threats.

I don't move. What the hell is going on here? Are they from ICD? Or are they members of the cult? Have the bad guys found out where I live? Do they want to put a stop to the investigation?

I look around. The only weapon I have is an empty beer bottle, sitting on the tiles next to my plastic chair. I check to make sure none of the intruders are looking through the door, then slowly crouch down. I reach out, trying to keep hidden. The bottle is too far away. I lean slowly forward, fingers stretching out. I touch the glass . . .

. . . and knock the bottle over. It topples and hits the tiles. I snatch my hand back and flatten myself against the wall as the noise rings out. No way they didn't hear that.

Sure enough, I sense movement behind the glass and glimpse a shadow approaching the half-open door. I tense as the bone-colored gun barrel appears, followed by gloved hands and then the body.

I grab the gun, yank it forward, and pull it from the guy's hands. He staggers, falling against the railing with a shout of surprise. His cry alerts the others. They rush toward us. Someone fires. The glass of the sliding door turns to dust. Another shot. I duck against the wall, and the bullet hits the guy I stole the gun from. He dissolves into greasy ash and drifts away.

I fire wildly into my apartment from behind the cover of the wall. A scream. Shouts of confusion. I keep firing, realizing I have to move now. Staying here will just give them time to get to cover, and then we'll have a standoff. No way I'd get out of that.

I take a deep breath, let off another barrage of invisible bullets, and dive into the room. I slide across the tiles and hit up against the back of my couch. On the other side is the coffee table and my flat screen. I hope no one's damaged it. I can't afford a new one.

Everyone's gone quiet. I take deep, calming breaths, then get to my knees and carefully shuffle along behind the couch.

It's still dark. The only light is coming from the Slip in my room—a blue, pulsing glow. The intruders are positioned between me and the front door, which means . . . the only way out is through the Slip. To wherever the bad guys came from.

Which is stupid in so many ways, but at least it means I won't get cut down in my own lounge.

I pause and listen. Still no sound. Nothing at all. These guys are good. My bedroom door is about ten feet away. Ample time for them to riddle me with bullets. This isn't a movie. No way I'd make it.

I need a distraction. This isn't a movie, sure, but distractions always work, right? I flatten myself down and peer under the couch. Lots of silhouettes. I feel around. An old pizza box. When did I have pizza last? A month at least. Gross. My hand hits something plastic. A game controller. That will do. Heavy enough. I pull it back, hesitate. Controllers aren't cheap. I don't really want to break it. I drop it and grab the pizza box instead. That will make enough noise.

I slide it out then throw it Frisbee-style against the far wall.

Shouted orders and the low, sonic-cannon sound of the guns firing. I scramble to my feet and sprint to the bedroom door. A shout behind me. I dive to the floor then hit up against my bed as the bullets go *phip-phip* into my wall, sending black veins crawling up the plaster.

I scramble to my feet, grab my gun, then my mask, and ram it onto my face. I leap through the Slip and run, ignoring the long corridor filled with sliding tentacles and freaky shadows.

I sprint as fast as I can. The exit Slip appears ahead, and I burst through—

Into Wonderland.

I stumble to a stop and pull my mask off, looking around in shock. This can't be right. It has to be some kind of mistake.

But I know it isn't. I'm ignoring the truth here because it's too big to face up to.

The people trying to kill me came from here. Wonderland.

ICD.

Fuck.

I realize I'm still standing in the arrivals room. Which means my attackers are going to be right behind me.

I run again. Straight for the elevators. I jab the button. Keep hitting it over and over till the doors open. I leap inside and stab the button for Department Zero.

The elevator takes ages to descend. I'm getting more and more panicked as I drop, wondering just what the hell is going on. A hundred different scenarios run through my head, none of them making any sense, and all of them feeding my paranoia and fear. Is my family safe? If the intruders know where I live, do they know where Megan and Susan are? My stomach twists with terror at the thought, and I can't shake it. What if they're there right now? At my old house.

The elevator bings, and the doors open. I see the muzzle flash and hear the explosion of gunfire at the same time. Proper gunfire. Old school. I dive forward, landing hard on the floor behind a desk. They're here too. Christ. What have I done? Why are they after me?

"More?" screams a familiar voice. "Bring it then, you curs! I'll take you all on!"

I frown. "Graves!"

A pause. "Is that you, Harry?"

"Yes! The hell you shooting at me for?"

"I thought you were one of them!"

"I'm standing up now," I call. "Don't shoot, okay?"

"I can't promise anything."

"Graves . . ."

"Fine. I promise."

I slowly stand up. Graves is hiding behind a metal filing cabinet, his gun leveled at me.

"What's going on?" I say, moving toward him. I stop, then turn back to the elevator just as the doors are closing and kick a wastebasket between them so they can't close on me.

"Why are you here?" demands Graves.

"Someone just tried to kill me. They came through a Slip. Into my home!"

"You too?" Graves lowers the gun and moves back to his desk. I follow him. My steps falter when I see the bodies lying on the floor, all of them wearing the same black tactical gear.

"Are they . . . ?"

"Dead? Yes."

"Did you . . . ?"

"Again, yes."

"Shit, Graves. This is bad. I think they're . . ."

"ICD? I know."

"You know? How?"

He stops rifling through the papers on his desk then looks at me as if I'm insane. "Because I recognize their faces."

"And you still killed them?"

"They had masks on! I didn't know who they were when I fought back!"

"Right. Sorry. So . . . what do we do? It's a mistake, right?"

He carries on scrambling through the papers on his desk. "No. We've been Lizbeth'd."

I pause. "What?"

"Lizbeth'd. Elizabeth MacLeod. An ICD agent. She was declared rogue a hundred years ago. She ran away and took a posse of agents with her. She was hunted down. The name just stuck."

"And?"

"And?"

"What happened to her?"

"She was killed! What do you think?"

"Right. And this is happening to us because . . . ?"

"I have no idea. The memo didn't say."

"You . . . got a memo saying you were going to be hunted down?"

"No, idiot. I hacked into the Inspectre's e-mail. Ages ago. It was helpful having access to the high-level stuff."

"Um . . ." I glance nervously at the elevator. "I didn't kill mine. I think they might have followed me back."

"Undoubtedly."

"So . . . you got a plan? You know what's going on?"

"What's going on is that after you went home for the day I reported to the higher-ups about what happened. I made my report. About the spear. About Nyarlathotep. About them summoning Shub-Niggurath."

"And?"

"And then one hour after I made my report we were declared rogue and someone tried to kill me. And you."

"Shit." I remember something. "Ash—"

"She's fine. I checked. I didn't mention her in my report. She wasn't with us."

I nod. "Okay. Good. So . . . what are you saying here?"

"You know what I'm saying."

"That someone in the ICD is in league with Nyarlathotep?" I scan the deserted office, my mind racing. "That they want us to stop chasing the spear?"

"And the Jewel of Ini-taya. Two sets of coordinates, remember? The spear is a powerful artifact, more powerful than I knew. I assume the jewel is the same. That massacre at the motel where I first met you? The coordinates? It's all been about these two items. It's why Nyarlathotep and his cronies were so keen to break cover. I always wondered. Coming out into the public eye the way they did . . ." He shakes his head. "I should have known it was big." Graves cries out in triumph and waves a file in the air.

"What's that?"

"The coordinates. The ones from your head. And Ash's research into the next world."

I start to ask him what he plans on doing, but he holds his hand up to stop me. He tilts his head, listening. I do the same. I can hear the trundling arrival of another elevator.

"Time to go!" shouts Graves. He grabs his mask, rams his own shotgun into his pants, and starts running for the bank of elevators. I follow, but we're not even halfway there when the elevator doors open.

Graves fires wildly with the handgun he's still carrying. The guys in black scramble for their lives, some ducking back into the elevator, others diving for cover behind the desks.

Graves keeps firing until his gun clicks empty. Then he throws it in their direction. I hear a clunk and then someone shouts.

"Ow!"

The silent bullets start peppering the area around us, turning parts of the office into entropy and dust, black veins creeping up the walls. I overtake Graves, slipping past his heavier frame.

"Hey!" he shouts. "I'm the senior officer here! I go first."

"Sorry, man. Youth before bulk."

I get into the elevator and hit the button for the arrivals room. Graves joins me, and we try to hide behind the doors as our attackers pop up from behind the desks and start firing into the elevator.

The bullets hit the wall behind us, the black veins crawling up to the ceiling, turning the metal to rust. The doors slide shut, and we start to rise.

"They'll follow us up," says Graves.

"So we've got ... what?" I ask. "Twenty seconds' lead?"

"Maybe thirty, if their elevator already started back up."

"So what *is* the plan?"

"The Jewel of Ini-taya. If it's even remotely as powerful as the spear, we need to get it before they do."

"But they're not connected. They're two separate things."

"The Spear of Destiny is not just a spear. It's *disguised* as a spear. Whatever it is, it's Elder Gods magic and somewhere along the years someone made it look like its current form. The jewel will likely be the same."

"Okay ... and? What do you think they do?"

"We know what they do. The spear was powerful enough to almost free Shub-Niggurath. We know what Nyarlathotep wants. To free all the Old Ones, to bring Cthulhu out of his underwater prison."

"And you think that's what these two things will do? If they're brought together?"

"That's what I *fear* they will do. If Nyarlathotep succeeds, then they will take over again. Understand? You. Me. This place. Your family. All of it. Everything. The Old Ones will devour it all."

"And the ICD knows this?"

"*Someone* does."

"Are we talking conspiracy here?"

"That's exactly what we're talking." He swings toward me, eyes wide. "I bet the Inspectre is involved! It makes perfect sense."

"*How* does it make sense?"

"The man's a complete buffoon!"

"That's not a reason. Sure you're not letting your personal feelings get in the way?"

"My personal feelings have nothing to do with the fact the man is an odious oink. He's involved. I feel it in my blood."

The elevator crawls up past the various departments and stops one floor below the gate room. The doors ping open, and we wait, just in case anyone wants to shoot us in the face.

Nothing happens.

"Take a look," says Graves.

"You take a look."

"I'm the boss. I order you to take a look."

"Not a chance. I don't think they've even started my medical coverage yet."

"Gads, you remind me of someone I used to work with. He was just as annoying. Short, too."

"I'm not short. I'm average height."

Graves shuffles toward the doors. "Keep telling yourself that." He takes a deep breath, then darts his head out into the hall and back in again.

"Anything?"

"No."

He steps out into the corridor, breaking into a jog. I follow, passing door after door as we head toward the stairwell at the far end of the passage.

Graves stops before the door and looks at me expectantly.

"What?" I ask.

"Your turn. I did the elevator."

"Oh for . . ." I lean past him and yank the door open. Nothing. Just an empty stairwell. "Happy?"

"Ecstatic." Graves pushes past me and climbs the stairs. I follow behind him, glancing across the graffiti that has been scribbled on the institutional green walls. There is a surprisingly large amount involving Graves.

"People don't really like you, do they?" I ask as we round the bend in the stairwell and come into view of the door to the penthouse level.

"I'm not here to make friends."

"Just as well."

Graves ignores me and gently pushes the door open. I strain to hear anything, but there's just silence. Graves pushes it wider and peers out.

A gloved hand reaches around the gap and puts a gun against the side of his head.

I react instinctively, slamming my foot hard into the door. It hits against Graves's assailant, sending him staggering back. Graves is still in the process of turning around in shock, and I lunge through the door and punch the guy hard in the stomach. He doubles over, his breath sucked from his body, and I bring my knee up as hard as I can, hitting him in the chin.

His neck snaps back, and he slumps against the wall. I turn around and face an amazed Graves.

"What?" I say. "I'm just getting real goddamn tired of people shooting at me today, that's all."

We make our way to the glass doors that lead into the penthouse offices. We crouch down and peer inside. Steel desks, computers showing screensavers. Abandoned. Stretching away into the distance.

"They've cleared out the room," whispers Graves.

"What's the plan?"

"We sneak in, enter the coordinates, and run to the Slip."

"That's it?"

"That's it."

Graves slowly pushes the doors open and crawls into the room. I follow, and we move slowly through the maze of desks, heading closer to the rows of pedestals where the Slips appear. Some of them are empty, others are pulsing a light blue color, as if they're in low power mode.

My senses are stretched, trying to pick up any sound of movement. The scuff of a shoe, an indrawn breath. But I hear nothing. Either these guys are really good or they all went downstairs looking for me.

Graves stops before a desk and slowly pulls the keyboard onto the floor. He types in the coordinates, pushing the keys as lightly as possible. Then he looks at me.

"Wait," he whispers.

He hits Enter, and one of the gates at the far end of the room flares to life.

Immediately, the room is a cacophony of shouts and orders. The leader of the tactical force orders his men out of hiding and into action. I look at Graves questioningly, but he's typing rapidly again. He hits Enter and starts crawling toward a second Slip that has opened up, this one close to us and far away from the first.

We make it to the Slip without bullets riddling our bodies. We put on our masks and crawl through the gate, into the tunnel of endless midnight, going God knows where in order to save the multiverse from being devoured by the Old Ones.

Just another day at the office.

CHAPTER FOURTEEN

We exit the Slip into a solid wall of heat.

I stagger into a cramped room, my breath sucked from my body. It feels like I'm suffocating, like I'm trying to draw something heavy and thick into my lungs.

My vision is weird, a green tinge over everything. It takes a moment for me to realize it's because the mask has gone silent. No information scrolls past my eyes.

I touch the catch beneath my chin and release the mask. Graves does the same.

"We've been cut off from Wonderland," he says.

"Completely?" I ask.

"Is your mask working?"

"No."

"Then yes, completely."

"What do we do?"

Graves flops down in a wooden chair and rubs his face. "I don't know."

I stare around the room. It's cluttered with old, dusty furniture. "Is this a safe house?"

"Yes." Graves throws the file at me and closes his eyes. "We'll have to do this old school. Read the briefing to me."

I open the file that Ash prepared. "The world of Imeskal, also known as the Sundered Lands."

"Catchy name," says Graves.

"Imeskal is a Class Z world." I pause and look at Graves. "What does that mean?"

"Don't cream your pants, but it means a magic-based world."

"Seriously?"

"Seriously."

"Like . . . Conan-type magic? Priests and wizards and stuff?"

"I don't know. You haven't read the briefing to me yet."

I go back to the file. "Religion is based around the Old Ones. The priests of the Old Ones rule over the monarchy and the government on all pedestals." I pause and look at Graves. "Pedestals?"

"Just read! My God!"

"Thousands of years ago, a war between the priests of different Old Ones ripped the world apart. The crust of the world was eaten away, leaving behind pedestals of land supported on huge pillars of rocks." I grin at Graves. "That is *so* cool." I go back to reading. "The Abyssal Sea is a world-spanning ocean, and the pedestals of land—some continent-sized—rise up from these waters. Various races and cultures have sprung up over the millennia, corrupted by the magic that was loosed in the war, much like radiation would change people in a Class A reality."

I turn the page, but there's nothing more. "That's it."

"That's it?" Graves opens one eye and sighs. "Not much help, is it?"

I put the file down. Rickety shutters block the windows. I pull them open. Blinding light barges into the room. I squint and peer outside. A dry landscape. Rocky plateau. A dark blue sky with distant thunderheads building up on the horizon.

I frown in confusion at what I'm seeing. The afternoon sun has dropped behind something in the distance. It looks like a huge land mass, a spire with a massive flat top, gold-limned and silhouetted against the sky like a thirty-mile-high letter T. I shift my gaze farther back. I can see more of these land masses—the pedestals mentioned in the briefing—in the distance, still shining in the summer sun, colossal pillars of rock supporting their own plateaus of land.

How goddamn cool is this? A real magical world to explore. I can't keep the grin from my face.

"You realize if we don't find the jewel all this—" Graves waves out the window, "—will be destroyed."

"I know."

"And our world. And *all* the worlds."

"I know."

"Then stop smiling."

"I can't."

"You can't? We're trapped here. You understand? Cut off from help. Cut off from the Slips. Stranded on a world we know practically nothing about. We have no guide, no ICD resources, nothing. We're on our own."

"Right."

"And you still won't stop smiling?"

"Nope."

"Wonderful," says Graves. "I'm working with an imbecile. Right then. I suppose our first task will be to try and find out where Nyarlathotep and his hounds have gone. They came through here about . . . what? Two days ago? They might even have this jewel by now."

"Wouldn't we all be dead then?"

"Good point."

He crosses to the door. He pulls it open to reveal a small, filthy man standing there, his mouth a wide O of surprise as he reaches for the door handle.

"Are you Jacob?" demands Graves.

The little man hurriedly performs a clumsy bow.

"Begging yer pardon, milord, but yes I am. I was tendin' the drifters and didn't hear ye arriving."

"Milord?" Graves frowns suspiciously. "How long have you been here?"

The small man squints his jaundiced eyes. "About . . . ooh, fifteen years?"

"Fifteen years? That's too long."

"That was my thinking too," says Jacob. "At first. Then after the first five years I just stopped wondering. You're the first person to come through since I've been here. Have to say I'm a bit surprised the gate still works."

"Right," says Graves. "Well it does . . . and here we are. Important ICD business. Can you take us into the closest city?"

"Of course! Come, come." He turns and leads the way through a narrow passage. "Misha will look after you."

Misha? I look at Graves, but he just shrugs and quickens his steps to catch up with the surprisingly spry Jacob.

"Who's Misha?" I ask.

"Misha. She's my special girl. Mothered all my drifters, she did. 'Course, she's gettin' on a bit now. Reckon one of her brood'll have to take over soon."

Which leaves me no closer to understanding.

Jacob arrives at a rickety door and pushes it open, letting the harsh afternoon light into the corridor. We follow him outside onto a small lip of land barely ten feet wide, leading to what looks like the edge of a cliff. I walk forward and peer over the edge. It's disorienting, but I realize I'm standing on one of those strange pieces of land balancing on top of the thousand-foot-high spires of rock.

I just catch a glimpse of a raging ocean far below, half-obscured by mist and clouds. I take a hasty step back, vertigo causing my head to spin. Jesus. How high up are we?

Traveling along the edge of the pedestal is a wooden framework bolted into the rock. Small piers travel out from the framework directly into thin air, supported underneath by slanted iron pilings driven into the rock.

But it's the sight of what is tethered to the framework that draws my attention. One of the strangest creatures I've ever see. A huge . . . I don't know what it is. A cross between a jellyfish and a tick. It bobs in the air like a balloon, a huge, bulbous thing about ten feet high, hanging from a cable that disappears out over the pedestal and into the clouds. The creature shimmers in the light, green and purple hues sparkling in a pearlescent sheen.

"This is Misha," says Jacob proudly, gesturing to the floating creature. "She'll take you across. She's the only one charged up, you see."

He gestures to the left where I see more of the creatures. But these ones aren't floating. They're about a third the size of Misha and sit in support frames, their skin thicker and less translucent.

"Why are they so small?" I ask.

"It's the sun," says Jacob eagerly. "The beasts absorb sunlight and fill with gas." He points at something I hadn't noticed, a man-sized slit at the back end of Misha.

"That is a birth sac," says Jacob. "What happens is, they reach sexual maturity and begin absorbing energy from the sun, you follow? They convert it to gas and float up." He waves into the sky. "It's a strange cycle. I've never been able to figure out what the point is. The higher they float, the more energy they convert into gas, and the higher they float. At a certain level eggs start gestating in the sac."

"These are Flying Polyps," says Graves. "The Old Ones used them as hunting beasts. They can channel the wind, use it to suck their prey toward them. Or pin them against the walls."

"They're not like that here," says Jacob defensively. "They're gentle animals."

"Gentle? They're mindless killers!"

"These ones have adapted. Come, come. I'll show you." Jacob steps onto the pier and then heads inside the slit on the back end of the creature. I look at Graves. He shrugs and follows.

I hesitate. Because, come on. Entering a floating creature through its vagina was *not* in my job description.

Graves pops his head out, and I can't shake the thought that it looks like he's being born. "Come on!" he snaps. "We don't have all day."

Nothing else for it. I enter through the slit, stepping gingerly into cool darkness. I look around in surprise. It doesn't look like the inside of a creature at all. More like a cockpit. The floor is made of the same bony material as the ridges around the slit, but there are winches and controls mounted on the walls.

Jacob reaches past me and releases the mooring rope, talking as he does so.

"After her eggs absorb enough sun, they rip this opening in the back here and pop out, drifting away to start their own lives. The mother—" he reaches out and pats the wall closest to him, "—keeps sucking up sun until—*bang*!" He claps his hands together with a sudden smack. "They explode." He squeezes past us and spins a small wheel. With a light swaying motion, the drifter turns slowly on its axis.

"People prefer to see where they're headed instead of watching what they leave behind," explains Jacob.

The drifter turns full circle. I can now see blue sky through the slit. Jacob gently turns another wheel, and with a slight lurch we begin moving along the cable that disappears into the distance.

"What we did," says Jacob, "is steal the idea from the slyth. The slyth are this world's version of . . . I suppose we'd call them elves."

I turn to look at Jacob. "Elves?"

"Sort of. They're thin and have pointy ears? But their skin gets translucent as they get older. So the oldest of them are see-through. You can see their hearts pumping, their lungs drawing breath . . . everything."

"That is *so* cool," I say.

"No it's not," says Graves. "And stop saying 'cool.'"

"You say groovy."

"Groovy is a timeless word."

"It's really not."

"It is. And before you ask, no, you cannot see these slyth creatures."

"Oh, come on! Why not?"

"Because we're not here on a sightseeing trip. We have things to do."

"God, you must be so much fun at parties."

"Hate them. Why would I want to travel to someone's house just so I can stand around in the kitchen?"

I open my mouth to give a witty retort, then stop. What can you say to that?

I turn away and stare out the opening of the drifter. I can hardly believe this. I mean, I've seen some weird shit the past couple of days, but this. Traveling through the air of a magical world inside a . . . living taxi. I can't help it. A huge grin splits my face again.

The wind picks up, blowing against my face, bringing tears to my eyes. I look around to find Graves staring at me with disgust. I turn back to the view before me. Maybe he's too jaded to enjoy this, but I'm not. Christ, I hope I never get used to this. How can you?

After half an hour of travel we pass into a thick cloud layer, the rope disappearing some ten feet ahead of us. The only sound is the slight hissing as the wheels slip over the greased cable. Wind ruffles my hair, and after a moment I realize I can smell something. Like . . . cooking meat.

I squint my eyes and lean eagerly forward. We must be drawing close.

And then, like a stage magician whipping aside a white cloth to reveal the trick hidden beneath, the clouds part and I see our destination for the first time.

"Here we are," says Jacob happily. "The city of Sheil."

Late-afternoon sun beats mercilessly down, sucking up heat waves that distort the air. The city sprawls over the whole plateau, some ten miles from edge to edge. Buildings and houses push up against each other, tighter and tighter the closer to the perimeter they get, so it looks like they're going to trickle off the edges. Everything is coated in tints of brown. Here a dark umber, there a dull sepia, here a deep ochre. Even the whitewashed walls are tinged with dust.

Thousands of greasy food stalls release thin stalks of wavering smoke. Pulley ropes travel the pedestal's circumference, winches and counterweights pulling massive baskets up from the base of the spire.

"The draku send up their cheeses and wine with those," says Jacob, noting the direction of my stare. "They live inside the spire."

I tear my gaze away from the sight before me. "What, inside the actual rock?"

Jacob nods eagerly. "Little people, they are. Shorter than me, even. Live their whole lives in those spires."

I laugh and look at Graves. "Dwarves!"

He points at me. "No!"

I turn back to the city. Strange, bat-like creatures fly through the air, some disappearing under the lip of the pedestal, others fluttering about seemingly at random. A flight of red birds, flying in perfect formation, dive toward the ground for some hidden treat, a bright flash of color against the muted tones of the city.

The buildings seem to rise higher as we approach. Three, four, sometimes five rickety floors pile one atop the other and lean precariously over tiny alleyways that seem far too small to be of any use to anyone. The shouts of street vendors as they ply their wares float up, the raised voice of good natures haggling and the shouted voices of those cheated from their money.

Jacob pulls hard on a lever, and the drifter judders and lurches, tilting suddenly forward. I grab hold of the sides as the opening we used to enter the creature swings sickeningly beneath me.

We dock at a wooden pier and climb out of the creature. People mill around, bumping into us, loud and sweaty.

"Thank you, Jacob," says Graves. "You can head back across now."

"Thank you, milord. Think I'll do some shopping first. Running low on toilet paper."

"Do they have toilet paper here?" I ask. "I always wondered what they did in these fantasy worlds."

"They do, yes. It's a bit rough, if you know what I mean, but it gets the job done."

"Wonderful," says Graves. "Now that's cleared up, can we get to work?"

Jacob waves and moves into the crowd.

"Right," says Graves. "We ask around about the Jewel of Initaya. If it's as powerful as the spear, people will have heard about it. But . . . make sure you're surreptitious, yes? Like a spy."

"A good spy? Or a bad spy."

"Bad spy?"

"Yeah," I say. "Like, James Bond. You heard of him?"

"No."

"He's a spy, but everywhere he goes, he's like, 'The name's Bond. James Bond.' And they all know exactly who he is."

"And this Jimmy Bond is still alive?"

"Well . . . he's not real, but yeah, he's alive. In the movies."

"That's ludicrous. I refuse to believe the viewing public would continue to watch something so stupid. I think you're lying to me. Now come."

Graves strides off into the crowd. I follow, trying to keep him in sight as we make our way through the afternoon streets. I stare around in awe. The warm wind flaps the multicolored awnings and shade cloths of a thousand barrows and stalls, the billowing snaps sounding like the crack of a whip. Hawkers try to entice me to buy cooked lizards on a stick, or greasy pastries that drip oil over the sellers' hands. One stall sells only metal cogs and gears, some rusted, some shiny and silver as if brand new. Another one is selling intricately carved dolls' heads, the detail in the features making them seem alive. I risk a brief stop by a barrow selling ancient-looking books and brittle scrolls. I study their faded leather covers, the elegant curling writing that adorns the spines.

"Pre-sundering, *astah*," says the deeply tanned owner of the barrow. "Only three hundred sterini."

I shake my head and get moving again. I turn a corner and almost collide with a rickety cage pulled by a three-legged creature with all the fur shaved from its body. I stare as it passes, then jump back as a hand tries to grab my hair. I bat it away and see an arm grasping from inside the cage. I peer through the bars and see that it is full of filthy humans. The one who had grabbed me is a young man with frightened eyes and a week's growth of beard.

"Help me, *astah*," he croaks. "I did nothing."

"Harry!" yells Graves.

I hurry to catch up with Graves. "Where are we going?"

"The place where the talk flows freely."

"A pub?" I ask hopefully. "I could do with a drink."

"No. Not a pub. Pubs are distractions. I'm talking about the docks. In this case, the air docks."

"Didn't we just leave there?"

"Not those. I'm talking about where food and cargo is brought into the city. I'm looking for workers, my boy. Workers who like to chat."

It takes us about half an hour to get to where Graves wants to go. The houses and shops are gradually replaced by warehouses and offices. We walk past alleyways stinking of rotting fish and filled with discarded bones. Packs of hungry dogs fight their way through the detritus, their ribs showing through mangy fur. The crowds slowly thin out, and for the first time since we stepped off the drifter I find myself able to take a breath without inhaling somebody else's sweat.

We eventually reach the lip of the pedestal. The warehouses stop suddenly in a neat line, and beyond them is about twenty feet of flat ground where men grunt and curse as they shift crates from pulleys and lifts, shoving them along the ground.

"These guys don't look like the talkative type," I say.

"Nonsense. Don't be classist, Priest. It's unbecoming. You go right and I'll go left. We'll meet up back here in one hour."

Before I can say anything, Graves strides off to talk to the workers. I sigh, then approach the nearest man who looks as if he knows what is going on. He's smaller than the others, and has a gaping hole where his eye should be.

"Uh. Hi there," I say, furiously concentrating on the man's good eye. "New in town. Me, not you. Obviously." I laugh, but it sounds forced and serial killer-ish. I wince. "Sorry. Look, I'm actually searching for information on a . . . piece of art or something. It's called the Jewel of Ini-taya. Don't suppose you've heard of it?"

The man stares at me for a moment, then turns and walks rapidly away. Rude. I approach another worker but get the same result, except this time accompanied by a quick flash of fear.

I ask again and again, but I get no answers, only variations on the themes of fear, insults, and anger. No one knows anything about the jewel. Or if they do, they sure as hell aren't telling me.

I make my way dejectedly back to the meeting point. I hope Graves had more luck. As I pass the dusty wall of a warehouse, I hear a voice.

"Hey. Hey, you."

I stop walking. The voice came from a little alley between two warehouses. I peer into the shaded pathway. "Yeah?"

"You the guy looking for information on the Jewel of Ini-taya?"

"Uh . . . yeah. Why? You know something?"

"Definitely. Come."

He gestures for me to approach. I hesitate, then do as I'm told. This is the only lead I've had. I can't just ignore it.

The man is wearing a dirty green cloak. He has a skinny face covered with patchy whiskers. He looks nervous, and I slow my steps, wondering if I'm doing the smart thing. Maybe I should go get Graves first, have some backup at hand.

The man's eyes flicker over my shoulder. I start to turn, but even as I'm doing so I know what is coming. Someone or something hits me on the back of my head, and I fall to my knees. Goddamn it. I'm going to get brain damage the amount of times I'm getting hit on the head in this job.

I try to get up, but I experience the curious sensation of being unconscious while awake. My mind is switched off, but I can still see. I watch the steady drip of blood onto the ground. Then it runs into my eyes, and I'm forced to close them as my body catches up with my mind.

§

I feel the breeze against my face first, a fresh breeze that carries the faintest hint of the sea. My head throbs painfully, pounding waves that radiate out from the back of my skull to encompass my whole being.

I gradually become aware of a voice somewhere behind me.

"What am I in for? I'll tell you! For telling stories! That's it!"

Someone mumbles a question.

"What story? Ah. Shall I tell you and damn you all? For it is blasphemy. It is a story of the creators, those we call the Elders, who weren't gods, but a cosmic race millions of years old. How they created their children: Cthulhu, Azathoth, Shub-Niggurath, Dagon, Yog-Sothoth.

"The story goes that one of these Elder Beings created mankind as worshippers for the Old Ones, to keep them busy, much like you or I would give our children wooden toys. Except, the Old Ones instead used mankind to fight each other, amassing followers, using us as sacrifices to gain power.

"Such were the battles between these Old Ones, such was the tremendous power unleashed, that the world started to fall apart. The Old Ones, realizing they had destroyed their world, took themselves into the void, fleeing the destruction. All except for Azathoth. He remained behind, hungry for power, hungry for worshippers.

"A cataclysm shook the earth. The world started to break apart, earthquakes split the land open, mountains thrust up from the bowels of the earth and fell again. The Old Ones had fought their wars and fled, but had destroyed the world in the process.

"But then something happened. Everything stopped. Just . . . stopped. The land was frozen in the middle of its own destruction. A spell of such power, even the Old Ones could not have done it. No, the Elder Gods had stepped in, stopping the destruction of their world, saving the creations of their own cosmic offspring. You see the results in the landscapes around you. The land eaten away, pedestals linked by half-eaten rock, the Abyssal Sea joining the world together."

"Hey!" A loud banging shakes me where I lie. "Keep it down in there!"

I crack open my eyes. There are wooden planks immediately above me. Too low to stand up.

A shuffling sound to my right. I turn my head, see about ten men, some wearing rags, some with days of beard growth. And bars. Metal bars.

I'm in a cage. I sit up abruptly, feeling the world swim sickeningly around me. I peer between the bars, wondering how long I've been out. The sun is lower in the sky, but not too much. Maybe an hour or two?

What the hell happened? I remember being hit on the head, but why the cage? We're still at the lip of the pedestal, but no longer at the docks. This looks like a richer area. Merchants with shiny cloaks and expensively tooled shoes. Drifters and other modes of transport are tethered against the air docks. Some move along tether lines, and a few are free-flying, heading out into the sky.

I try to move my feet and hear a metal sound. I look down and see that we're all shackled together.

Wonderful.

§

Half an hour later we're herded out of the cage onto the dusty stone. A small man with a waxed moustache and a sweaty bald head leads us away, crooning to us as if we're animals he's being careful not to startle. I find the sound incredibly disturbing, almost perverse.

"Come now, my little chicks," he whispers. "Be good for Uncle. He will make money from you, yes? Uncle is good to you. That's right. Keep walking."

Make money from us? So, not Nyarlathotep then. Or the ICD. I'd be dead by now if it was them. That's something, at least.

On the *other* hand, it sounds like I'm about to be sold as a slave, so not ideal. Swings and roundabouts, really.

The man leads us to an open square and onto a raised wooden platform. He padlocks us to an iron pole and then leaves. The heat of the day hasn't lessened. In fact, it seems even more humid. Sweat drips down my back and face, and my head throbs painfully.

An hour later, the slaver arrives back from his lunch break or wherever the hell he disappeared to. He staggers slightly, his cheeks and nose touched by faint blossoms of red. I feel a surge of jealousy. The bastard's been in the pub. I want to go to the pub. I want to drink cool, chilled beer. Instead I'm about to be sold as a slave. Life sucks, man.

The sale begins. There's no show, no pomp and ceremony. The slaver simply walks down the line and points to each slave in turn and waits for the bids to come. If none do he simply mutters, "One for the mines," and a young boy makes a mark on a piece of paper as he follows behind.

All but two are sold before it's my turn. The slaver hits me in the chest with his cane and yawns, staring enviously down at those in the crowd buying beer from an enterprising old man pushing a heavy cask around on a wheelbarrow.

No one looks ready to bid on me. I scan the crowd, noting the disinterest. What the hell? I'm a prime specimen. Why isn't anyone bidding on me?

The slaver waits another ten seconds, and is about to move on when a cloaked figure pushes his way through the crowd and lifts his hand, holding four fingers up. The slaver looks around to see if there are any better offers, then nods at the cloaked figure and moves on to the guy to my right.

Now that it's done, outrage resurfaces. Just like that? Now I'm someone's property?

The bidding finishes, and I'm finally unlocked from my chain. A smaller length is attached to the shackle, and the slaver hands it to the person who bought me. Money exchanges hands, and I'm led off the platform. Another bunch of slaves arrive. I give them a once-over with my newfound expertise. They're a sorry-looking bunch that will probably all end up in the mines.

I study the figure who purchased me as he leads me along the rim of the pedestal. He doesn't look too strong. I think I could probably take him. I tense, ready to yank the chain from the man's hand.

"Don't even think about it," he says in a low voice. A low, *familiar* voice. I hesitate, frowning.

"Graves?" I ask incredulously. "Is . . . is that you?"

The hooded face turns toward me. A hand reaches up and lowers the hood, revealing the grinning face of Havelock Graves.

"Didn't take long for you to get into trouble, did it?" he says.

I fight down the rush of relief, summoning up outrage and fury instead.

"Why the hell didn't you tell me it was you?"

"I just did."

"Before!"

Graves shrugs and fishes a key out of his pocket, using it to unlock my shackles. "Thought this way was more fun."

The shackles fall away, and I resist the urge to punch him in the face yet again.

He sets off, striding through the crowds.

"Did you at least learn anything?" I ask.

"Yes," says Graves. "That we need to leave this city."

"Why?"

"Two reasons. One, because it's ruled over by priests of Azathoth. In fact, this whole country is, and they're not the nice priests. They're the kind you like."

"*Evil* priests?"

"Very evil. Sacrificing–human beings evil."

"And two?"

"Two is that the jewel we're looking for is on a pedestal a few hundred miles away called Roflake. Held at the headquarters of the Priests of Azathoth. Apparently, it's a holy relic."

"Wonderful."

"There's more. A group of robed strangers came through the city yesterday. New priests, some of the people thought. But wearing different colored robes. They were asking about the jewel too. And there were strange sounds in the city last night. Howling. Hissing."

"The Hounds of Tindalos."

"Exactly. And they were asking about passage to Roflake."

"Right. So . . . I guess we're going to Roflake?"

"Unless you have a better plan?"

"No—"

We've been walking while we talk, the crowds providing a constant background hubbub, a comforting accompaniment to the afternoon. But all of a sudden the sound falls away, a circle of silence spreading outward, with us at its epicenter.

I stop walking and look around. We're still walking along the edge of the pedestal. Piers jut out from the rocky lip, some of them holding drifters, others empty.

I hear Graves swearing softly beneath his breath, and I turn around.

Nyarlathotep stands in the center of a rapidly emptying plaza. Six Hounds of Tindalos stand around him. I've never seen them this close, in daylight. They don't quite seem real. Their shape is almost geometric. Every time they move it's like an optical illusion, like parts of them fade in and out of reality. The only thing that stays constant are their mouths, snarling, filled with black teeth.

Nyarlathotep smiles brightly. "Hi there. Nice to see you again."

"Hi yourself," says Graves.

"I hear you guys are asking about the Jewel of Ini-taya?"

Graves straightens up. "We are, yes," he says with a wide grin. "My son is doing a class project. Find out what you can about scary religious artifacts." Graves rolls his eyes. "He was supposed to do it weeks ago, but you know how kids are. Always leaving it to the last minute."

"Funny." Nyarlathotep cocks two fingers and points them at Graves. "I like you. You seem like you'd be a really cool guy to get drunk with."

"Oh, I am."

"Listen, I'm a nice guy. I believe in the sanctity of life and stuff. I'll give you one chance. Stop searching for the jewel. Get out of our way, and you can live."

"For how long?" asks Graves.

"What?"

"Well . . . you're going to free the Old Ones."

"Ah, yes! I see what you're saying. Good point. A few months, tops. But it's better than nothing, you know? Like I say, you seem like a groovy dude, and I'm happy to let you carry on if you get out of our way."

"Sorry," says Graves. "I mean, I am. Truly. Even more so now that I heard you use the word *groovy*."

"It's an amazing word, isn't it?"

"Spectacular," agrees Graves. "But the problem is, it's my job to stop nutjobs like you."

Nyarlathotep frowns. "Nutjob? Hey, come on. That's hurtful, man. I'm just doing my job, you know? I'm like you. You have any idea how long I've been serving the Old Ones? Millions of years, that's how long. I mean, sure, they can get a bit much sometimes, but the universe is rightfully theirs, you know? Mankind is just sort of . . . a parasite. Sucking the blood out of everything."

"And what do you get if you free the Old Ones?"

"A holiday," says Nyarlathotep promptly. "I haven't had a proper holiday in millennia."

I stare at Nyarlathotep in amazement. "You're going to wipe out humankind so you can have a holiday?"

"For sure. Cthulhu promised me a world of my own. All beaches and islands. Tropical climate. Apparently cocktails grow on the trees there. Can you imagine?"

"As lovely as that sounds," says Graves, "I still can't let you get away with it." He shrugs. "Sorry."

"Oh, no apology needed. I expected as much. My hounds? Attack!"

The hounds howl and leap forward. Graves whips aside his cloak and brings up his gun, firing at the closest. But the hound is fast. It bursts into black smoke, then reforms a few feet farther on. The bullet misses, hitting a sandstone building in the background and crumbling it to dust.

Graves turns to me. "Run!" he shouts. He takes his own advice and sprints toward a drifter tethered to a pier.

I run after him, the hounds close on my tail. Graves is already untying the mooring rope as I throw myself through the opening and grab hold of the wheels I'd seen Jacob operating.

Graves lands at my feet as the drifter lurches away from the pier and drops through the air. I grab the support rail and turn around. I can see the edge of the pedestal above us through the drifter's opening.

Nyarlathotep and the hounds appear, peering over the edge. I lock eyes with the priest. He looks slightly irritated.

"You can't escape!" he shouts. "Once the hounds have your scent, they'll follow you wherever you go!"

Then he shoves one of the hounds over the edge. It falls the short distance to the drifter and lands on top of the gas sack. There is a soft *bang*, and then the drifter drops and sways sickeningly.

I fall to the floor. Graves grabs hold of a wheel and tries to stay on his feet. He yanks some more levers, trying to even out the drifter's flight, but I can hear the hiss of escaping air.

"The hound punctured the sac!" I shout.

The hiss grows louder, and a moment later I hear a howl as the hound slides from the drifter and tumbles into the air.

The drifter drops again, but this time it doesn't stop. I hold on for dear life as Graves tries unsuccessfully to steady our descent with spins of the wheels and the venting of gases.

I stare out the opening as it spins through cycles of sky, then sea, then the rock of the pedestal's vast pillar. Over and over again. I can't help noticing that every time we spin around, the pillar of rock is growing closer and closer.

I turn to warn Graves, but he's already staring through the opening, sweat dripping from his face as he concentrates.

The pinnacle draws closer. We're going to hit. This is it. Strawberry jam smeared all over the rock.

Then Graves's face clears, and he twists a valve hard. The drifter picks up speed and drops violently.

I twist around and suddenly the rock is right in front of us. But just before we hit, Graves turns off all the valves and we plummet straight down the side of the cliff face.

And stop.

In midair.

But not for long. Whatever we land on has a lot of give, and we bounce back up again. This is repeated a few times until we eventually come to a complete stop.

I breathe a sigh of relief and slide toward the opening. I poke my head out and see the ocean thousands of feet below me through the crisscross pattern of rope.

Graves has landed us in some kind of safety netting attached to the pinnacle walls. Broken boxes and other pieces of detritus lay caught up in the net.

Graves steps off the drifter onto the thick rope, straightening his clothes and looking around with satisfaction.

"Not bad," he says.

"Not bad?" I look at him, amazed.

"We're alive, aren't we?"

Before I can say anything else, Graves sets off toward the cliff face, the net bouncing with his movements.

"There's an opening here," he calls. "Leads into some sort of tunnel."

I follow. Nothing else I can do, is there?

CHAPTER FIFTEEN

I follow Graves as he walks into the dim interior of the spire, moving along a wide, roughly carved passage through the rock.

"Shouldn't we be running?" I ask, looking nervously over my shoulder.

"Relax. They can't get down here. The overhang is too wide. The hounds would just fall into the ocean. We're safe. For now."

After about ten minutes of walking the path opens up into the hollow center of the pedestal. My steps falter, and I look around in awe. The sense of space and size as our surroundings recede away into the echoing distance is . . . *immense.*

I walk forward, coming to rest against a rock balcony that over-looks the huge central shaft. All around the walls, easily two miles away from our position, I can see hundreds of living levels, thousands of lights twinkling in the space. I lean over the balcony and stare into the depths. The shaft drops below me, narrowing to a pinpoint miles below.

"Close your mouth," says Graves. "You'll attract flies."

I wave helplessly around us. "How can you be so . . . blasé? Look at this! It's amazing!"

"My friend, I come from an alternate with dragon gods. I've seen people resurrected from the dead. I've seen gods torn apart by magic. What we are currently looking at is a hole dug in a mountain. Forgive me for not falling over in amazement."

I study our surroundings again. There are people everywhere, and they're short, like . . . hobbits. Or dwarves. But they're not mining for gold, as far as I can see. Most seem to be farming. Whole levels are given over to growing crops, while some of the lower levels hold markets and shops, lit by flickering torches.

Lifts and winches carry the dwarves up and down the shaft. Some of them are nothing more than one-man baskets that look incredibly flimsy, while others are made of wood and easily thirty feet square. Graves walks toward one of these larger lifts, pulling open the gate and stepping inside.

The lift operator looks up from the book he's reading. He does a double take when he sees us, then heaves himself to his feet.

"All the way down," says Graves. "We have an appointment with the barge clans."

"Who?" I ask.

"Not now, Priest."

The lift operator holds out a hand. "One sterini."

Graves scowls at him and turns his back, fishing around inside his shirt for a small purse hanging around his neck.

"Where did you get that?" I ask.

"None of your business."

Graves pulls out a single coin and hands it over. The lift operator nods curtly, then carefully places a bookmark in his book and gently closes it.

The lift lurches and drops. Our speed soon picks up, a cool breeze rushing past my face. I lean over the rail and stare into the blackness. The sound of rope whirring through the winches is all I can hear.

I can't help a huge grin from appearing on my face. My God, I wish Megan and Susan were here. Just to show them how much more is out there. How much more than our stupid little arguments. My pathetic pride that couldn't just . . . accept the fact she needed to spend some time alone. No, I had to let my ego react. Turning what should have been something simple into the end of our relationship.

I'm not sure how much time passes, but I gradually become aware of the ground rising up to meet us. The operator pulls a lever, and the lift slows abruptly, forcing us to brace ourselves against the edges. Then the lift hits the ground with a none-too-gentle thump.

Graves and I step out. We're standing next to a vast lake, so dark it's like liquid midnight. Waves lap against the shores.

"This way," says the operator, leading us around the shore toward a towering arch in the spire wall that opens out onto the sea. We mount a wooden dock, passing beneath the arch, and venturing outside again I can smell salt water and seaweed battling with a sickly sweet incense.

The lift operator leads us to a pier that branches off from the dock. Tethered just beyond it are floating platforms, a hundred feet square, covered with people and shelters and brightly colored cloths.

"The barge clans," says the lift operator. "Good luck. And watch your purse. They'll have it off you before you know it."

He turns and walks back the way we came.

"Right!" Graves claps his hands together. "Time to negotiate. Follow me and keep your mouth shut. If you utter even a single sound you will throw my negotiations into chaos. Bartering for a price as I'm about to do is a very delicate procedure, requiring the utmost cunning, guile, and of course my stunning good looks."

I stare at Graves, wondering if he's trying to make a joke.

He isn't.

§

"Can I offer you anything? Wine, perhaps? It's the finest red from the south island pinnacles. Very rare."

"Thank you, yes," says Graves.

I'm standing just inside of what I'm told is the Matriarch of the Barge Clan's cabin. Every surface of the room, be it wooden chairs or wrought-iron tables, is covered with ornaments, trinkets of every kind imaginable. It reminds me of those junk shops Megan used to drag me into, where she'd spend ages just picking things up and studying them. She never even bought anything, something that used to drive me crazy.

But I get the feeling the items here are worth a bit more than the bric-a-brac she used to look at. Small jewels are tossed carelessly next to porcelain dolls. Bolts of red-and-purple silk are piled high in a corner. Against the far wall is a massive canopied bed. Some kind of thin material hangs down the sides and sparkles with the slightest touch of the lantern's light.

"Here you go," says the Matriarch, handing over a crystal glass to Graves.

"Thank you."

"Does your . . . companion want a glass?"

Graves glances over his shoulder at me. "No. He's a terrible drunk. Gets very emotional. Starts crying. Best to leave him be."

"As you wish. Now, tell me. What can the humble barge clans do for you?" asks the Matriarch, settling herself down in a cushion-filled chair. She uses the hand that isn't holding her glass of wine to rearrange the pillows into a more comfortable position.

Graves looks around for somewhere to sit, but there is only the one chair in the room. I watch with amusement as he attempts to gracefully fold his legs beneath him and sit on the floor. He eventually manages to flop down onto one of the larger cushions without spilling too much of his wine. "There's time for that later," he says. "Let's talk about you. You really are *incredibly* good-looking for someone of your age."

I wince and look away.

"There's a silence," says Graves. "Why is there a silence?" He looks over his shoulder at me. "Harry, did you do something?"

I look at him in amazement. He turns back to the Matriarch. "Did he do something? Yes? No?"

The Matriarch doesn't reply, just stares at Graves over the top of her glass.

"What?" asks Graves.

"I'm trying to decide whether to have you thrown into the ocean or to stab you where you stand."

"I knew it!" Graves turns and points at me. "You *did* do something, you cretin. What did I say about interrupting my negotiations?"

I open my mouth to argue, but he holds up a finger. "Silence!"

I sigh and turn my attention to a nearby table. It's covered with books. I pick one up. It has an octopus-headed creature embossed on the cover.

"Now," says Graves. "Let's get back to talking about how beautiful you are."

"Let's not. You there."

I look up. The Matriarch is staring at me.

"Uh . . . yeah?"

"What do you want?"

"Passage."

"To where?"

"Uh . . . Roflake?"

"What can you offer me in return?"

I gesture at Graves. "He's got a purse on a string around his neck."

She turns to Graves, who is staring at me with a hurt look on his face. She holds out her hand. He sighs and pulls out the purse, opening it up to take coins out. The Matriarch grabs the whole purse from him and hefts the weight in her hand. "This will do."

"That's all I've got!"

"Then it's lucky for you that it's the exact amount I charge."

"You don't know how much is in there," Graves points out.

The Matriarch gives him a look. "Seriously? You're really going to argue this?"

"Fine! Take it all. Do you want the shirt off my back too?"

The Matriarch reaches out and touches his shirt. Her face twists with distaste. "No need."

She gets to her feet. "We leave within the hour. We're traveling toward our yearly Gathering, where all the clans meet up to pay respects to our Elders. To chart the course of the year ahead."

"Sounds wonderful," says Graves, stifling a yawn. He looks around. "I'll take this cabin."

The Matriarch laughs. "You can find a tent out on the deck. Now leave."

"You can't talk to me like that! I'm a paying customer!"

"No. Unless I'm very much mistaken, you are someone on the run."

Graves opens his mouth, then snaps it shut again.

"I thought so. No luggage. Disheveled appearance. Panicky." She walks toward the exit. "Like I said, we leave in an hour."

As she passes me, she reaches out and trails her fingers across my face. Then she's gone, leaving behind a scent of eucalyptus and citrus.

I lock eyes with Graves.

"Traitor!" he shouts. "Backstabber!"

I sigh and walk away. I'm rapidly realizing this is the best way to handle Graves.

Sigh and walk away.

CHAPTER SIXTEEN

A lanky youth with black hair gestures for us to follow him as we emerge from the Matriarch's cabin.

He leads us along the edge of the barge. The thing is massive. I reckon it would take a good half hour to walk its perimeter.

We receive curious looks from the bargers as we pass them by. Most are busy cooking lunch and brewing hot drinks. The smells go straight to my stomach. When was the last time I ate? Last night? No. All I'd had was a beer before I fell asleep on the patio. I can't help noticing that although some of the bargers smile at us, they are predatory smiles, the smiles of the hunter to the hunted. I've seen that smile before. On the faces of hustlers spotting a new mark.

Fresh meat. That's us.

The boy stops by a canopied section of the deck right next to the rails. Red-and-yellow cushions and thick blankets are rolled neatly on the wooden planks.

"You stay here, yes?" says the boy.

Graves looks at the pillows with disdain. "Boy, I require a bed and a roof over my head."

The boy looks at me. I shake my head, as if saying, *He's not with me.*

"You joking. Very funny," says the boy. He points at the canopy. "Roof." He points at the blankets. "Bed." Then he turns and leaves us standing there.

I duck underneath the awning and grab the biggest cushions, spreading them onto the floor in the shape of a bed before Graves takes them all. I see by his glowering face that this was exactly what he was planning.

"My God," he complains as he yanks a cushion toward him and sits down. "I sincerely hope they at least have some alcohol to share."

§

Later that afternoon, I find myself leaning on the sun-bleached railing and staring out to sea until my eyes sting from the salty air. I rub them and lower my gaze, watching the barge slide through the water without the slightest sign of rocking. Waves swell and head toward us from all sides, then simply stop and sink back into the sea as if they hit an invisible wall. It doesn't even feel like we're moving.

I've realized I'm not going to be able to talk to Susan tonight. Not going to be able to read her a story. Out of everything that's happened since last night, this is the worst. I haven't missed a day talking to her since I moved out. I promised her. Promised her a day wouldn't go by when I didn't call. Now she's going to think I lied. And Megan . . . God knows what she's going to say. The hurt, wounded part of me wants to say she'll use it to score points with Susan, but I know that's not true. Megan isn't like that. I know if I could get past my stupid pride, that we could still have a good friendship. She's told me that. But it sounded like such a cliché. *I really want us to be friends, Harry. We still have a connection. One I won't have with anyone else. Don't ruin it with your insecurities.*

And how did I respond? I walked away without a word and haven't talked to her properly since. That was months ago now. She used to text. Used to ask how I was doing, but even that stopped. She's given up, and I can't blame anyone but myself. I pushed her away. I was hurt, and I acted like a petulant kid.

I turn and spot Graves lounging on the deck with his eyes closed. He lifts a bottle of wine to his lips and takes a deep drink. Looks like he found his booze.

I stroll toward him.

"Any idea how long we'll be on the barge?" I ask.

"You're blocking the sun," says Graves, eyes still shut.

"Sorry about that."

He raises a hand to shield his eyes and squints at me. "You're still blocking it."

"How long?"

"Move and I'll tell you."

I step aside.

"I've no idea," he says, closing his eyes again.

"How can you just lie there?"

"What do you want me to do? We evaded capture by Nyarla-thotep. We're on the move instead of standing still. This is forward momentum. It's good. Just . . . try and relax."

"Do you think we'll be back in our alternate by tonight?"

Graves laughs. "I sincerely doubt it. Why?"

I shove my hands in my pockets. "It will be the first time since I . . . since Megs and I spilt up that I haven't said good night to Susie."

"Oh." Graves appears at a loss about what to say. "Think of it as a valuable lesson to the child. She has to start coping with disappointment some time. The sooner the better."

I sigh. I'm doing that a lot lately. I look around in frustration. "Any idea how this thing moves?"

"Apparently, they have a shaman who does it. An old woman who lives in a hut down the other end of the barge. Why don't you go and bother her?"

Somewhere, someone starts to play a cheery, fast-paced song on the flute. A moment later another person joins in with a drum.

"Down the other end of the barge," Graves repeats. "I'm sure she'll be glad of the company."

I trudge around the huts and awnings, looking for the cabin, but I can't see it anywhere. I ask the bargers for directions, but they won't tell me. I get the feeling they don't trust outsiders. I eventually ask a small girl with raven black hair and a blond streak at the front. She gently takes me by the hand and leads me to a small hut hidden behind a maze of tents and awnings.

I knock gently on the door. There's no answer, so I knock again, harder.

Still nothing. I turn away from the door, and it suddenly jerks open to reveal a tiny old woman blinking owlishly at the light.

"What is it?" she demands.

"Ah . . . nothing," I stammer, taken aback.

"Nothing?" she snaps. "You knock on my door for nothing?" She leans forward into the light. "Who are you? I don't know you. Did I smack your rear cheeks when you were born? I don't think so." She holds up her wrinkled hands. "These beauties never forget a birth. So. I ask again. Who are you?"

I don't know whether to laugh or run away. "I'm a visitor. My . . . companion and I are traveling with you."

"Oh? Nobody told me. You must've had somethin' good to convince that old bitch to let you aboard. What you want with me?"

"I just wanted to talk. To find out how you make this barge go."

"Is that right?" The old lady smooths down her wild nest of gray hair. "You want to talk to Mad Arin about her magic." She smiles, then suddenly lashes out a hand and grabs hold of my shirt. "You're not tryin' to steal Mad Arin's secrets, are you?"

"No! No," I splutter. "I promise."

Arin lets go of my shirt and smooths it carefully down again. "Good. Just checkin'. Come in, come in."

She bustles into her dark cabin and kicks piles of clothes out of the way. She tips a chair over, dumping the pile of books that had previously occupied it onto the floor, and looks around in bemusement. "Sorry about the mess. It's the cleaner's day off." She looks over her shoulder at me, then bursts into cackling laughter. "'Cleaner's day off.' Ah . . . that's priceless, that is."

I stand in the center of the chaos that is Mad Arin's room. She scuttles about, walking around or hopping over piles of old clothes. Every available surface is taken up by ornaments and curios, all totally different in their make and style: here a carved man with a stomach double the size of the rest of his appendages; here a doll made of straw that seems to twitch as I look at it. One shelf holds only jars with a cloudy liquid inside. When I look closer I see tiny faces looking back at me, as if someone had caught sprites and pickled them.

Arin interrupts my inspection of her cabin. "So you want to know how it's done?"

"Sure."

She leans forward as if imparting a great secret. "Our ways can be traced back to the Elder Gods."

"The Elder Gods? The ones who . . ." I think back to what Graves had told me. ". . . who locked away the Old Ones? Cthulhu and his brothers and sisters?"

"That's right. The Elders were speakers of the First Language, see. The true tongue, as some call it." Arin pauses to marshal her thoughts. "The words we use now have no true power. They're watered down so much—it's like piss compared to the finest wine. But if you know the true names of things, the names in the First Language, ah, there you have power. To speak something's true name is to control it."

I think about this. "So you know the true name of the ocean?"

"Smart boy. Aye, I do. I speak its origin poem, and it does as I ask."

"But that kind of power . . ." I shake my head. "Why do the barge clans not rule this world?"

"Because we don't want to? It's hard enough getting us to take responsibility for our own kind, and you want to lumber us with the entire world?" She shakes her head. "No thank you. Besides, we don't know the true words for everything. All the clans know the word to calm the oceans, the word to control the wind, but after that it's a different story. Each clan jealously guards what words they know. I know four true words, and that's a lot. Other clans have more, but the most I think is seven. And there will be overlap between clans. We search for them all the time, but no one has discovered a true word in over a thousand years. Maybe they're gone forever."

"Is that why your people are always traveling around?"

"In a way. You see we . . . You really want to hear this?"

I nod.

"Fine then. We travel around because we're searching for what we call *Idia*."

"What's that?"

Arin leans back again and stares thoughtfully at the ceiling. "Idia is our name for the first Word. It is the origin word of all creation, the very first moment in time. But more than that, Idia . . . is a . . . a feeling," she says. "A moment of rightness. You know when sometimes—not often, mind, but sometimes—you get a feeling of . . . oneness. A feeling that everything is right with the world and your place in it. It's that fleeting moment of complete inner peace, yes? When everything clicks and you think, *This is how it should always be.* Maybe you get it watching the clouds turn dark and heavy with an afternoon storm. Or you get it on a summer's afternoon, sitting outside with a gourd of good wine. Or walking across the snow plains of the north. Just you and the whiteness and the sky, forever. Or watching your children playing among the grapevines as the sun sets behind them." She smiles. "That is what we seek."

I frown. "And where do you think this *Idia* is?"

"Oh, we know where it is. It's inside us. Sometimes I think we travel so we can run away from it. So we don't have to face it. But see, there's the opposite side of the coin, and some of the clans seek that instead. We're bound to stop them. That's why we go to this Gathering. To find out who has turned to the other side."

"I don't understand."

"The opposite of Idia. The word of Undoing. The Elder Gods had to create this word when they battled the Old Ones. They used it to undo the creation of some of them. It's how they managed to get them locked away. Threatened them with undoing."

"Why would anyone want to know the word?"

She looks at me as if I'm simple. "Power, stupid. Power over everyone and everything. Still, no need to worry. It's said the word died out with the last of the Elder Gods." She frowns. "Even though some say the Elder Gods might come back." She shakes her head suddenly. "Anyway, enough of this! Such talk is best kept for under the stars and after a skin or two of wine. Come. Move. Arin has work to do."

"Do you need to recite the origin poem again?" I ask, genuinely curious.

"Not exactly. I'm going to have a nap."

A nap doesn't sound too bad, actually.

§

I'm dreaming. I know it instantly, but I don't give a crap, because the feeling of wind against my face as I fly through the air, the damp feeling of clouds brushing my cheeks, is like nothing I've ever felt before.

Bit of an odd choice of subject, though. I'd have thought scantily clad women would be more my subconscious's idea of a good time. It's certainly *my* idea of a good time. Maybe I'm flying to an exotic locale, a secluded beach or a private forest glade.

And then I'm plunging down through the clouds. I burst through and see this odd world spread out below me.

I'm soaring down, past one of those impossible plateaus of land. Down the supporting spire of rock, all the way to where it drops into the ocean. And then I'm skimming across the water. Faster than is possible. I see the Barge Clans up ahead, but before I even get there I sense something is wrong. As I draw closer I see bloated bodies bobbing in a polluted sea. Birds hop from corpse to corpse, pecking at water-decayed folds of gray skin.

A blink and I'm before another spire of rock, this one a hundred times thicker than the one that supported the city where we arrived. As I fly to the top, I see the miners who let us use their lift. They're climbing the rock, spilling from holes in the spire and crawling topside.

I rise past the lip and see them fighting with others. Thousands upon thousands are dead. And at the head of both armies are monstrous beings, a hundred feet tall, tentacles and limbs slashing the air. One has a hundred eyes and snapping jaws; the other is difficult to look at, a being made of angles and refracted black light.

I'm high up again, in bright sunlight. I look down and see desert. But then I notice that the ground is moving. Tall, thin people moving like a tide of sand to the edge of the plateau. I swoop lower and see drifters tethered there, floating in the air. The people—and I notice something odd about their skin; it is almost translucent, pale and thin, and invisible at the same time—are climbing into the drifters, and they're heading down, to fight a war.

Then all I see are bodies, a carpet of rotting meat, and the screams of the dying fills the air. The sky rains ash. The clouds are heavy with ravens. They circle in packs, black against gray.

And through this sea of carnage wades another colossal being. This one with tentacles on his head and wings on his back. The creature is incomprehensible in power. It hurts my mind just to look at it.

Cthulhu.

As if sensing my thoughts, the massive creature turns to me. But not just me, because suddenly I'm not alone. I turn to look.

Graves stands next to me, plus the Matriarch and what looks like every clan member currently onboard the barge. Even Mad Arin.

The old woman looks at me, puzzled. "How are you doing this?" she asks.

As if these words are a signal of some kind, I feel myself yanked backward in my dream. I'm flying again, and the world is dark. Stars burn brilliantly in the freezing sky. I look wildly around and see that

I'm approaching the darkened city from my dream last night. From up here, I can see just how monumental the city is. How vast and alien, buildings cut in angles and shapes that are not for the human mind.

In the center of the city the towering monolith watches over everything, carved from what looks like black obsidian. I'm pulled toward the top of this tower.

Where something waits.

I look behind me. I'm alone, but at the same time I know that everyone else is with me, just . . . unseen. I try to change direction, but something keeps drawing me—all of us—toward the coldly glittering tower.

I can sense a presence, a hunger. Curiosity. I strain against the pull, but there's nothing I can do. It draws me in, faster and faster. The monolith grows larger. I can feel the presence watching me, reaching out with its mind—

"Wake up!"

My eyes snap open. My breath catches in my throat, and I inhale a great, panicked gulp of air. I scramble to my feet, looking wildly around. I'm surrounded by bright red light. I think for a moment that it's blood, but then I realize it's just the sun shining through the red silk of the overhang. My stomach lurches and heaves. I feel like I'm going to throw up.

Graves is seated next to me, looking at me with wide eyes.

"On your feet!"

It's the same voice that woke me up. I peer out of our shelter and see the Matriarch standing a few paces away, surrounded by guards armed with spears. She doesn't look happy.

Graves and I step out of the shelter. It's about an hour from dusk now. Afternoon. I couldn't have been asleep for long. I squint against the low sun, realizing the barge isn't moving. In fact, no one is moving. Everyone has stopped whatever they were doing to watch the scene unfolding before them.

"What was that?" snaps the Matriarch, looking directly at me.

"What?"

"You know what. That . . . vision. Dream. Whatever it was."

"You saw it too?"

"We all did. You pulled every single person aboard this barge into the Dreamlands."

I frown. "Into the what?"

"The Dreamlands," says another voice.

Mad Arin approaches. The Matriarch and the guards step respectfully aside to give the old woman space. She stops in front of me and peers into my eyes, frowning.

"How did you do that?"

"I . . ." I look helplessly at Graves, but for once he's silent. "I honestly have no idea what you're talking about. I fell asleep, I had that dream, and then she woke me up." I point at the Matriarch.

"That wasn't a dream," says Arin. "That was the Dreamlands. You pulled all of us in with you to witness what you saw."

"But . . . I don't even know what the Dreamlands are," I say.

"It is an alternate dimension. Born from the power of the Elder Gods. Some say the Dreamlands are the real world and all this . . ." she gestures around us, ". . . is the dream."

"Which is of course, nonsense," says Graves. "Mumbo jumbo and superstition."

"Oh? Then how do you explain what just happened?"

"I don't," says Graves. "I choose to ignore it."

"Good for you. I, on the other hand, choose not to. Something is happening here, and it involves the two of you." She thinks about it then nods to herself. "You must stand before our Oracle."

"Sorry," says Graves. "Got people to see, magic artifacts to find. No time to stop and chitchat."

"We're not asking you for permission," says the Matriarch.

"Outrageous! You can't keep us here against our will!"

One of the guards taps him in the chest with a spear point. "This says otherwise," he says.

"I will not put up with this!" shouts Graves. "I'll report you to the authorities. I'll write bad reviews about your hospitality."

"I'm afraid it is necessary," says Arin. "Didn't you see that? Those creatures. They were the Old Ones. Freed from their prisons."

"In a dream!" snaps Graves. "It wasn't real."

"It felt real to me," says Arin. "It won't be so bad. You are still going in the same direction. You will just be stopping off for an afternoon visit before you go on your way."

"And if this Oracle decides she doesn't like what she sees?" Graves asks. "If she decides to keep us prisoner?"

"We will deal with that when the time comes. For now, relax. Enjoy the journey. Tonight we will have a feast. To show you we are not bad people."

Graves turns and points an outraged finger at the Matriarch. "I want my money back. The service on this barge is abysmal."

"Sorry," says the Matriarch with a grin. "No refunds."

§

Later that night, the barge clan is throwing a feast. Not for us. I think it's just what they do. Music and wine and fires lit in metal bins. Lots of singing and dancing and good-natured fighting.

I close my eyes and let the sounds of feasting wash over me. The sounds, the laughter, the music, and, barely discernible, the sound of the ocean moving aside, a dull *whoosh-whoosh* sound as the barge slides through the waters.

Megan would love this. She always liked to have a good time. It's in her blood. She didn't even need booze to do it. Not like me. She just naturally enjoyed life. I could never understand how she did that.

"Cheer up, it might never happen," says Graves, heaving himself down next to me.

"I think it already has."

"Stop talking," snaps one of the bargers seated next to me. "The Medula Onta is going to tell a story. It is a great honor for you both."

"The Medula-what?" I ask.

"*Medula Onta*. The Speaker of Words."

She gestures. I follow the direction of her gaze and see Mad Arin standing before a large fire pit. She raises her hands in the air, and silence flows out from her, spreading through all of the clan members.

She waits until all eyes are upon her. Then she begins speaking.

"Before, when we all lived on the unbroken land, strangers would visit our clans in the woods and forests, and we would spend the night eating and sharing stories, sharing *cultures*. This practice has fallen by the wayside of late." Here she looks pointedly at the Matriarch of the clan. "Some think we should keep to ourselves, trapping our souls in these bags of skin and preventing them from joining with others. For that is the reason behind sharing our past, our legends. Joining with others. We take away a part of someone else, we carry a small amount of them with us, an understanding, the memory of a moment shared."

It seems that she looks directly at Graves and me as she speaks.

"With that sharing we gain a small amount of knowledge of another people, and hopefully that knowledge leads to greater respect, to greater tolerance of those we thought were nothing like us. For we are all the same. We all seek happiness, peace, love. We all dream of growing up; we all think fondly of our youth. We all cry. We all hope. We all live. We all die. Tonight is my gift to our visitors, and I hope they will carry this tradition with them on their travels."

She waves her hand over the massive fire. It is the width of two men lying head to toe, and I can feel its heat even from where we sit.

And then, as I watch, Arin suddenly leans forward and plunges her face into the flames. I gasp and leap to my feet, but the woman by my side grabs hold of my arm.

"Sit!" she commands.

I look around. No one else seems worried. Not even Graves. But then he looks bored by the whole thing, casually inspecting his nails for dirt.

A moment later Arin pulls her head out of the flames, her face unscathed. She opens her mouth, and a small flame dances on her tongue. At the same time, the massive fire dies down to the barest flicker, an orange carpet that glows and pulses. She spits the small flame out of her mouth, and it lands in the pit. As I watch, it forms into the shape of an egg.

"The origins of things are important," says Arin. "I know the origin poem of fire so I can control it. But knowing the origin of things does not always mean control. Sometimes, it means understanding. This is why I tell you this night about the origin of language. The origin of the universe."

She waves a hand, and a flame flicks out of the fire pit and forms into the shape of an eagle, swooping through the air. It weaves in and out of the spectators, drawing wondrous gasps. I grin as it swoops past my face. Graves bats it away in irritation.

"The world eagle flew through the dark skies before time was created. She was the first of the Elder Gods. Everything existed as one instant, an eternal moment that contained within it the whole history of everything that could or *would* exist. The world eagle watched over this moment. She carried it within her beating heart. We, sitting here right now, existed in that moment, in that time before time. We were part of the world eagle. She has already foreseen this meeting."

The eagle swoops around and flutters to a halt in front of me. I reach out to touch it. The eagle pecks out with its beak and flies away. A few of the barge clan laugh at this, but none louder than Graves.

"One day the world eagle laid an egg, and it became the sun. This was another of the Elder Gods, the second. They began talking, the first words ever spoken between two beings, and from these words the cosmos was created. Their words fell to create stars. When they saw this they laughed and cast more words into the blackness. These words created the world and all that exists within it. And when it was time to part, their words of farewell fell even heavier and created the first race, the Old Ones. They are many and varied, but among them are the most important: Cthulhu, Azathoth, Shub-Niggurath, Dagon, Yog-Sothoth."

The fire eagle expands to form a round sphere, then expands again and flattens out to show a fiery landscape of trees and mountains, all made from flickering orange fire.

"The sun decided not to give the knowledge of words to the Old Ones. They were not happy with this. Cthulhu appointed himself as leader of the Old Ones. He signaled for the world eagle to come to him, and using gestures, he begged for a ride. The eagle agreed, but when he sat on her back he trapped her with a harness he had fashioned from fallen moonlight. When night came, Cthulhu forced the world eagle to fly to the sun.

"The sun spoke in her sleep, and Cthulhu stole the words from her mouth and put them into his bag. He returned to the earth, but unknown to him, his bag had a hole in it and some of the true words fell across the land. But even though he had lost some of these true words, he still had most, and he shared them with the other Old Ones.

"When the sun awoke and discovered the theft she was furious. In her fury she spat out the word of Undoing. She shouted it at the earth and split the land open. The Old Ones were swallowed up, pulled into another dimension as punishment. This place is called the Absolute Elsewhere, and it is eternal and cold.

"The sun reserved a special punishment for Cthulhu. He was the most powerful, the first born, and the sun trapped him in a prison beneath the ocean. A place called R'lyeh.

"But this was not enough for the sun. This Elder God put Cthulhu to sleep forever, and locked his prison, throwing away the keys."

Arin suddenly claps her hands, and the flames in the fire pit shoot upward again. I start from my reverie. I was so caught up in the story that I was unaware I was watching pictures made of fire. I rub my eyes.

Arin looks at her audience. "I am the Speaker of Words. This is the story I tell," she says formally. "If it be good, or if it be not good, it matters not. Take some elsewhere, and let some come back to me. So we share. So we grow."

CHAPTER SEVENTEEN

The next morning the barge shifts direction, turning toward a large mass of land that Arin tells me is Roflake. I lean on the railings and let the cold salt breeze wipe away the last vestiges of sleep. The rising sun hasn't crested the pedestal's horizon yet. It shines through the thousands of pillars that hold the continent up, the light silhouetting them and making the whole pedestal look like some sort of twisted tree.

Something bothers me about this whole business. About Nyarlathotep and his cult, about the spear and the jewel. About the ICD attacking us. We're missing something. Something I can't quite put my finger on.

I go over and over it in my mind as the morning progresses, but I'm no closer to finding an answer. The barge makes a series of slight turns until it is headed directly for a specific spot beneath the plateau, a twisted rock archway formed by the shape of the spires.

I have no idea what is so special about that spot until we draw close enough for me to see the gently undulating carpet of color in the shadows underneath the land mass, thousands of barges linked together by ropes and bridges.

The light dims as our barge tracks its way beneath the pedestal, moving through the channels kept open through the mess of barges. Good-natured shouts and curses follow in our wake.

I study our surroundings with intense curiosity. It isn't just barges that takes up space here. Collapsed spires form low islands in the sea. These spires are covered with buildings: huts, shops, and even homes. The short people from inside the spire, the dwarves, as I've come to think of them, operate out of stalls that sell mushrooms and dried meat, expensive foods from topside and bright swathes of material.

Graves eventually joins me at the railing, yawning and rubbing his face.

"How much longer do you think we'll be stuck here?" I ask.

Graves smacks his lips, grimacing. "A few days, if we're lucky."

"And if we're unlucky?"

"Forever."

I hesitate. I've been wondering whether to tell Graves this or not, but I suppose I should. It might be important.

"Listen, I didn't want to say anything in front of this lot, but the city that I supposedly took everyone to? In this Dreamland place? I've seen it before."

Graves turns to stare at me. "Where?"

"Remember back at that castle? When Himmler was trying to use the Spear of Destiny? When I touched the spear, I had this . . . flash. Of a city, of stars in a night sky. And then that night when I went home, I dreamt the same thing. An old, abandoned city under a starry sky." I take a deep breath. "I don't like the way those dreams make me feel."

"How do they make you feel?"

"Utterly . . . insignificant. A mote of dust in the eye of the universe."

"But that's exactly what we are."

"Well . . . sure. But we spend our entire lives trying to ignore that fact. When I have those dreams, I can't escape it. I want to just . . . crawl into a hole and die."

"Well . . . There's nothing we can do about it now. And who knows? Maybe this Oracle they're taking us to see is the real deal. Maybe she can tell us what it means. Because I certainly don't know. And that's the first and last time you'll hear me say that."

"It all just feels a lot bigger since we've come to this world. More serious. Like back when we were getting the spear it was important, but still workable. Now it just feels hopeless. And the worst thing is there's nothing I can do. We're powerless here."

"Like I say, let's wait and see what the Oracle says. Plenty of time for wallowing in self-pity later."

The barge is guided deep into the center of the floating city. We finally stop next to one of the broken islands formed by a collapsed spire. This one is larger than the others, easily a mile across. Streets have been leveled out of the rock, permanent structures built using stone and mortar instead of the wood I see everywhere else.

The Matriarch appears behind us. She steps off the barge and is soon deep in conversation with someone waiting on the island. He runs off, and we wait another ten minutes or so before he returns with a message for the Matriarch.

She gestures for us to follow, leading us away from the wet rock at the water's edge. A single main street leads to the center of the island. At some point a second pillar of rock dropped from the distant underside of Roflake and landed on the island. Where the pillar met the ground it shattered into vast pieces, forming a huge cave-like structure.

The Matriarch leads us inside this structure, along a tunnel lit with a soft gray light. We follow the passage through a series of twists and turns until the light starts to brighten, like the arrival of dawn.

We enter a large, circular chamber. There's an ancient woman sitting cross-legged in the middle of the room, bathed in a directionless white light. I stare at her. I thought Mad Arin was old, but this woman looks like she has a couple of hundred years on Yoda. Her face is a map of deep wrinkles. Two dark, glittering eyes peer out at us.

"Which of you claims to enter the Dreamlands?" she demands.

Graves gives me a shove. I stagger forward, hands clasped before me like a naughty schoolkid.

"I don't claim anything," I say. "Mad Arin said I was able to do it."

The Matriarch steps forward. "It is true, Oracle. We were all drawn into his dream."

The Oracle waves her hand impatiently. "It is impossible. No one can do such a thing. Not even I. This is something only the Old Ones could do."

"This is why I thought you should meet him, Oracle," says the Matriarch respectfully.

The Oracle turns her attention to me.

"Come forward. Sit by me." She gestures, and a young girl who I hadn't even noticed moves forward to lay mats on the floor. Graves and I sit down.

"Now," she says to me. "Do you know what the Dreamlands are?"

"Just what your Speaker of Words told us," I say. "That it is the soul of the universe?"

The Oracle nods. "Just as you have a soul encased in your body, and your soul is who you really are, so the multiverse has the Dreamlands. The Dreamlands came first. They were the home of the Elder Gods, the home of the Old Ones. Our plane is the shadow cast by this realm. We are the physical body; the Dreamlands are the soul, the spirit."

The small girl comes back with a tray and presents a cup of steaming liquid to Graves. He takes it and sniffs as she passes a cup to me.

"Is there alcohol in it?" he asks.

"Lots," says the Oracle dryly.

Graves tips it back and drains the cup. I sip mine more slowly. Some kind of tea. Sweet, but with a bitter aftertaste.

The Oracle waits until I've finished. She smiles.

"Now we wait."

"For what?" I ask.

"For the *berlini* bark to do its work."

Graves frowns at her suspiciously. "What are you talking about?"

I stare into my cup. I blink, my eyelids suddenly feeling incredibly heavy. I'm dimly aware of someone appearing at my side, taking the cup and gently laying me down on the mat.

Then I close my eyes.

§

The sky is black and filled with pinpricks of brilliant light. A gibbous moon hangs low, a sickly yellow in color.

I blink and look around. I'm standing on the muddy shore again, yellow light glinting on the cold mud.

Graves stands to one side with his arms folded. "You tricked us!" he shouts at the Oracle.

The Oracle shrugs. "I did what I needed to do."

"Are we asleep?" I ask.

The Oracle cocks her head. "Our bodies are, yes. But in a way, you are more awake now than you have ever been." She winks at me. "But now's not the time for such conversations, eh?" She studies our surroundings. "So it is true. You have the ability to bring people into the Dreamlands. Very interesting."

"I don't know how I'm doing it," I say quickly.

"So you say," she says mildly.

I look in alarm at Graves, but he gives an almost imperceptible shake of his head.

"And this is the city you visited," says the Oracle.

I turn and see the angular cityscape jutting against the night sky. The buildings hurt my eyes, like looking at an Escher painting when drunk.

"I . . . do not like this place," says the Oracle.

"No," says Graves. "I feel like my brain is being twisted around and inserted back through my eyeballs." He turns to glare at me. "Where have you brought us, idiot?"

"I have no idea!"

"That tower," says the Oracle.

I turn and look at where she's pointing. And as if the mere act of looking is a signal, the three of us are suddenly standing on the tower, staring down over the cityscape.

"Stop doing that!" shouts Graves.

I don't answer. We're standing on a walkway that circles the structure. Black arches lead inside, but I really don't want to go in there. There's something . . . *other*, if that makes sense. I can feel it, lurking in the darkness.

The Oracle, however, has no problem at all, and she strides through the closest arch as if it's happy hour at the local pub.

Graves glares at me as he strides past. "I regret the day I met you. I just want you to know that."

A crystal growth takes up the center of the huge room inside. There is no pattern to the structure, facets and protrusions sticking out randomly, crystal clear and segmented, refracting the little light that enters the tower.

"What is that?" I ask.

The Oracle is peering inside. I follow her gaze and see something beyond the crystal. Some kind of dark skin. Scales, shifting around.

"What's . . . what's in there?"

And then a sudden movement. The chamber is lit up in purple-and-black light as the creature opens an eye as large as the Statue of Liberty.

My eyes snap open.

I'm back in the chamber, lying on the mat that had been laid on the floor.

I push myself shakily to my feet. The girl who had poured our tea is checking on the Oracle, handing her a glass of water.

She pushes it away, turning her attention to us. "This is worse than I feared," she says.

"Why?" asks Graves. "What was that?"

"That was Cthulhu himself, in his prison of R'lyeh, the city beneath the sea."

"That wasn't beneath the sea," I say. "There were stars."

"That was the dream reflection of R'lyeh. The true version, if you will. What is your plan?"

"We're supposed to be getting this jewel from the priests. It's part of this. I think part of a key or something. There are people after it."

"The ones who wish to free the Old Ones?"

I nod.

"Then we must help you. You must get this key before our enemies."

CHAPTER EIGHTEEN

An hour later and we're ready to go. The Oracle has chosen ten clan members to see us back to the surface, and I have to say, I'm feeling pretty safe. They're a hard-looking bunch. Six men and four women, all of them carrying long spears. On top of this, they've got bows and quivers of arrows strapped to their backs and thin blades scabbarded at their waists.

Even Graves eyes them warily as we approach them. The Oracle is talking to the eldest of the ten clan members, a thin, hard-faced woman who looks to be in her forties.

"This is Teshani," says the Oracle. "She will be in charge of your safety."

"I still protest," says Graves. "I do not need looking after."

Teshani looks him up and down. "How old are you?"

Graves draws himself up taller. "That, madam, is none of your business."

"Because with the white hair and everything, you look ancient. Seventy at least."

"Seventy! Are you insane? I do *not* look seventy." Graves turns to me. "I don't, do I?"

"Nah. A well-preserved sixty?"

Graves's eyes widen, and he sputters his outrage before turning his back on us and striding toward the ramp.

"Good luck," says the Oracle softly. "Your destination is the temple of Azathoth. A labyrinthine complex of halls, passages, rooms, scriptoriums, and cells."

"Sounds cool."

"It is not," says the Oracle.

"Oh. Okay."

"The jewel you're after is one of their holy relics. It's said the head of the priesthood—they call him the Eli—keeps the jewel in his bedchambers."

"He keeps their holiest treasure in his bedroom?" I ask incredulously.

The Oracle shrugs. "That is what I hear."

"So . . . how do we find his rooms?"

"Just keep climbing. He has the highest room in the temple." She hands over two satchels. "Water. Disguises for when you reach the temple. Weapons. Good luck. You will need it."

"Thank you," I say. The Oracle nods and leaves us.

I pull the satchel onto my back and study the ramp that is going to be the first leg of our journey back to the surface. It's been cut out of one of the support spires, spiraling up around the pillar before stopping at a wooden rope bridge that connects to another distant spire.

It looks like we have a lot of walking ahead of us. Which sucks, because I hate exercise. I think I'm allergic to it.

Teshani and her troop set off, heading up the ramp at a rapid pace. Graves is leaning against the wall, sulking. I toss him his satchel, and we set off after them.

After about twenty minutes we arrive at the top and cross the rope bridge to a narrow shelf of rock that curves around the next pillar. A long ladder has been carved into the rock, handholds chopped away and then smoothed out so the stone won't cut into the skin.

This leads up to a tunnel that cuts straight through the middle of two thick spires, the insides of the tunnel illuminated by flickering torches. I run my hands over the walls, wondering how they were carved.

"Bore worms," says Teshani, seeming to read my mind.

The tunnel is easily three times my height. "Must have been really big worms."

"These were babies."

The second tunnel exits onto a stone arch so narrow that we have to walk across it single file. I make the rookie mistake of looking down as we go, my stomach flipping as I fight down a wave of dizziness. The clan Gathering is well underway by now. I can just hear the sounds of laughing and singing from far below.

Our path leads us through another bore worm tunnel that slants steeply up through another spire. We need safety lines attached to our waists for this one, since the incline is too sharp to simply climb up on our own. A sullen-faced woman fastens our lines and then sets a taut wire, which disappears up the tunnel, to vibrating. A moment later I feel a tug on my midsection as someone above responds to the signal.

We're all winched upward at a walking pace. When we reach the other side, we remove our harnesses. A broad shelf of rock with a more gentle slope climbs into the darkness before us.

I lean over to get one last glimpse of the barge clans before they disappear from view. Let's face it. When the hell am I going to see anything like this ever again? Especially because once we get back home and resolve all of this, I'm quitting.

It's something I decided on the barge. I wasn't a hundred percent sure, but now I am. This is crazy. I'm all for seeing amazing things, but when they take me away from Susan, just . . . no. I can't do it. What the hell is she thinking? That I'm just ignoring her? Is Megan worried about me, or does she think I've gone on a bender or something?

I frown, realizing I've been staring down but not actually seeing anything. I can still see tiny glimpses of color where the torches illuminate the multicolored cloth strung up between the barges.

I'm about to turn away again when something catches my eye, an odd movement that doesn't quite fit in with everything else. I squint, trying to see what it is.

There. Some sort of disturbance, barely visible from this height. Nothing specific, but a ripple of shadowy, violent movement. I let my eyes unfocus, and I catch another burst of activity in my peripheral vision. A shadow moves across the barges far below, snuffing out fires and torches as it passes. And now that I know what I'm looking for, I can see other patches of darkness, all of them sweeping across the floating barge city, leaving behind chaos and darkness in their wakes.

Then the screams start to filter up toward me.

"Teshani!" I shout.

She hurries over, scanning the scene far below us. Graves appears at my shoulder.

"The Hounds of Tindalos?" he asks.

I nod.

One of the hounds leaps up the ramps and slopes we just used. I watch in amazement as the creature soars twenty feet through the air, grabs hold of an underhang, then pushes itself off to soar another thirty feet before latching onto a stone spire with its vicious black claws.

It turns its head around almost 180 degrees and looks directly at us, the tentacles on its face reaching through the air.

Even from this distance, it knows it has spotted its prey. The hound tilts its head back and lets out a high-pitched howl that raises the hair on the back of my neck. I look down and see that the other patches of shadow have stopped moving.

Then they start bounding toward us, scrabbling up the rock spires like spiders darting along a wall.

Teshani yanks me away from the edge and shoves me up the ramp. "Go," she says. "Run."

She turns back and grabs Graves by the collar.

"Hey, I want to see the . . . oh—"

He's cut off as the first hound leaps past the ledge and lands directly in front of him. It rears up to its full height, its head twitching this way and that, blurring and shuddering as it shifts through the angles of reality. I stare at it in horrified fascination: gray-and-black skin riddled with red, swollen veins. Yellow eyes with orange slits for pupils, and a mouth so wide it looks as though it has been ripped into the face. Tentacles wave in the air, dripping black fluid onto the ground.

"*Run!*" shouts Teshani.

She lunges forward with her spear, stabbing the hound. The creature whirls to face her, swinging its hand down and snapping the spear's shaft in half. Teshani stumbles back as the others move in, keeping the creature at a distance with their spears while trying to land a killing blow.

The hound jerks and hisses, obviously in pain. But an attack that would have left a normal person dead doesn't even slow the thing down.

It reaches out and touches the closest fighter. The man stiffens, then jerks his head back and screams. His face melts, his skin sloughing off his bones, turning to a puddle of blood and purple, rotten flesh.

The other fighters stare at their comrade in horror as his body drops to the ground. Then Teshani runs forward, leaps into the air, and swings her sword, slicing through the hound's neck. The creature's head flies through the air and disappears over the ledge.

Teshani boots the creature in the chest, and the body tumbles away into the darkness.

Teshani turns to the others. "Move!"

No one needs a second warning, even Graves. We all turn and sprint up the ramp. I search ahead of us as we run, but can't see any end to our path. It looks as if it was supposed to be the final part of our route, that it leads all the way to the surface.

Which means there's nowhere for us to hide.

Another hound clears the edge of the ramp. It sniffs the ground where the blood of its brother was spilled, then comes after us, bounding up the ramp on all fours. Teshani shouts an order, and five of the fighters stop running and spread out in a line, spears and swords at the ready.

The hound attacks. The clan members have learned now to stay out of reach. Four of them jab and slash with spears, keeping the hound at bay while the last one circles around with a sword, looking for an opening to take its head.

I stumble over a rock, and Teshani grabs me before I fall to the ground.

"Eyes front," she commands.

I manage to keep my eyes forward for about ten seconds, and then I have to look back.

I wish I hadn't. The hound is dead, but so are two more clan members, and another hound is heading straight for the remaining three. Teshani also sees this because she curses loudly and moves us toward the craggy wall at the left side of the ramp.

"Wait here," she says. She grabs a lantern from one of the clan members, then sprints ahead, peering at the wall and running her hands over the rock. Searching for something.

She obviously doesn't find it, though. She hurries back to us.

"There is a cleft in the wall somewhere along here. It leads into an old network of bore worm tunnels. Find it." Teshani nods at two clan members, a grizzled man and a girl who looks to be in her twenties. Teshani hands the lantern to the girl. "You two, stay with them. Get them to the top. You," she says, pointing to the last remaining fighter, "with me."

Then she turns and runs.

We watch the two of them sprint toward their comrades, trying to reach them before the hound does. As they draw closer, Teshani skids to a stop, leans back, then throws her spear. It sails through the air and hits the hound in the face, lifting the creature from its feet with the force of the impact.

The clan members cheer. But the cheer falls away as three more hounds claw their way over the lip and straighten up to sniff the air.

The girl who is holding the lantern shoves me in the back.

"The name's Tal. You listen to me now, yes?"

I nod.

"Good. Let's go."

"But . . ."

"What did I just say? We have our orders."

I reluctantly tear my gaze away just as Teshani glances over her shoulder. She salutes us, then turns back to face the hounds.

We move quickly up the ramp and find the split in the rock face about thirty feet from where Teshani had thought it was.

To my eyes the entry looks like the shadow cast by an outcrop of stone, but Tal pushes the lantern inside, enabling us to see rough walls leading into a thin fissure.

We move into a narrow passage. The eldritch screams of the hounds follow us as we move forward. My heart thuds fast in my chest. How are we going to get away from these things? Five fighters with years of training could barely keep one of them at bay. What chance do we have?

The opening soon narrows so much that the sharp stone digs into my back. Finally, we can go no deeper. We've reached a dead end.

Tal swears. "Wait here," she says, and turns back to retrace our path. I peer around Graves's shoulders and see that she's knocking the end of a dagger against the wall. She disappears around a bend in the tunnel, but I can still hear the *clink-clink* of the metal on rock.

We wait. My breath sounds ragged and uneven in my ears, but not as bad as Graves's. The guy is wheezing and coughing, sounding like he's in pain.

"You all right?" I ask.

Graves says nothing.

"Seriously, it sounds like you're about to throw up a lung. You're not having a stroke, are you? Because I'm not giving you mouth to mouth."

Graves just glares at me, and I shut up. The sounds of fighting outside filter into the tunnel. Shouts, cries of pain, the snarls of the hounds. I think they're getting closer.

A moment later I hear rock crumbling to the floor. My head snaps back, and I stare at the roof, making sure it isn't collapsing on us. But the sound came from somewhere else.

Tal appears around the bend and gestures for us to follow. Graves leads the way back, and we find the girl standing before a hole in the wall. Dust swirls thickly in the air. I wave it away and peer through the gap. It leads into a huge tunnel, this one twenty feet across.

"Bore worms?" I ask.

Tal nods and steps through the tunnel. She holds her lantern up, moving in a slow circle as we follow her in.

"Are these safe?" asks Graves.

"I think safe is something of a relative term right now, don't you?" says Tal.

"Fair point, well made," says Graves.

We follow Tal up the slope of the passage. Pebbles and loose rocks shift underfoot, forcing us to move slower than we'd like. At one point I trip and throw my arm out to steady myself. My fingers brush the rock, and a whole section of wall detaches itself, spilling down toward us like an avalanche. I barely have time to dive out of the way before the rock piles up where I was standing.

"Be careful!" snaps Tal.

Graves shakes his head in mock disgust, wagging a finger at me.

I make sure not to touch anything else after that.

Half an hour later, I'm thinking we might just get out of this alive when I hear the noise. It comes from far behind us, the sound of grinding rock, then stone falling. Everyone freezes.

The howl of a hound echoes up the tunnel toward us.

"Run," says Tal.

We sprint as fast as we can along the passage, trying to keep from sliding on the loose stones. But it's a waste of time. The approaching hound sounds like a galloping horse. We'll never outrun it. Never.

"Stop!" I shout. "It's too close."

Tal puts the lantern down to our left, lighting up the small area of tunnel. Then she and the other fighter spread out in a line across the passage.

I lick my lips. Tal passes me one of her swords, and the other clan member does the same for Graves. The hound is getting closer, scrabbling across the rocks, its breath hissing and gurgling in its throat.

"Get ready," whispers Tal. She has her spear gripped firmly in her hand, the back end resting on her shoulder. I focus on the bend in the path. The light from the lantern flickers up across the smoothly worn stone, arching around to the roof. But the tunnel beyond is just a dark circle.

The sounds grow louder. I strain my ears, trying to judge how many are coming. One? Two? More?

We wait. The seconds move at an agonizing pace.

Then everything happens at once.

A shadow slides around the corner. The hound's face is revealed, eyes narrowing in the lantern light. Tal throws her spear directly at the creature's head. The hound sees it coming and jerks back, bringing a clawed hand up to bat it away. The blade enters its gray flesh and keeps going. The creature's hand disintegrates in a mist of blood and pulp as the wide spear pushes out the other side, leaving the hound staring at a stump that pumps black ichor against the wall.

I leap forward while it's distracted and bring the sword clumsily down on its raised arm, severing it at the shoulder. The creature howls in pain, swinging for my head with its remaining hand. I duck and lunge to the side, rolling to my feet just in time to see the hound's head flying through the air to thump up against the wall.

Graves lowers his own sword and grins at me. "Did you see that? How amazing am *I*?"

Tal shoulders him aside and retrieves her spear from where it fell beyond the light.

"Sliced and diced!" says Graves. "Right through its neck." He holds the sword up to the lantern light. "Maybe I should get one of these for official ICD business. I like the feel of it."

"Quiet!" commands Tal.

"I was only—"

"Silence!"

Graves clamps his mouth shut. We wait. The silence stretches.

Then the howling starts up again. My heart hammers in fear. They're close. The first one must have been a scout, to see where we were. The sounds of scrabbling and falling rocks echoes toward us, the eager snarling and snapping of the creatures loud in our ears.

Tal turns to face us, the light crawling across the left side of her face. The defiance and anger is gone. Now she just looks defeated. "We can't—"

She doesn't say anything more. A hound lunges from the darkness and swings its black claw, slicing the top half of her head clean off.

Her fellow clan member screams in rage and rushes past us, thrusting with his own spear. The hound barely even looks at him. It swings a backhanded blow that sends him flying through the air to crash against the wall. Rocks and stone fall on top of him, dislodged by the impact of his body.

Graves and I rush forward, swinging our swords before the hound can turn its attention to us. Graves drops to the ground and slices his weapon into its leg. The creature stumbles forward, its arms flying out to steady itself and dislodging more rocks in the process. The rocks tumble into the tunnel, smacking up against the hound's legs, pushing the creature to its knees. Graves darts in and stabs it in the chest while I swing my own sword as hard as I can, cutting its head from its body.

We stumble back away from the falling rubble. The sounds of the other hounds approaching are growing louder.

"We can't fight them all," says Graves.

He's right. We'd die if we even tried. I look around for something to help us, my gaze coming to rest on the wall, where a large pile of rocks has fallen. The same thing has happened on the opposite side, where the clan member hit the wall.

"Help me here," I say. I put my sword away, then move the lantern back about ten feet. I pick up Tal's spear and position myself close to the hound's body.

"What are you doing?"

"Come here. I need to get on your shoulders."

Graves looks at me as if I'm mad, but he crouches down and helps me climb up. He slowly straightens, staggering and groaning.

"*My God*, how much do you weigh?"

"When the roof starts to fall, move us back," I say.

"Fine— Wait, *what*?"

I ignore him and ram the spear into the rock ceiling. Dust sprinkles my face. I ram again, harder this time. I hear something shift, stone scraping against stone. A howl comes from just ahead. I glance down and see the first hound round the corner, galloping on all fours. Shit, shit, shit. I thrust the spear up, again and again. Stones fall onto my head. Graves moves back a step. I force my eyes to stay open against the dust and push again.

This time a huge chunk of rock drops down. Graves lets out a yelp and falls backward. I tumble from his shoulders, landing on my back and hitting my head hard on the ground. Stars explode across my vision. Waves of sharp agony pummel my skull, getting stronger and stronger. I stare dazedly at the clouds of dust billowing around us, noting how the light from the lantern makes them glow. Everything sounds distant and muffled.

Then someone grabs my arms, and I'm sliding back across the ground. My hearing sharpens suddenly, and I hear a terrific crashing noise from somewhere, and screams of pain and rage. I shake my head, trying to clear the cobwebs.

I stop moving.

"Really," gasps Graves. "You need to lose some of that weight! I must insist. In fact, I'm going to bring it up at your first review."

I push myself into a sitting position. Dust swirls everywhere, but I can just see the collapsed ceiling that now blocks the tunnel.

"You nearly killed us," says Graves accusingly.

"I saved us," I respond.

"Possibly. But you nearly killed us in the process."

Graves stops talking as a chunk of collapsed rock is displaced from the mound blocking the tunnel. It rolls to the ground, followed by another, then another.

The dust clouds are slowly dissipating, drifting up the passage. Graves and I stare at the spot where the rock fell.

A black claw punches through. The front of the rock wall shifts, then slides away as a hound lurches into the open. I can just see a small tunnel inside the rockfall, where larger pieces of stone have kept a passage open beneath the collapse.

The hound puts its head back and howls. It spots us and starts running the twenty feet in our direction. I look frantically for the spear, but it's gone. I try to yank the sword from my belt, but the hound is already ten paces away. Graves lurches to his feet, searching for his own sword.

There is a sudden rush of movement behind the creature.

My mouth drops open as Teshani emerges at a full sprint from the collapsed tunnel. She darts to the side, and actually uses her speed to *run up* the wall until she is the same height as the hound. Then she shoves off with her feet, sails through the air with two stiletto blades extended, and slices them through the hound's neck.

She lands in a crouch as the hound's body drops to the floor. The severed head hits the ground and rolls to a stop directly in front of me. I stare at it in amazement.

"Bad*ass*!"

"Which one of you *bastards* just brought a roof down on top of my head?" demands Teshani.

Graves and I quickly point at each other.

§

The three of us trudge up the tunnel, relief at being alive tempered by the deaths of those who had been sent to protect us. The clan members gave their lives to make sure we survived. It makes everything so much more real. So much less fun. I know that sounds like a shitty thing to say, but what I mean is it brings the consequences of everything home. Makes me realize this isn't just about me getting home to see Susan. This is real. Nyarlathotep is responsible for people dying. Which means we have to take it a lot more seriously.

"Lucky I came back," says Teshani. "You two would have been dead without me."

Graves snorts. "Please, woman. We were fine. We'd just killed about half a dozen of those things in hand-to-hand combat before you came along."

"How many?" asks Teshani.

"Er . . . a few."

"How many?"

"Fine! Two!"

"That last one would have got you, though."

"No way. I was ready," says Graves. He holds up his hands. "These are lethal weapons. Registered in five states."

"Five what?" asks Teshani.

"Doesn't matter."

I shift my gaze to the path ahead. A gray light is filtering in from somewhere.

"We're here," says Teshani.

We quicken our pace and soon see the light outlining thick thorn bushes that block the way out of the tunnel. Graves enthusiastically hacks and slashes at them with his sword, shouting like a kid.

We emerge on the slope of a rocky hill. Behind us, the hill rises up until it merges with a range of mountains, but in front of us the ground drops away to meet a craggy rock plain covered with human-sized boulders.

Teshani points into the distance. "That's your destination. It's called the Chalice. Good luck." She turns away.

"Aren't you coming with us?" I ask.

"I was told to escort you to the surface. I have done that. Now I must return and see what other damage the hounds have wreaked."

Without another word she turns and ducks back through the opening.

Graves and I turn back and stare into the distance. We can just see a small jumble of buildings and a tower piercing the gray clouds.

"Well," says Graves. "You got your fantasy, your magic, your mad priests, and now you've got your temple." He glances over at me. "Aren't you lucky?"

CHAPTER NINETEEN

Eight hours later, Graves and I are sitting behind a massive rock watching the sun drop below the distant lip of the pedestal. It throws shafts of light up past the distant edge of the plateau, illuminating the undersides of a few stray clouds in gold and red.

It has been a long day, let me tell you. We had to stay out of sight the entire journey, picking our way across the desert-like landscape while keeping the larger boulders between us and the temple.

I'm sweaty, irritable, thirsty, and hungry, and all I want is a cold beer and my cheap plastic patio chair and to say good night to my kid. This isn't what it's like in the books. In the movies. There's never any mention of the chafing from so much walking. The painful rash that develops between your legs. No mention of searching for a suitable place to relieve yourself. No mention of the hunger, the headaches from dehydration.

But I suppose we're here now. That's the important thing. We're only going in when night falls, though. More cover then.

The sandstone wall of the temple compound stands about a hundred yards away, the gates standing wide open. The massive building Teshani called the Chalice towers into the sky, lanterns and candles flickering in the windows. What was it the Oracle said? *A labyrinthine complex of halls, passages, rooms, scriptoriums, and cells.* I don't know what a scriptorium is, but I'm kind of looking forward to finding out.

"How long?" I ask.

"Another hour or so," says Graves. He leans back against the massive stone and folds his arms across his stomach, closing his eyes.

"What are you doing?"

He squints up at me. "Taking a nap. You have to get rest when you can in this job."

He closes his eyes and is soon snoring away. There's no way I can sleep. I watch the sun vanish, the sky turning from blue to purple to black. The stars come out, bright and clear, unfamiliar constellations strewn above me. I wonder what we're actually going to do if we get this jewel. Do we destroy it? *Can* we destroy it? And what about the spear? How do we get that back? Because it can't be left in the hands of the cult. It's obviously too dangerous.

How does it even work, anyway? How do a spear and a jewel unlock a million-year-old prison? How will it release the Old Ones?

Questions for another time. It's dark now so I nudge Graves's foot. He blinks and looks around, yawning hugely and scratching his balls.

"Time to go?" he says.

"Reckon so."

He pulls open his satchel. I do the same and take out what I assume is my disguise, a neatly folded square of charcoal gray material. Graves has one too. We shake them out to reveal one of those robes I'd seen the priests wandering around the city in when we first arrived. The Oracle also supplied two daggers each. Small enough to hide but wicked sharp.

I slip my robes over my head, pulling the hood up to conceal my features. I turn to Graves. "What do you think? Neutral evil or chaotic evil?"

"What are you talking about?" asks Graves.

"Doesn't matter."

"If you're finished messing around, follow me. And remember, the key to a good disguise is to act like you belong. *Become* your subject. *Be* the person you are pretending to be."

"You want me to pretend to be an evil cleric?"

"Yes."

"Cool. I've read enough Robert E. Howard. Let's do this."

We hurry across the rocky ground, coming to a stop against the wall just to the side of the gate.

I peer into the church grounds. A flagstone courtyard, empty. Marble stairs that lead into the temple structure itself.

Graves straightens up and makes sure his hood is positioned correctly, then casually walks into the courtyard, heading straight for the huge doors.

I follow, and we enter the Chalice building. The atrium is brightly lit, revealing a mosaic in the floor that depicts some sort of epic battle with lots of fireballs and lightning and stuff. We climb the stairs leading to the second floor. Graves pauses by the wall and peers into the corridor beyond.

"For someone supposedly 'in character' you're acting very shifty," I say. "Unless this is how the priests normally walk around in their own temple? Like you're on your way to a midnight rendezvous?"

Graves straightens up without answering. Then he strides out into the passage. I grin and follow.

We move along the corridors, passing expensive tapestries and old, faded paintings. Deeper into the temple, up back stairs and along more passages. The corridors eventually all blur together, but we gradually make our way higher, moving to where we were told the Eli or whatever he is called has his bedroom.

I mean, what's with that, anyway? What kind of crazy-ass priest keeps the holiest relic in his bedroom? What an idiot. He deserves to have it stolen. We're actually doing them a favor. They can see how crappy their security arrangements are.

I've taken the lead by now, Graves dragging his steps as he pauses to admire each of the tapestries.

I turn a corner and come face-to-face with one of the priests. I falter, smile, and nod, hesitate, panic slightly, glance over my shoulder to find that Graves is nowhere to be seen, face front again, smile one more time, just for good luck, then carry on walking past the priest.

"You! Stop."

Shit. I turn around. This priest has silver embroidery sewn around the hems and sleeves of his robe, patterns that make him seem like he's high up on the food chain. And he has a deranged look in his eyes. This one's definitely of the "mad priest" variety.

"What are you doing up here? This area is off-limits. You cannot disturb the Eli's sleep."

"Uh . . . yeah. Sorry, man. I was . . . I got lost, you know?" I rack my brain for anything remotely similar in my life that could in any way prepare me for this. The only thing I get is the thousands of movies I wasted my life watching. "I . . . was looking for the bathroom."

"The what?"

"The bathroom? No?" I think about it. "The . . . water closet?" He stares at me blankly. "The crapper?" Still nothing. "The john? The restroom? The throne. The potty. The commode. None of these ringing a bell?"

"I think you should come with me."

"Love to, pal. Really. Sounds amazing. But I've got virgins to sacrifice and evil magic to conjure."

I try to walk away, but he slaps a hand on my shoulder. Oh, well. Had to happen sooner or later.

I brace my feet and whirl around, pushing the priest hard in the chest. He stumbles back with a shout of surprise and hits the wall. I lunge forward before he can recover and grab hold of his robe, pushing my forearm into his neck.

He struggles, trying to pull his robe from my fingers. I hesitate, then release him and shove him as hard as I can in the face, banging his head into the wall.

The priest bounces and staggers forward, a smear of blood left on the stones behind him. I reach into my robes and pull out one of the daggers.

The priest grabs hold of my wrist before I can do anything. My eyes snap up, locking gazes with him. I almost let go. I see no intelligence there, just a crazed, feral look. Before I can even react, the priest lifts a foot and boots me hard in the stomach.

My breath explodes from my lungs. I stagger backward. The priest comes with me, still holding onto my wrist with one hand. I twist my arm and try to pull his fingers apart with my other hand, but his grip is like stone. Surprisingly strong, these insane priests.

I give up trying and pull the second knife from my belt. I swing it clumsily, aiming for his neck. He sees it coming and tries to jerk away. The blade rips through his cheek and comes out the side of his mouth.

I let go of the dagger. The priest howls in pain and pulls me in close, then balls his fist and hits me as hard as he can in the side of the head.

I collapse to the floor, dropping the first dagger, and this time he lets me go. I lie there dazed, telling myself to get up, to move, but my body doesn't want to obey. Everything is spinning. I try to push myself to my feet. I can hear the priest moaning in pain behind me. He tries to speak, but it comes out as a muffled scream as he opens his torn lips.

Then my head is yanked back. I find myself staring into something from a *Friday the 13th* movie. Blood and saliva drip onto my face. The priest raises the first dagger I dropped.

I reach up and rip the second dagger from his cheek. The priest roars, and then I quickly thrust the blade deep into his chest.

He looks at me in confusion, then collapses to the flagstones. He hits face-first, and I can hear his nose breaking as it smacks into the stone floor.

I push myself shakily to my feet and stare at the corpse. Then I throw up into the corner.

"Not bad," says a voice.

I wipe my mouth and turn to see Graves leaning casually against the wall.

"What the hell, man? Why didn't you help?"

"You were doing fine on your own."

"He nearly killed me!"

"*Nearly* being the operative word. Relax, idiot. I would have stepped in eventually."

I straighten my robes. I want to punch him, but my hands are trembling so much I don't think I'd manage it. I stare down at the body. I can't believe I just did that. Stabbed a man to death. I mean, sure. I used the Elder Gods' guns on things, but they just made the target . . . go away. There was nothing left to look at and realize what you've done. This, though. This was actual death. Actual murder. I mean, sure, I killed Crew Cut, but that was instinct. I couldn't stop that if I wanted to. This . . . was different.

"It was self-defense," says Graves, as if sensing my thoughts.

I glance at him, and he nods over my shoulder. "Nearly there."

I take a deep, shaky breath and turn. He's right. The passage leads to a single open door with a narrow set of stairs leading up.

We climb the stairs, moving as quietly as possible. I'm worried about guards, but when we reach the top there's nobody there. Just a doorway leading into a huge antechamber with couches and tables and a wooden desk facing an arched window. Seems that when you're the head honcho in a world, you grow a bit lax on the security front.

"I don't suppose it would be out here?" I ask.

"We were told it's in his bedchambers."

Of course. There are three doors leading out of the antechamber. The first opens into a tiled room with a sunken floor filled with steaming water. I close the door as Graves opens the next. He closes it again.

"Library," he says.

That leaves one. We approach the door, and Graves carefully pushes down the handle, edging the door slowly open.

I peer over Graves's shoulder. The smell of incense is heavy in the air, thick and cloying. Rich tapestries hang from the walls. Cushions and thick carpets are strewn everywhere, and in the center of the room is a massive four-poster bed with gauze curtains hiding the occupant.

We sneak inside. Graves gestures for me to search the right side of the room while he takes the left. I nod and move off, checking the sideboard, looking behind the tapestries, searching the shelves of gold ornaments depicting Cthulhu and his brothers and sisters. There really are quite a lot of them, and they all look like monsters from the deepest part of our primal brains. Just looking at them makes my skin crawl.

No jewel, though.

Graves glances over at me and shakes his head. He hasn't found it either.

Our eyes turn to the bed. We move slowly toward it, and I gently part the curtains, seeing Graves doing the same on the opposite side.

The high priest is lying on top of the sheets. Naked. He's ancient and wrinkly and, frankly, pretty disgusting to look at. His massive, hairy belly pokes up like a mountain.

But it's what he's lying next to that draws our attention.

It's a huge head.

No body. Just a head. It's about three times the size of my own, but the proportions are odd. Like some kind of space alien left out in the sun to wither and dry out.

And it has a jewel embedded in its forehead.

I stare at it in awe. The jewel seems . . . alive. It's black and oily, and it looks like there's something inside it, slowly writhing.

The head is on my side of the bed. I look uncertainly at Graves. He's staring at the head with a pale face, looking seriously freaked out. I gesture for his attention, miming if I'm supposed to lift the damn thing up or not.

He seems hesitant, at first, but he finally nods, once, and steps back away from the bed.

I reach down and pick up the head.

As soon as I touch it, the eyes snap open. They're black and filled with stars. I almost drop it in shock. The mouth opens. The forehead creases in a frown. It's about to scream. I don't know how I know that, but I do. I quickly try to slap my hand over its mouth.

In doing so, I accidentally brush the jewel. . . .

Darkness. A breath of cold wind that brushes my face with an almost audible sigh. The breeze becomes sticky, tangible. It pushes against my face, pressing into my skin so that it's like walking through a cobweb. The pressure against my face increases, turning into pain. I open my mouth to scream, but then with an almost physical snap, it pushes through my skin and enters into my very being.

I cry out. Pictures flash before me, but so quickly I only have a sense of the vastness of them, of the sense that if I *did* actually manage to focus on them I'd be driven mad. They're blood red and liver purple, glistening and sharp. A battle—between the Old Ones and the Elder Gods. The screams of a million dying madmen, the taste of raw flesh and corrupt earth. The touch of the images is ragged and sharp, a tongue made of shards of glass that licks over and over, pulling up strips of skin and muscle, breaking against my bone.

Then a voice speaks to me, and it is the joyful babble of a lunatic as he kills innocents. It is the rending scream of a man woken up to find his family murdered and a bleeding knife held in his hand. It is the cajoling voice of madness, the encouraging whisper that speaks of foulness and murder.

It is the voice of a god.

The presence sifts through my mind, searching for knowledge. I can't remember the questions. They fall away from my thoughts with the blood that drips from my ears. The presence pillages my mind, pushing, twisting, leaving trails of vileness that I know I'll never break free of.

Then the presence is gone, and I'm left with a sense of dark, alien space. Cold and brittle stars. Freezing cold. Eternity. Dreaming. Hungry.

§

I try to lift my head, but it won't budge.

Why can't I move?

Then the memories roll over me. Touching the jewel. Opening my mouth to scream. Guards, yelling. Pain.

I pull my arms. Nothing. I force open my eyes and swivel them left and right. Chains. I'm chained to something. I finally manage to lift my head, and then I peer over my shoulder. A . . . giant pillar of rock, by the looks of it, that disappears up through the roof.

I look around. I'm in some kind of arena. Or an amphitheater, the kind used for lectures. Tiers of benches climb up to doors. I'm at the bottom, the rock pillar situated on a sandy floor.

Well. This is just peachy. I look left and right, but I don't see any sign of Graves. Did he escape? Is he dead?

This is bad. I strain against the chains, but there's no give. The rock is digging into my back and arms, cutting into my skin.

I hear a creaking sound from somewhere. I look around to see one of the doors at the top of the amphitheater slowly opening. I tense, adrenaline surging through my system. I strain against the chains again, but it's no use.

"Psst!"

I snap my head up. Graves is peering around the door. I blink stupidly at him, wondering if I'm hallucinating.

He makes sure I'm alone, then enters the chamber carrying his rucksack against his stomach. It looks heavy.

He makes his way down the steps, looking furtively over his shoulder.

"What the hell happened?" I ask.

"What do you mean?" says Graves. He puts the bag down and starts fiddling with the chains. "You started screaming. Woke the high priest up; then you passed out. The guards came running and took you into custody."

"And you?"

"I hid. Under the bed."

"You hid under the bed?"

"No choice. I knew one of us had to stay free. And your little distraction meant they left the room unattended, meaning I could get hold of . . ." He kicks the heavy satchel. "This."

"Is that the head?"

"It is indeed. They left it in the bedroom when they took you off, you naughty thief. Perfect plan, all round."

Graves disappears behind the huge pillar, and a moment later I slump forward, only just managing to stop falling face-first into the ground.

"Get up, idiot. No time for napping."

I push myself to my feet. I stretch and wince, trying to get life back into my limbs.

Graves grabs the satchel and leads the way back up the stairs. "Nearly done," he says.

"Yeah." I follow him to the door. "Now we just have to figure out how to get the hell off this world."

Graves's shoulders sag slightly. "God. Five minutes, Priest. Is five minutes too much to ask without you inflicting reality on me?"

We retrace our steps back through the temple. We still have our robes, so nobody gives us any trouble as we pass.

We arrive back at the first entrance hall. We pause and peer over the balcony, but there don't seem to be any surprises waiting for us. We hurry down the stairs and across the hall, stepping through the doors and back out into the humid night air.

We start to run, which doesn't really make sense. It's not as if we can run all the way across the desert, but still, you like to get a head start when you've just ripped off a holy relic from mad priests.

We don't get far.

As soon as we pass the massive rock that we hid behind earlier in the day, there is a flare of blue light and the air around us rips apart. We skid to a stop as the tear spreads, completely surrounding us in a circle of torn reality.

And then Nyarlathotep steps through the rip, accompanied by Dana and four Hounds of Tindalos.

He pauses a few steps away and smiles widely.

"I like you guys, I really do. You're the kind of enemies I want in my life. So incompetent that you do all the actual work for me. But don't feel bad. Seriously. Not your fault." He nods at the bag Graves is holding tightly to his chest. "Is that the jewel? Bigger than I thought, but no matter. It's cool." He claps his hands. "You did it, guys! Well done. Saves me having to storm the temple with my hounds. You saved a lot of peoples' lives there, so good for you. I respect that. Now. Be good little monkeys and pass it over."

Graves grips the bag tighter to his chest.

"Come on, man. Let's not ruin what we have here. I won. You lost. Dana. Fetch. There's a good girl."

I notice that a brief look of hatred flickers across Dana's face. It's so quick I wonder if I imagined it. But she walks forward and stands before Graves and myself.

Graves still doesn't release the bag. Nyarlathotep sighs and clicks his fingers. The hounds stalk forward, their geometric planes shifting and refracting the moonlight.

Dana holds her hands out, and Graves reluctantly hands over the bag.

"Thanks!" says Nyarlathotep brightly. "Glad we could resolve this without any bloodshed—oh wait, we didn't. Because I should probably kill you now, right? No offense, you seem like groovy guys, but you're just starting to get a bit annoying, you know? Dana?"

She takes a knife out of her belt and smiles at Graves.

"Just put your hands up, yeah?" says Nyarlathotep. "Make it easy for her. I mean, the size difference between you guys is immense. She probably won't be able to take you on—"

Dana whirls around and flings the knife straight at Nyarlathotep. He squeals and brings an arm up to defend himself, and the knife goes hilt-deep into his bicep. The hounds growl uncertainly. I look at Graves, and he shrugs, his hand moving slowly to his gun.

"What the hell, Dana? Was that, like, a really bad throw or something?"

"Yes! It was! I wanted to kill you."

"What? Hey now, you don't mean that. You're hyster—"

She reaches into her robe and pulls out a wand. She points it at Nyarlathotep. "I swear to the *gods*, if you dare say I'm hysterical, I will rip your throat out with my teeth."

She flicks the wand, and four blue fireballs surge out its tip and hit the hounds.

They burst into greasy flames. The creatures howl and run in circles, rolling around and trying to put out the flames. But they can't. I hear the shattering of glass, and then the hounds explode into shards.

"Why did you do that?" shouts Nyarlathotep. "You know how expensive those things are? Seriously, what's with you, Dana? Should I set up a meeting with HR? We can discuss—"

"Discuss? Discuss what? How I'm sick of you? Ordering me around, treating me like a slave. I'm a person, you moron. An actual real person."

"Hey, I know that."

"You don't! I've never met anyone so patronizing. So . . . casually misogynistic. You're a relic from a bygone era. You should be put down."

Nyarlathotep's face clears. He smiles. "I know what it is. It's . . . you know . . ." He lowers his voice. ". . . that time? Of the month?"

I wince. Graves's breath rushes inward. Dana freezes and straightens up. Nyarlathotep looks over at us and grins. "You guys know what I'm talking about? Right?"

Graves and I both take a sudden interest in the stars.

"Guys?"

"Don't talk to us," says Graves urgently. "We don't know you."

Dana walks slowly toward Nyarlathotep, her whole body vibrating with fury. "I'm going to take this jewel and the spear. I'm going to free the Old Ones. And I'm going to be the favored one."

"But that's my job."

"Not anymore."

Graves has been using the distraction to slowly take his entropy gun out. He brings it up and fires, but Nyarlathotep sees him and yanks Dana in front of him. The invisible bullet hits her in the back. She shrieks, not in pain, but hatred, and she lifts the wand and releases one last fireball, straight into Nyarlathotep's face.

He staggers back, shrieking in agony, his face a ball of fire. Dana drops to the ground, the black veins spreading over her face, aging her until she's nothing but a skeleton that turns to dust.

Nyarlathotep grabs the bag containing the head, and he dives into the Rip, trailing smoke and the smell of burning flesh behind him.

"Not cool, guys. . . ." comes his distant voice as he sprints away through the tunnel. "This . . . really hurts."

I look at Graves. "What now?"

"We follow after."

So saying, he slaps his mask onto his face and leaps into the Rip, just as it's starting to close. I grab my own mask from the satchel and quickly follow.

CHAPTER TWENTY

The Rip snaps shut behind us. I've never been in the tunnel without a functioning mask, so I have no idea what to expect. I mean, it's still there, covering my face, but it's not linked to Wonderland. Surely that will have an effect.

It's dark. A soul-level, primordial darkness that speaks to the collective memory of humankind. A darkness that drove us into caves, that made us gather around fires in primitive family units to fight off the night.

Something slithers in my peripheral vision. I turn quickly. Lightning flickers. I see strobe-like images of tentacles and claws, flashes of old bone and serrated teeth. Horned gods dancing in ancient forests that stretch from one coast to the other.

Fear surges through me, ancient, primal. I tense, readying myself to run, but Graves grabs me by the arm.

"Control it," he says softly. "They can sense your panic."

"What are they?"

"Ancient fears. Given life by humankind's collective unconscious. They only exist here now, between the worlds."

"I didn't feel this before."

"You think we use those masks because they make us look dashing? The Elder Gods were the only ones who knew who they were. Understand? They had evolved beyond fear. Beyond self-doubt, narcissism. They accepted their reality utterly, and when they could do that they gained control over it. The masks that we use—parts of the Elder Gods—hide us from the echoes in the dark. Now, enough questions. We need to move."

He gestures ahead. Nyarlathotep and the remaining hounds are stepping through the end of the tunnel into bright sunshine. I feel a surge of happiness at the sight. Sun. Normalcy.

Graves starts moving at an odd, skipping trot. I follow at the same pace, wondering why we don't just run for it. Especially as I'm sure something is following us and oh, look—the Rip is starting to close up, healing itself and knitting back together.

"Graves—"

"Slowly," he says. "We have to time this properly."

He moves faster, then slows, then suddenly speeds up again. The Rip has almost closed up in the middle, streamers of sunlight shifting and dancing across the inside of the tunnel. Invisible creatures surge and hiss away from the light, pulling back into the darkness. We're not going to make it. We're going to be shut in here forever, with no way to contact Wonderland—

"Run!" snaps Graves, and he leaps ahead of me, sprinting the remaining distance to the opening.

I'm stunned into immobility at first, watching his back recede. Then I feel something wrap around my ankle, and I shriek and surge after him, moving faster than I've ever moved in my life.

Graves dives through the Rip. The opening is tiny, barely two feet long and getting smaller. I throw myself forward, sailing through the air like Superman and landing like . . . well, like me, the most unathletic person I know.

I hit the ground hard and roll onto my back just as the Rip winks out of existence. I groan and blink in the afternoon light, staring up at the blue sky. A second later the surrounding sounds filter into my awareness. Traffic. Horns blaring. A distant gunshot.

My eyes widen.

It . . . it feels like . . .

I scramble to my feet, looking around in amazement.

Home.

We're back beneath the overpass, where I shot the creepy old monkey man.

"How are we here?" I ask.

Graves is peering along the deserted street. "Hmm?"

"How are we here? And where's Nyarlathotep?"

"Oh, he's gone. Why do you think I was hanging back in the tunnel? You think I like it in there? What was the first question again?"

"Is this . . .? Are we back in my world?"

Graves frowns. "It appears so, doesn't it? Didn't really see that coming, to be honest with you. Bit of a shame, really."

I stop staring at my surroundings and instead stare at him accusingly. "You're about to say something bad. I know it. *Why* is it a shame?"

"Think about it, moron. Nyarlathotep has the two pieces he needs. He wants to free Cthulhu. Which reality do you think he's going to go to?"

"The . . . one where Cthulhu is held prisoner?"

"Check out the brains on Harry. Got it in one, sport. And if Cthulhu is released it's good-bye planet earth. He'll use it as his all-you-can-eat breakfast buffet."

"But . . . we're going to stop them, right?"

He looks at me in relief. "Are we? Great. How?"

"I don't know!" I shout. "Don't you?"

"Oh. No, not really."

I press my fingers against my temples. "Jesus Christ, Graves. I swear to God I'm going to shoot you unless you start being helpful."

"Hey! I got us here, didn't I?"

"No. You didn't. We were ambushed, and the priceless artifact was stolen from us. Again."

"Yeah, but . . . we're *here*."

"Where an ancient cosmic god is about to be freed from his prison, killing all seven billion people on this planet. My family included."

"Well . . . sure. If you put it that way. But she's your ex. She doesn't really count, does she?"

"Graves . . ." I take a step toward him.

He holds his hands up. "Relax. We'll think of something." He looks around. "Problem is, we're still cut off from Wonderland. Which is a pain in the ass."

"Well . . . don't you have a safe house here? Can't we use it to communicate with Ash?"

Graves looks at me with wide eyes. "You know, that's actually the most intelligent idea you've had since we met. Well done, you—wait, where are you going?"

"To see my family."

He hurries to catch up. "You can't. We have more important things to do."

"No. We don't. Last time I was here I was attacked and people tried to kill me. I haven't seen my daughter in days. I would like to make sure she's still alive, if that's okay with you. *Then* we can go to the safe house."

"Fine. But make it quick. 'Hello, dear, daddy's still alive. He hasn't been devoured by an ancient cosmic entity yet.' Then we're off, okay?"

§

We "borrow" an old Ford and use it to drive to my house.

There's nobody home. I can sense it even before I walk up the drive. The house has that vacant, empty feeling. Abandoned.

"We're too late," I whisper, my heart thudding painfully in my chest.

"Oh, don't be absurd," says Graves. "Why on earth would they target your family? They know nothing about what's going on."

"To get to me."

"Wow. Paging Dr. Ego. I think you have a rather overinflated opinion of your importance, good sir. Me, on the other hand. If *I* had any family, I would fear for their safety on a permanent basis. Because I, as opposed to *you*, am *incredibly* important. Whereas you're not." He waits a bit. "But I am."

"Yeah, I got it."

I try the door. Locked.

"What do we do? Should we call the police?"

"For what!? You're being absurd!"

I peer through the window. Everything looks normal.

"Come on," says Graves. "We don't have time for this. We have an apocalyptic-level event to prevent."

"Have you got a plan yet?" I ask.

"I'm working on it, okay?"

"Because I have an idea."

"Oh? Careful not to get ahead of yourself. Two ideas in one day, you're liable to burn out that little brain of yours."

I wait.

"Well? What is it?"

"You sure you want to hear it? Because I'm good if not. I mean, you're probably right. It's most likely stupid—"

"Priest, just tell me the damn plan!"

"Fine. What I'm wondering is what happened back at the motel."

"The . . . ?"

"The motel. When all this started. The . . . carnage. The one you came to investigate."

"You mean when you murdered my coworker?"

I sigh. "Yes. Then. Did you ever find out why that weird glass ball was there at that motel? The one with the coordinates?"

"Well . . . no. We were demoted, remember? Because you murdered—"

"Yes, yes. But don't you see? That kicked all this off. *Why* were the coordinates there? At that motel? And for there to be a massacre, it meant there had to be two different groups. I can see Nyarlathotep and his cronies being there. They wanted the jewel and the spear, after all. But who else? Who was the fight *between*? It wasn't you guys, was it?"

"ICD?" says Graves thoughtfully. "No. We got the call after the fact."

"CBC?"

"No. If they were involved we wouldn't have even been called out."

"So who was it?"

Graves stares at me for a moment. "You know," he says slowly. "I think if we can find out what happened at the motel, it might give us a lead. Somewhere to start."

I blink at him.

"Don't look so vacant!" shouts Graves. "Think about it. And keep up, please. Who else was at the motel? There were two sides fighting. And if the other side wasn't us, who was it? There were human body parts there. So if they didn't come through a Rip they must have come from here. Your reality. Which means someone here on earth knows about Cthulhu. About Nyarlathotep. It's imperative that we find out what happened that day!"

"Harry?"

I whirl around and see Megan and Susan standing at the bottom of the drive.

"Daddy!"

I run to Susan and then swing her up into my arms, holding her tight against my chest.

"Harry? What the hell are you doing?" says Megan. "Where have you been? You haven't called. We even went round to your apartment. We—Your daughter was worried."

I lock eyes with Megan. I can see it there. See what she won't say.

I put Susan down, carefully stroking her hair back into place. "I . . . had to go away for a bit. Um . . . new job."

"New job? What is it this time?" asks Megan. "Street cleaning? Funeral director."

I stare at her, silently pleading with her not to do this in front of Susan.

"Actually," says Graves, strolling toward us. "Harry is helping me." Susan squints at him. "You look funny."

"Indeed I do, small human. It's part of my charm."

"And who the hell are you?" asks Megan.

Graves pulls out a leather wallet and flashes a very shiny and official-looking badge at Megan. "Havelock Graves. ICD."

Megan glares at me. "What have you done now?"

"Oh, you misunderstand. Harry here is part of my team."

"Part of . . . ?"

"My team. A highly trained team that solves crimes. His past training in law enforcement and his local knowledge made him eminently suitable for the job. We've been on assignment, and I forbade him from using phones. It was more for your safety than his."

Megan looks at me. "Is this true?"

I'm staring at Graves in amazement, but pull my gaze back to Megan and manage to nod.

"Are you a policeman, Dad?" asks Susan.

"Uh . . . yeah."

"Indeed, tiny person, he is. But now we must go. We have an urgent case to solve! It involves monsters and naughty men with narcissistic tendencies and a desire to ruin the world. Harry, let us away!"

With that, Graves turns and strides toward the Ford.

"Sorry, honey. Dad has to go. I'll come round later, okay? When this is all over."

I give Susan a kiss on the head. I glance once at Megan, then set off after Graves.

I'm halfway to the car before Megan calls out. "Harry, wait."

I pause as Megan approaches.

"Sorry. About what I said. The street-cleaning thing. That was a low blow."

I shrug. "It's fine. I haven't exactly been the most . . . ambitious guy, have I?"

She smiles slightly. "No, not really." She lightly touches my arm. It feels like a shock of electricity. "But congrats. I'm happy you've got something in law enforcement. It's what you've always wanted to do."

"Yeah." I think about telling her the kind of law enforcement I'm actually involved with, but decide not to utterly ruin the moment. (See? I'm learning.)

"Harry!" shouts Graves. "We have somewhere to be."

I nod to Megan and wave at Susan, then jog to the street. "Thanks," I say as we get into the car. "For saying that."

Graves shrugs. "It's the truth. No need to thank me. Now, let's go and stop that incredibly annoying death cult from releasing an ancient god, shall we?"

§

Graves drives us through Central LA, whistling. He seems to be in a better mood now that we have a plan. He turns left into Rossmore, then right on Melrose, taking another right into South Western, lurching to a stop against the sidewalk before we hit Koreatown.

I look out the window, at the dealers lounging against the shop fronts, smoking and passing bottles around. The passersby laughing and shouting insults. The fight with broken bottles going on a few feet away. Yup. Definitely home.

"Nice neighborhood," I say.

Graves looks around without much interest. "Is it?"

He gets out the car and heads toward a pawnshop before leaning forward to peer through the dirty glass door.

"Why are we here?" I ask, hurrying to catch up.

"This is the safe house."

"Charming."

"It doesn't need to look nice," says Graves. He pulls the door open, and a little bell jingles. "It's supposed to be low-key. That's the whole point."

I follow him in. The smells of old leather, cigarette smoke, oil, and ramen noodles hit me in the senses. The scents hang heavy and dense, weighed down with stale air and old smoke. The shop is a cluttered mess of old typewriters, tube televisions, watches, and gold jewelry. It's some sort of time capsule, as if it was locked down in the eighties and hasn't been opened since.

"Dante!" Graves shouts. "Where are you?"

"We're closed!" a voice shouts from behind a curtain of plastic beads.

"No you're not!"

The curtain parts, and a face wearing the thickest glasses I've ever seen peers out. Noodles hang from his mouth. He blinks owlishly at us, then sucks the noodles up with a loud slurping sound.

"Havelock Graves?"

"The same."

"I thought you were dead."

"Still hale and hearty. As you can see."

"No, I definitely remember you being dead. Few years back. Something to do with a vampire dragon."

"Oh, that. Yes, that was me. I got better."

"Good for you."

The little man steps into the front of the shop. He's wearing a dirty Hawaiian shirt, stained cargo shorts, and pink flip-flops. He's also holding a huge tub of steaming noodles. "How long were you dead for?" he asks.

"Couple of weeks, apparently. Listen, we need to use the link to Wonderland. That okay?"

"Uh . . . Sure, man. Why wouldn't it be?"

"No reason," says Graves, heading through the curtain. "That's Harry Priest," he calls out. "He's the rookie."

Dante shuffles forward and peers up at me for a long, uncomfortable moment. "Want some noodles?"

"I'm good, thanks."

"You sure? I've got sweet and sour or peri-peri."

"Thanks, no."

"They're *really* good. I get them imported from Japan."

"My God, man!" shouts Graves, his head emerging back through the curtain. "He doesn't want any noodles!"

Graves disappears again and leaves me with Dante. The guy stares at me as he eats his noodles. Doesn't take his eyes off me.

"You want a pickled egg?" he asks eventually.

"No."

"Some jerky?"

"No. Seriously, thanks, but I'm not hungry. I mean, I *am*, but not for that."

He blinks at me. "I need a wee."

"Have fun."

He nods, then disappears through a door off to the side. A moment later I hear the flushing of a toilet.

I wait, but Dante doesn't reappear. I suppose I should be grateful, but when five minutes pass I start to get uneasy. I move toward the door and knock.

"Dante? You okay in there?"

No answer.

I knock harder. Still nothing. I try the handle, and the door swings open to reveal a cesspit of a toilet, green fungus covering the walls, chipped and broken tiles, a sink that might have once been white but that is now gray and black with grime.

And an open window.

I stand on the toilet and peer out. A sun-bleached alley lies beyond, litter and old crates strewn across the asphalt next to a rusted Dumpster filled with old mannequins and computer monitors. No sign of Dante anywhere.

This can't be good.

I hurry back to the bead curtain just as Graves comes back through.

"I found a name," he says. "One of the victims from the motel."

"Dante's gone."

"What do you mean?"

"I mean he's done a runner. Jumped out the back window."

Graves's eyes widen. He runs to the front of the shop just as a Slip flares to life outside, and the Inspectre steps through the doorway with a small army of tactical officers spreading out behind him.

"Shit," says Graves, turning and shoving me toward the rear of the shop. "Go, go."

We move past the beaded curtain and down a tiny passage into a cluttered office. Graves takes his entropy gun out, shoots an antique-looking computer system (complete with blinking green cursor), and pulls the back door open. He stops and grabs an old revolver that's sitting on the desk, then darts outside.

We move along the rear wall of the shop and pause at the mouth of the alley, peering into the street beyond. The Slip is gone. Off to our right the ICD agents are bursting through the door into the pawnshop, screaming and shouting. Graves waits a second, then sprints for the car. He gets behind the wheel, and I slide into the passenger seat. Graves starts the engine and pulls off slowly, not wanting to draw attention.

We head south until we hit the suburbs, driving past identical houses with identical, neat lawns and immaculate sidewalks. A David Lynch nightmare.

"So," I say eventually. "Dante. What a dick."

"I can only assume they threatened his family."

"Really? 'Cause he's not the kind of guy I see as having a family. Unless you're talking like sitting blow-up dolls around the dinner table or something."

"You don't even know the man!"

"Am I wrong, though?"

A pause. "No," says Graves eventually.

"So what now?"

"We carry on. I got the address of one of the victims from the motel. We'll see if there is anything to be found there."

"No," says a voice from behind us. "You won't."

I turn in my seat and see an ICD agent wedged down in the rear footwell. He's pointing a gun at me, but holding it really awkwardly, his elbows pushed hard against his ribs.

"Hey, Graves. There's a guy on the floor back here."

"What's he doing?"

"I don't know. Hey—you. What are you doing?"

"Guaranteeing my promotion. See, all the other guys. They always go in guns blazing. But I spotted your car outside and decided to hide in it, just in case you managed to sneak past."

"That's . . . actually pretty smart."

"Thanks. I like to plan ahead. No offense. I'm going to shoot you now. I only need one of you alive, and I think Graves is the most valuable—"

Three gunshots explode in the car, and the guy bucks and screams, blood spraying everywhere before he slumps back, dead.

My ears are ringing. I look at Graves, shocked, as he tosses the gun he grabbed from Dante's desk into the glove box.

"What an idiot," he says.

CHAPTER TWENTY~ONE

The address Graves got from Dante's computer system is a fenced-off apartment block that looks more like a motel than anything else. A U-shaped, three-story building facing into a concrete courtyard with rusted swings and a broken seesaw. The gate is closed and locked, but the chain-link has more gaping holes than a politician's excuse for being photographed at a strip club, so it's easy enough for us to get inside.

"Are you really expecting to find anything?" I ask. "It's been a couple of weeks since the massacre at the motel."

"If you have any better ideas, I'm very keen to hear them," says Graves as we move across the pitted concrete. "At the very least, we might find out something about the victim, something we can use to make sense of how he was involved."

"And you're sure he wasn't ICD?"

"Not according to the search I did at Dante's place. The victim was called Maurice Stableford, and it looks like he was a born-and-bred earthman. Like yourself."

"That's what I'm not getting," I say as we climb the stairs. "If he's got nothing to do with ICD, and if he was from this alternate, then how the hell did he know to be at the motel?"

"That's what we're here to find out," says Graves, stopping before a door. There are remnants of police tape stuck to the frame, but it looks like it was ripped away ages ago.

Graves tries the door, but it's locked. He takes out a small leather purse from his jacket and extracts two thin pieces of metal that he proceeds to insert into the lock. Five seconds later and we're inside.

"Shocking security," he says as he studies the cramped entrance hall. "Imagine a poor, defenseless woman living here, prey to the whims of the psychos who roam the streets."

"Defenseless women?" I say. "This is LA, Graves. The women here are tougher than me."

"That doesn't take much," mutters Graves as he moves into the lounge.

It's pointless, though. The place has already been cleaned out. There are empty spaces on the walls where paintings have been removed, a few computer cables lying around on the dark brown carpet.

"Looks like nobody's home," I say.

"That's a very annoying habit, you know," snaps Graves. "Stating the obvious in a manner you think is amusing. You're not funny. Or clever."

He disappears through a door into the bedroom. I give him the silent finger and check the door to my right. It's the bathroom. I use my foot to open the door all the way, peering hesitantly inside.

No old-man monkey waiting for me this time. I check the medicine cabinet. No prescription drugs with helpful names and addresses. Just old, disposable razor blades and expensive moisturizing cream.

I open up the cream and sniff. Then put some on my finger and rub it into my face. Traveling between alternate realities really dries you out.

I head to the kitchen, pulling open cupboards in the hope of finding something helpful. Just a couple of chipped cups. No handy scribbled note stuck to the fridge with a forwarding address. No postcard from a close friend or work partner, handily chatting about why they were at the motel.

Some people are no help at all.

I head back into the lounge, and something catches my eye. A tiny blinking light by the front door. I stroll over to see what it is, crouching down and peering at the little contraption.

It's an infrared beam set up across the doorway.

Which means it would trigger when the door opens.

"Son of a—"

That's as far as I get. I see a flash of movement from the hallway outside the apartment. Then a blinding, nausea-inducing flash of pain.

Then a nice, pleasing darkness.

§

I wake up to the sound of arguing. Goddamn it, but I'm going to need to see a neurologist once this is over. I must have some kind of brain injury by now.

"I don't care if your father is a pastor, institutional religion is the cause of more wars and deaths than anything else in human history."

Graves's voice. I blink in confusion.

"No. You can't generalize like that," says another voice, a man's. "If religion was applied like it was meant to, then we'd all live in peace."

"Exactly. But there's just the little problem of humankind, isn't there? You all tend to get in the way of the spreading of the good vibes."

Are we in a bar? The last time I heard religion being argued about like that was in a bar. As I recall it ended up in a fight with bottles being applied at speed to peoples' heads.

"No religion. No politics," I mutter.

The talking stops. I lift my head and woozily look around, studying my surroundings.

It's not a bar—it's some kind of dreary room. And Graves and myself are tied to old wooden chairs. I shake my head and focus. It looks like a private investigator's office from the seventies. Three old desks, dirty windows, and a metal fan that creaks and whines as it turns slowly, wafting the tepid air around the room. Two of the desks have ancient computers on them, tiny CRT monitors and keyboards that are so old they've gone that horrible bone-yellow color.

The other desk has a typewriter on it. There's a young girl seated behind the typewriter, and she's halfheartedly hitting a key over and over, a bored look on her face. She's in a stylish suit, her purple-and-blue hair pulled back in a severe ponytail.

Clack, clack.

Behind the other desks sit two very . . . beige-looking men. That's the only way I can describe them. They almost fade into the furniture they're so nondescript. One looks to be in his thirties, the other in his fifties, and both look as if they've stepped out of a 1950s clothes catalog. Old-fashioned brown suits and Brylcreemed hair set in the exact same side parting.

"Hey!" I shout. "I know you! You're the people who have been spying on me!"

"Don't be absurd, Harry. You're not important enough to spy on."

"No, he's right," says the woman. "We've been watching him since the motel."

"Thank Christ for that," I say, relieved. "I thought I was going mad."

"Someone talk to me," says Graves. "I don't understand what's happening here."

To be fair, the two dudes look like they have no idea either. They look out of their depth, their eyes wide and staring. I instinctively turn to the girl.

"Who are you?" I ask.

She sighs. "Agent Anderson." She points at the younger of the men. "That's Agent Winston, and the other one is Agent Smith."

"Thank you," I say. "You've succeeded in explaining absolutely nothing at all. Are you feds?"

"No," says Anderson distastefully. "We're . . ." She hesitates, and a look of embarrassment crosses her face.

Winston straightens up proudly. "We are agents of the Society for the Prevention of the Takeover of the Old and Unseen. Or PTOU for short."

"P-too-ee?" I say, sounding out the letters. It sounds like I'm spitting.

Anderson sighs. "Yeah. Not our choice, believe me. I've petitioned to have it changed, but oh, no—" she uses her fingers to air quote, "—tradition."

"Who do you report to?" demands Graves.

"The Miskatonic University," says Smith. "In Arkham."

"'That is not dead which can eternal lie, and with strange aeons, even death may die,'" says Winston.

"'That is not dead which can eternal lie, and with strange aeons, even death may die,'" repeats Smith.

Both look to Anderson.

"I'm not saying it," she says.

"Come on, Agent," begs Winston. "It's our pledge of office. You have to repeat it if one of us say it. It's in the rule book."

"Shove your rule book. I'm not saying it. It's stupid."

"Agent Anderson," says Smith severely. "You must repeat the pledge. Otherwise I will be forced to report you."

"Go ahead. No one knows this little club still exists."

Smith splutters in outrage. "How dare you! Of course they do. We are all that stands between humanity and the depredations of the Old Ones. We are the last line of defense against an alien race trillions of years old."

"The three of us?" says Anderson. "We don't even have Internet in here. Not even dial-up. When was the last time you were contacted by the head office?"

"Well..."

"When?"

"Just the other—"

"When?"

"1986."

A silence descends.

"Right," says Anderson. "It's been great and all that. But I think I have to draw the line at kidnapping weird old guys."

"Hey!" I say. "I'm not old."

She looks at me with pity. "What are you? Forty?"

"Uh . . . yeah."

"I rest my case."

She grabs her phone and brandishes it in the air. "We can't even get a signal in here! Lost tribes in the Amazon can get a signal, but us? Oh, no! Not us."

"I'm confused," says Graves. "Miskatonic University is from the Lovecraft stories. It was never real."

"It's real," snaps Smith.

"Yeah," says Winston. "Our remit is to battle and defend human-kind from the eldritch horrors of the Absolute Elsewhere. We are the last line of defense, protecting the world from being devoured by ancient, unknowable gods from beyond the stars."

I look around the tiny office. "And you do all that from here?"

"Look," says Graves. "If this is true, if you're not just sad mental cases with a Lovecraft fetish, then we're on the same side! We're trying to stop Nyarlathotep from releasing Cthulhu from his prison in R'lyeh."

Smith pales. "What do you mean, releasing?"

"Did I stutter? Nyarlathotep wants to release Cthulhu. Wants to let it take over the multiverse or something."

"He wants to release Cthulhu?"

"Jesus! I just said that."

"But . . . to do that he'd have to wake Cthulhu up, wouldn't he?"

"I'd imagine so," says Graves. "That's how it usually works."

"No," says Smith. "No, no, no. That can't happen. You hear me? It can't!"

"All right. Keep your hair on. Just let us go and we'll stop them."

"Relax," says Anderson. "If he doesn't have the star-mover or Cthulhu's consciousness then we're fine."

"The what?" asks Graves.

"It is what Nyarlathotep was after. When the Elder Gods imprisoned Cthulhu, they took away his consciousness so he would stay sleeping forever. They put it into a jewel and threw it randomly into the multiverse."

"The Jewel of Ini-taya," I say. "That's why I had that . . . episode when I touched it. I was actually connecting with Cthulhu."

"You've seen it?" demands Smith.

"Seen it, stole it, had Nyarlathotep take it from us."

"And . . . the star-mover?"

"What's that?" asks Graves.

"It looks like a spear," says Anderson.

"It is not a spear," snaps Smith. "The Elder Gods locked Cthulhu away in his prison hundreds of millions of years ago. The lore says that, 'That cult would never die till the stars came right again, and the secret priests would take great Cthulhu from His tomb to revive His subjects and resume His rule of earth.'"

"Which cannot happen," adds Winston. "Obvs."

Graves points at Winston. "Did you just say obvs? Because if you did I swear to God I will strike you down where you stand!"

"The star-mover was created to . . . artificially induce this process of the stars coming right. Like a combination lock. The spear advances the starscape until the correct sequence is arrived at and it opens Cthulhu's prison."

"Which cannot happen," says Smith. "Seriously, I cannot stress this enough. We are on the cusp of an instant genocidal extinction here."

Graves clears his throat. "Why do I get the feeling you're not telling us something?"

The three agents exchange uneasy looks.

"I demand you tell us what is happening," shouts Graves. "Now!"

Smith sighs. "What do you know of the Old Ones?" he asks. "And the Elder Gods?"

"What everyone knows. The Elder Gods created the Old Ones, but imprisoned them when they got a bit too . . . bitey. The Old Ones are locked away in the Dreamlands—also known as the Absolute Elsewhere—but their minions are always trying to free them."

"That's . . . not quite everything. You see, our society was founded in 1899 by someone from your organization. Elizabeth McLeod."

"Elizabeth McLeod?" Graves frowns. "I know that name. You're mistaken. She was a traitor. She was hunted down and executed for changing sides."

"That's the story the ICD put out," says Smith. "The reality was different. Elizabeth discovered something she shouldn't have and was hunted down because of this knowledge. By her own people."

"Sounds familiar," I say, glancing at Graves.

"And just what is it she was supposed to have discovered?" asks Graves.

"Not just her. She had a partner. Her husband. A man called Howard Harrison."

Graves waves his hand negligently in the air. "Yes, yes. I know the story. Very tragic. He was forced to hunt down the woman he loved because she betrayed humankind."

"No," says Smith. "If anything, it was the other way around. It was Elizabeth who first discovered the secret. She shared it with her husband, and he fled here, to this very world, to attempt to gain favor with the Old Ones."

"How? How would he gain favor?"

"He created a device that could open up a gate to the Dreamlands. That would take him into R'lyeh itself. It was the first step in the plan to free Cthulhu."

"That's impossible," says Graves. "It can't be done."

"Who says?" asks Smith.

"Well . . . everyone."

"Everyone with a vested interest in keeping the truth hidden," says Smith. "Harrison partnered up with Nyarlathotep, and they did indeed create a machine that would open up a doorway."

"Then his wife found out," says Winston eagerly. "She came here to stop him. He had already gathered a number of followers and coconspirators, you see. Nyarlathotep was instructed through his dreams to aid Harrison. Of course, by this time, Harrison was an empty shell. He was totally under the control of the Old Ones. They have a way of getting inside your mind, you see. Once you open the door to them even a tiny bit, they shove it open and take over."

"So what happened?" I ask.

"Elizabeth brought her own followers, and they fought against this cult. She was the one who ended her husband's life, saving the entire multiverse from destruction. Nyarlathotep fled, but ever since then he has never stopped searching for a way to unleash his god. For the past century he has sought out the spear and the jewel . . . to finish what he and Harrison started."

"Elizabeth founded our organization," says Anderson. "To prevent that from happening. She stayed here and joined Miskatonic University. Since then our society has been keeping an eye out for anything suspicious. See, the truth that Elizabeth discovered, the truth that she shared with her husband, that . . . ultimately drove him insane, is something that can never be known. . . . A secret your organization is willing to kill for."

"Yes, yes. Very dramatic. What is it? What is this big secret?"

"That none of us are real," says Smith simply. "We are all the dreams of Cthulhu as he slumbers in his prison."

A moment of silence. Then Graves bursts out laughing. "What a load of crap."

"It's true!" says Smith defensively. "Cthulhu was the first of the Old Ones. And what we call the Dreamlands was the original universe. None of this, none of the alternates you travel to, existed. But when the Elder Gods imprisoned Cthulhu and extracted his consciousness, the unleashing of his power fragmented reality, shattered it into thousands of pieces. His dreaming mind created the multiverse and everything in it."

I rub my head. It's really hurting. "So . . . you're saying we're all fig-ments of some octopus god's imagination?"

"Exactly so."

"No," says Graves. "I'm sorry, but I don't accept that."

"You must. Because if Nyarlathotep succeeds with his plan, if he manages to wake Cthulhu up, he will stop dreaming."

"Then . . . what happens to us?" I ask.

Anderson makes a little explosion gesture with her hands. "Poof."

"Poof?"

"Poof. All gone. The entire multiverse will be a vague memory in Cthul-hu's mind while he scratches his balls and has his morning cup of coffee."

"This can't be . . ." says Graves uncertainly. Then he stares into the distance.

"What?" I ask.

"When I reported what was going on to the higher-ups. When I told them what Nyarlathotep was planning. That he wanted to wake Cthulhu . . . They looked very shifty. Some would say . . . suspiciously so."

"That's why people have been trying to kill us?" I say. "To stop us from finding out the truth?"

"That is what eventually happened to Elizabeth," says Smith. "She was lured to a meeting in Central Park and murdered. Luckily, her killers—the ICD—did not know of the organization she formed, so we were free to continue her work."

"I don't get it," I say. "Nyarlathotep knows what will happen if he wakes Cthulhu?"

"Oh yes, indeed."

"Then why is he doing it?"

"Who knows? But if we want to still exist tomorrow, then we must stop him."

"How? We have no idea where they are."

"Of course we do. The same place where he and Harrison first tried to cross over into the Dreamlands."

"You know where the gate is?" asks Graves. "The machine he and Harrison built?"

"Of course."

"Where?"

"At Griffith Observatory."

§

It's getting dark as we wind up the Hollywood Hills in Smith's ancient Cadillac, which spews black smoke and dust behind us as we go. I can see the Hollywood sign from my position squashed up against the left window, Anderson's elbow digging savagely into my ribs every time we go over a bump.

"I don't see why we couldn't take two cars," I say.

"In hindsight," says Smith, glancing at me in the rearview mirror, "we maybe should have. This car doesn't handle hills very well. Or flat surfaces, actually. Even down hills is a bit tricky."

The sun has dropped behind the hills by the time the huge dome of the Griffith Observatory appears ahead of us, a shadowy silhouette jutting up against the orange-and-gray sky. I've been here a couple of times before, when Susan wanted to look at the stars. I remember it being a lot busier.

"Is it closed?"

"It's an observatory, idiot," says Anderson. "It's open at night."

"So why is it deserted?"

It is. We're the only car in the parking lot. Anderson shoves open the door.

We follow her out, and Smith opens the trunk to reveal an arsenal of weapons. Shotguns, revolvers, machetes, katanas, broadswords, machine guns, even a few spears. Anderson grabs a shotgun and throws as many shells as she can into a Hello Kitty backpack, slinging it over her shoulder.

Graves and I don't bother. We have our entropy guns. Smith takes a machine gun and extra magazines, while Winston takes as many revolvers as he can shove into his pants.

"You guys ever done this kind of thing before?" asks Graves.

Smith and Winston share a look.

"Uh . . . not as such," says Winston. "I was once involved in a pretty serious crime situation."

"How serious?"

"A robbery. At a pet shop."

"Jesus Christ," mutters Graves. "Right. You two—" he points at Winston and Smith, "—stay at the back." He points at Anderson. "You on my left, and Priest, on my right. Shoot first, ask questions later."

It's almost dusk as we make our way up the wide road to the observatory. Everything is silent as we approach the sward of grass in front of the building. There's a monument up ahead, a tall, geometric pillar situated on the grass before we even get close to the building itself. I remember this from when I brought Susan. They called it the Astronomers Monument, and the six figures carved into the base are various famous astronomers. I can only remember Galileo, though.

"Stop," whispers Smith.

Graves glares at him. "What?"

"We're here." He gestures at the pillar. "That's the machine."

We all turn to look at the pillar.

"See that metal thing on top?" whispers Smith. "It's called the armillary sphere."

I squint up at the brass spheres. As far as I can remember it's some kind of astronomical instrument made up of interlocking metal rings that represent latitude and longitude. Before we actually discovered the telescope it was what astronomers used to find out celestial positions and stuff like that.

"That's the gateway to the Dreamlands?" asks Graves. "You're sure?"

"Hundred percent. Harrison built it through Griffith J. Griffith. The gateway was created first, and the observatory built around it later on."

There's something odd about the monument. As far as I can recall it's a bright white color. But right now, in the fading light, it looks . . . gray.

"It doesn't look like anyone's here," says Anderson.

"'The lady doth protest too much, methinks,'" comes a distant voice.

"Oh my God. . . ." I whisper.

Then a hundred voices take up the call. "'This above all; to thine own self be true.'"

"Goddamn it!" I shout.

The voices stop.

And the hundred monkeys with old-man faces clinging to the pillar all turn to look at us.

"Watch these bastards!" I shout. "They quote Shakespeare at you!"

Anderson drags her gaze away from the monkeys. "They what?"

"You heard me!"

The monkeys slide down the pillar and sweep toward us, chattering with anger, their old-man (and old-woman, now that I see them closer) faces twisted with rage.

I fire into the crowd. I hit one of the monkeys, and it withers and turns to dust before me. But it's like firing at the wind. There are too many of them.

Anderson unloads her shotgun. Smith and Winston (random thought, they should have hired someone with the name Wesson; infinitely cooler) fire their own guns. We manage to take down six or seven before the monkeys surround us, a hopping, leaping, furious simian wall that grips our arms and murmurs Shakespearean quotes into our ears like a lover whispering sweet nothings.

Our guns are wrenched from our grips and tossed to the ground. The crowd of simians parts, and Nyarlathotep strolls through, hands reaching out to stroke the monkeys as he passes. Three massive Shamblers walk behind him, their tick-faces rippling and sniffing at the air. Nyarlathotep himself looks hideous. Like he's dipped his face in acid. I can see the bone through his cheeks. His lips are gone, his teeth permanently visible in a skull-like grin.

Nyarlathotep stops suddenly, looking at us in surprise like a children's TV show presenter doing a double take for the camera. "Hi, guys!" he says brightly. "Didn't expect to see you back here so soon. You'd think you'd have learned your lesson by now. What is this, man? Like, the fourth time I've managed to surprise you?"

"Third!" snaps Graves.

"Sorry. My mistake. Third. Anyway, I suppose you can stay and watch. I've been told it's going to be quite a show." He sighs and looks up at the monument. "Nearly a hundred years I've been waiting to activate this baby. But patience is a virtue, as they say."

"Doesn't that hurt?" I say.

"I won't lie to you. It does. But not as much as the betrayal."

"You can't blame Dana," says Graves. "You can't treat people like that."

"I can do what I want, man! I'm a minion of the Old Ones."

"Please," says Winston urgently. "You can't do this. Do you realize what will happen if you free Cthulhu?"

"Why, yes. I do have some idea, thanks for asking. Really appreciate that. Taking an interest. You're a good man."

"No," says Winston. "You don't. If you free him. If you wake him up . . . we all die. We are Cthulhu's dream. The entire multiverse exists in his mind as he sleeps in his prison."

Nyarlathotep's eyes widen. "Wow, really?"

"Yes! Really."

"So . . . you're saying I should just leave him where he is. Lying in his prison, sleeping away the millennia?"

"Yes!"

"Yeah, okay."

Winston pauses. "Really?"

"No! Idiot! You think I don't know all that? I *want* him to wake up. I want to vanish in a puff of existential smoke."

"Why?"

"Because I'm tired of running around at their beck and call. You have any idea what that's like? Having all the Old Ones in your head? And I do mean all of them. Arguing, ordering me around, telling me to do this, no, do that, no, this! And every night the same dreams. Them, reciting instructions for me. Every. Single. Night. Forever. All this shit I see every day? All the stuff your mind is supposed to process when you dream? I don't have that. I think I went insane about a hundred millennia ago. I'm basically just operating on nightmares and coffee. Anything they want, I have to do. I'm the eternal dogsbody, and I'm, like, sick of it. It's like being an unpaid intern for eternity. I just want everything to end."

"Why not just kill yourself?" I ask.

"No way, man! Suicide is the coward's way out."

"Whereas killing untold billions and wiping out hundreds of thousands of alternate realities isn't?"

"They'll thank me in the end."

"I really don't think they will." I frown. "But what was all that about retiring to a world made of beaches or whatever it was?"

"Lies. Lovely, cunning lies. I mean, it's not as if I was going to tell you I wanted the entire multiverse to end, you know?"

"Sure . . . I can see that."

"So glad. Groovy." Nyarlathotep turns and gestures. The Shamblers move forward and grip our arms, and the monkeys run back and scamper up the monument. They play around with the metal spheres on top of the pillar, and the spheres start to spin, slowly picking up speed. Nyarlathotep spreads his arms wide and starts shouting in a guttural language.

"Ph'nglui mglw'nafh Cthulhu R'lyeh wgah'nagl fhtagn."

The monkeys chitter and scream as the globes spin faster and faster. They're moving so fast they're actually forming a solid-looking structure. There are alien words spreading out in the blurred circles. Words that change and flicker as the globes pick up speed. Like those old-fashioned kids' lights that spin round and round, showing a moving picture of something creepy on the wall.

A crack of lightning arcs out of nowhere and hits the top of the monument. A dark cloud billows up and out, a reverse cyclone, spreading, probing. Nyarlathotep's chanting grows louder, his face lit up by the flashes of lightning.

"Ph'nglui mglw'nafh Cthulhu R'lyeh wgah'nagl fhtagn!" he screams.

"I really think we should be doing something here!" I shout.

"Like what?" answers Graves.

"Yeah, I'm with the old guy," says Anderson. "Standing around while the end of the world happens is so *Raiders of the Lost Ark*."

I can't help it. I laugh out loud. Anderson then casually drops to the ground, slipping through the grasp of the clumsy Shambler. She hooks her foot under her shotgun, flicks it up into the air, grabs it, and shoots the creature in the face.

I stare in awed amazement as its tick-head explodes, spraying black-green ichor everywhere. The Shambler falls to the ground, and Anderson sets off, heading straight for Nyarlathotep.

I shake my own jailer off and dive for my gun. I grab it and roll onto my back, aiming it at the one gripping Graves.

"Wait!" he shouts. "Not while it's holding me, you buffoon!"

I sigh and pick up a revolver instead, using it to shoot the Shambler in the leg. It spins to the side, releasing Graves, and then I shoot it with my entropy gun, watching its head wither and shrink like a grape into a raisin, then implode with a little sad squelching sound.

I lurch to my feet and race after Anderson.

But before we can get to the monument the spinning globe throws up a massive black umbrella of darkness that surrounds Nyarlathotep and his monkeys. The bulbous shadow grows larger, like a bubble, pulsating and growing.

Then it suddenly snaps out of existence, taking Nyarlathotep and his hench-monkeys with him.

Graves stumbles to my side, looking around at the now-empty park in front of the observatory. The silence is deafening.

"Congratulations, everyone," he says, flopping down onto the grass. "We've failed. Light 'em if you've got 'em."

"We haven't failed," says Smith, appearing at my side. "Not yet."

I turn to look at him. "What do you mean?"

"After she killed Harrison, Elizabeth went about building her own gateway, should it ever be needed. But . . . it's not the same as this one. She couldn't perfect it. It can get someone into the Dreamlands. But . . . not wholly. More like . . . the *dream* of someone can enter. But they're able to function like a normal person. It doesn't work on everyone, though. Those that are not properly attuned can . . ."

"Can?" I ask.

"Die. By brain aneurism."

Graves pushes himself up onto his elbows. He looks at me and smiles. I step back, not liking the look in his eyes one little bit.

"Graves?"

"Yes, Harry. So nice of you to volunteer." He glances at Smith. "This fine fellow here has sucked myself and others into the Dreamlands a few times already. I'd say that means he's properly attuned. Isn't that right, Harry, my boy?"

"Uh . . . No. I mean. Maybe. But I don't know how." I glance at Smith. "It was after I touched the spear and again after I touched the jewel. I was there, but I have no idea how I did it."

"You ever seen *Blade Runner*?" asks Anderson.

I blink, thrown by the change in topic. "Uh . . . yeah."

"You know the building where they shot some of it?"

"The Bradbury Building? Yeah. Who doesn't?"
"You ever been there?"
"No."
"Then it's your lucky day."

CHAPTER TWENTY~TWO

The exterior of the Bradbury Building is a bit disappointing, if I'm being completely honest.

After watching *Blade Runner* I imagined this towering block soaring up into the sky, Art Deco designs covering its surface. But the reality is a lot more boring: a brown, terracotta building located in South Broadway. It's only five stories high, and most of it is taken up with offices and shops. Not even apartments. What a crock.

Okay, the inside is a bit more impressive. I'll give it that. Open balconies and filigreed stairs lead up to the different floors, the LA night sky visible through the glass ceiling. Wrought-iron staircases prevent people from falling to their deaths, and the marble flooring echoes our footsteps back to us.

It doesn't feel like it belongs here in LA. It's too clean. Too ... European. It almost feels like I'm walking onto the set of *Chinatown*.

"This way," says Smith, leading us to a section of the wall beneath the wide staircase. It looks the same as any other section of wall, exposed bricks all neat and clean. Smith looks around to make sure no one is watching, then touches four bricks in rapid succession.

A section of wall swings inward with a quiet sigh. Smith ushers us quickly through, then follows. The wall swings closed again, plunging us into darkness.

Winston clicks on a small flashlight, revealing stairs winding down into the darkness. We move slowly, no one saying a word. About twenty minutes later we arrive at a doorway and Smith touches the bricks again. The door swings open, and he leads us through the opening.

The flashlight reveals a long passage flanked on both sides by huge brass cogs that glow golden in the light. We move along the corridor single file until it opens into a room whose walls are totally covered with weird machinery. Gears and pistons. Brass levers. Old-fashioned dials. And massive glass containers filled with a milky liquid. The machinery is all linked by thick tubes to a brass framework suspended from the roof.

Anderson flicks a switch, and fluorescent tubes stutter to life. Winston spins a huge wheel on the wall, and the metal framework lowers itself jerkily to the floor, hitting small indentations in the concrete. I notice for the first time that it's human-shaped.

Anderson and Winston walk over to a row of levers and pump them vigorously. As they do so, the wheels and cogs on the walls begin to turn, grumbling and complaining. These in turn pass their motion onto others. Small cogs drop into larger cogs, and the motion is carried forward until all the wheels in the room are spinning. A rhythmic swishing sound fills the air, and the smell of warming oil wafts through the room.

"Right," I say. "Awesome seeing your secret torture chamber, but I think I need to go now."

"I admit it's a bit . . . old-fashioned," says Smith, "but it was built over a hundred years ago, remember?"

"What is it exactly?" asks Graves. And hearing the doubt in his voice just makes me all the more terrified.

"It's a way for him to enter the Dreamlands," says Winston. "Instead of waiting to fall asleep and hoping he can get in, this will pull his consciousness from his body—"

"*Rip* his consciousness," says Smith.

"Right. Rip his consciousness from his body and sort of . . . scatter it into the ether, sending his mind into the Dreamlands. This whole building was built as part of the machine. It's designed to funnel a person's consciousness out and send it in the correct direction."

"Yeah. I just really don't like the sound of that," I say.

"It will be fine," says Smith. "Hopefully."

Graves pulls Smith aside. "It's not as if we have much choice, do we? Come on. In you go."

"No."

"No? Are you mad?" Graves shouts. "The entire universe—the entire *multiverse*—is dependent on this. Don't you be selfish now."

"Did you hear what they said? Rip my consciousness from my body? Does that sound healthy to you?"

"Harry," says Graves seriously. "If not for yourself, then do it for your daughter, Esmeralda."

"Not even close."

"Heather?"

"No."

"Agnes?"

"No." I sigh, looking around at the others. "I really don't have much choice, do I?"

"None at all. And the quicker you get into the Dreamlands and stop Nyarlathotep, the sooner we can put this case to bed and take our rightful place at the top tier of the ICD. Come along. Hop to it."

I climb reluctantly into the framework, trying to get comfortable as I lie down on the metal frame. Anderson uses cracked leather straps to secure my legs and arms against the cold metal.

"No gross jokes about bondage," says Anderson.

"Don't worry. Are the straps really necessary?" I ask.

"Afraid so. There's no telling how a person will react when this thing kicks off. Put your head back."

I do as I'm told, and Winston lowers a metal cap onto my head. I can feel hundreds of tiny pinpricks resting against my scalp. I swallow nervously.

"Just relax," says Anderson softly. "It will be fine. And . . . just so you know. You're pretty brave. For an old weirdo."

I smile at her. "Thanks, kiddo."

"Don't call me that. Ever."

"Sorry."

"Ready?" asks Winston.

"Not even remotely."

Winston nods and pulls a lever down with a lot more gusto than is needed, as if he's auditioning for a part in *Frankenstein*. The tiny needles resting against my scalp suddenly push in, jabbing through my skin, burning my scalp.

The fluid in the jars bubbles and belches in response.

My back arches in pain and fear as I feel myself being slowly drawn from my body. That's the only way to describe it. It's an incredibly horrible feeling, as if I'm being sucked up a straw.

I'm aware of everything, the ever-increasing bubbling in the tubes, my skin tingling, being pulled tight against my bones, my very essence being somehow drawn through the needles and traveling along metal piping, up through the walls of the building like blood through veins. I feel like I'm stretching, stretching so far that my awareness not only encompasses the entire building, but the city as well. I'm aware of the traffic, the bustle of LA, the ebb and flow of life, babies being born, people dying, animals scurrying through garbage, rats and wild foxes. Birds wheel through the sky in sudden agitation.

And finally I'm out, erupting through the skylight that was built for exactly this purpose, to draw a person up from her or his body.

I'm out into the sky as pure energy.

My essence tries to escape, to spread itself out so thinly that I would no longer be me, just a vague remembrance of something that once was. But I rein it in, focusing my mind on Susan, remembering why I'm doing this.

I close my eyes (although I don't actually have eyes). I block everything out: the sounds of traffic, the wail of police sirens, the barking of dogs, the smell of exhaust fumes and greasy food.

I feel a calmness wash over me. I think of Graves, of Susan, of the Inspectre, of Ash, and everything that brought me to this place, trying to hold onto who I am, remember what it is that makes me, me. I think of the Dreamlands, of Cthulhu and Nyarlathotep. I think of that city I saw, the towering prison of black glass.

And when I open my eyes again the world has changed.

It's like a demented dream. There are islands everywhere, but they're not rooted to the earth. They float freely in the air, hundreds of islands that drift around each other in a complex dance.

But it's not just that they float. Some of them are upside down, some doing slow, balletic turns in the night sky, as if gravity is simply something to be ignored, like a letter from the IRS.

I float close to an island that has a waterfall soaring over the edge. The water sails gracefully into the sky, then simply vanishes when it reaches a certain point. Some of the islands are covered with heavy rain clouds, clouds that taper away to nothingness beyond the border of each isle. One of them off to my right is under a constant barrage of multicolored lightning. Red, purple, yellow. It arcs down into the rock, sending chunks and debris flying into the air.

"This is insane," I whisper.

I stare around, wondering where I'm supposed to go. None of these look like the weird city I'd seen in my dreams.

I think myself forward, and start moving, drifting faster and faster through the Dreamlands. I turn in slow circles as I move, checking every piece of land I pass, searching for one that looks vaguely familiar.

Then finally, after what seems like hours of floating, I see it.

Deep within the heart of the floating land masses is an island much larger than the others. It's covered with a massive ocean that is held in place by a perimeter of mountains.

And rising up from the center of this ocean is the city of R'lyeh.

I head toward it, soaring over the mountains and then over the ocean. Huge, lumbering creatures swim just below the surface, vast shadows that make me climb just a little bit higher in case any of them decide to try and pull me out of the sky.

I slow down as I approach the city walls and land on the now-familiar muddy shores. I turn in a circle, the icy stars impossibly bright above me, glittering on the ancient ocean that surges over my feet, almost as if it is trying to pull me into the inky depths.

I stare back out over the ocean, tracking back the way I've just come. Strangely, I can't see any of the floating islands anymore. Just the stars in the night sky and a sickly, jaundiced moon that casts yellow-green highlights on the black water.

I shudder and turn my back on the ocean. The city is a black, jagged silhouette. As before, my eyes hurt if I stare at the buildings too long. The angles and edges just seem . . . wrong, as if they aren't meant for human minds.

I walk toward the city walls. The silence is absolutely complete. I can't hear Nyarlathotep or the monkeys. Or *anything*, for that matter. It's like sound is being sucked away.

I feel odd in my body, trembling inside. As if I've had way too much coffee. I stare up at the structures towering over me, taking in the odd angles, the way the buildings turn in on themselves, twisting into never-ending modernist sculptures.

The huge tower is still there. It must be a couple of miles away, towering over the city itself. My hands are twitching. Adrenaline surges through my body, trying to get me to react. To fight or run for my life. But I can't do either. Hell, I don't even know what I can do. I stare at the city, feeling a deep upwelling of fear. I'm supposed to go in there. I'm supposed to find my way through those demented streets in order to stop Nyarlathotep from waking up Cthulhu. But I have no idea how.

I stop before the wall. A massive gate stands open before me. I reach out to touch the black surface, but my hand is repelled by an alien force. As if the city is trying to push me back.

Nothing else for it. At least I've got my entropy gun, something I'm incredibly glad about. Seems making weapons out of the bodies of deceased Elder Gods was a good idea after all. I hope it does the same damage in the Dreamlands as it does in real life.

I step into the tunnel that leads through the wall. I stumble, pushed off balance by the weird energies shoving and pulling at me. I break into a stumbling run, stopping only when I finally make it through the tunnel.

I stare around in fear and awe. The buildings are . . . colossal. Twisted and impossible, covered with hideous images of torture, scenes that go straight through my eyes to the back of my brain. I blink, and it seems as if the angles shift subtly, buildings changing shapes and moving every time my eyes are closed, a feeling that puts me instantly on edge, fearful, wondering what is going to happen next. I feel like an ant. Like I'm nothing. Like I'm an unwelcome guest tarnishing the city with my presence.

Keep it calm, Priest.

I take a deep breath. Then another. At least I shouldn't get too lost. Just head for the last place any sane person would actually want to go. The massive glass tower in the middle of the city.

Yeah. Great plan.

I force myself to start moving, passing into a wide boulevard. The buildings loom to either side, leaning over me so that only a tiny glimpse of the stars is visible. I keep walking, moving along alleys and streets, turning corners and walking around the buildings until I feel as if I'm walking in circles.

I've been walking for about ten minutes when I hear a noise up ahead.

I freeze, my ears straining.

There it is again. The scuff of feet on the ground. My fingers curl around the gun, holding it ready. I move slowly forward. I can hear murmured voices now. Is it Nyarlathotep and his cronies? Maybe they haven't made it to the tower yet. Can I just end this now? Shoot that bastard in the head? Or at least shoot the jewel so he can't use it to wake Cthulhu?

I raise the gun to my shoulder, put my back up against the building (it feels oily, viscous, as if I'm constantly in danger of sliding away), and finally dart around the corner, quickly aiming the gun around to find my target.

Graves, Anderson, Winston, and Smith all turn to stare at me.

"Oh, very well done, Harry," snaps Graves. "Honestly, you can't do anything right, can you?"

CHAPTER TWENTY~THREE

"Me?" I say, glaring at Graves. "What the hell are you talking about now?"

"You drew us in here with you," says Graves. "Again!"

"Oh." I look around, then turn back and shrug. "Not my fault."

"I think you'll find it is your fault. You have endangered our lives, you cretin."

"Oh, shame!" I snap. "So you have to take part in saving the world with me! I'm so sorry for unknowingly summoning you to help humanity in its hour of greatest need." I stare at his hand. "What's that?"

Graves looks down. It's a large cocktail glass. He looks pleased and lifts it to his lips.

"There's a bar in the Bradbury Building," he says. "We were having margaritas."

I stare at him in amazement. "Margaritas?" I look at Anderson and the others. At least she has the good manners to look embarrassed.

"That's his fifth," she says.

"I was thirsty!" shouts Graves. "I wanted one last taste of booze just in case you failed miserably to save humanity. Besides, facing those monkeys was traumatic!"

"I know!" I shout "I was there!"

"No need to take that tone," says Graves in a hurt tone of voice. He takes a sip of his drink and smacks his lips. "Not bad."

I close my eyes and count to five. "Right," I say. "You're here now. Which I'm glad for. Although God knows why."

"So what's the plan?" asks Smith. He's looking pretty nervous.

Jumpy and sweating. "Maybe I could stay here and guard the rear? Make sure nothing comes after us?"

"Nice try," I say. "But you're all coming with me." I point to the huge tower that dominates the skyline. "Cthulhu is up there, so that's where Nyarlathotep will be going. The plan is kill Nyarlathotep or destroy the jewel." I glance at Graves. "Right?"

He sips his drink and shrugs. "This is your rodeo, partner. I'm just along for the ride."

I sigh and look around. We're all standing exposed in a wide, empty plaza. Tall pillars surround us, thin shards of black slate crunching underfoot. Some sort of ivy crawls up the pillars, gray and greasy-looking.

No one seems inclined to move. "Let's go then," I say, and start walking.

We move along the avenue leading away from the plaza. Everyone is twitchy, except for Graves, who is sipping his margarita and looking around with casual interest.

The city has an oppressive air. It makes me feel... depressed. Empty. I shiver. I suppose that makes sense for the ancient prison of the leader of the Old Ones. It's not exactly meant to be a fun day out at the park.

As we move deeper into the city, there are strange statues everywhere. Nobody else seems interested, but I pause to examine one. They're made from black glass, sculpted into stylized representations of men and women. But it's as if they have been placed randomly throughout the city. Some stand on street corners, others in the middle of roads, and some in the gaping doors of ruined buildings. I wonder what they're for. Art isn't exactly something you expect to see in a place like this.

We pass a long street lined with more of the statues. The others are walking slowly, so I turn off the road to study the glass statues. They are all different to each other, as if each one had been carved by a different artist. One has a rough style, using the chips of the chisel to form shadows and character. Another has smoothed features, the glass carved in gentle slopes and curves so that not one line of tool work is visible. The statues are covered with the same gray creepers that hang everywhere, chaining them together in a line.

I can't shake the feeling that they're alive. I reach out and touch one, but nothing happens. It just feels like cold glass. Like touching a window.

I notice a small alley angling off from the street. There's something odd about it that catches my attention, and it takes me a moment to realize what it is: the alley looks clean. No rubble. No shards of obsidian. No dust.

I glance back along the street. The others are strolling along like it's a day at the beach. I can easily catch up with them.

I stroll over to inspect the alley. I was right. The alley has been swept clean. Banks of dirt and pebbles line the walls to either side.

Interesting, I think, and follow the alley as it rounds a corner. The lane narrows even farther, then turns a second corner before feeding into a courtyard. The courtyard is roofed with the shadowy vines; the sickly vegetation coaxed up twisted pillars and knitted together to form a dark canopy.

I step into the square and note a small house directly opposite me. It stands out because the neat pathway leads directly to the front door. I frown and walk slowly forward. How is that possible? Surely no one lives here. Or do they? Is there someone here who can help us?

I glimpse movement from the corner of my eye.

I turn around to find a wooden stick flying straight at my face. I swear and drop to the ground, the stick clattering into the wall behind me.

I catch sight of a small figure scurrying away from me beyond the veil of ivy. I push myself up and run after my attacker. I see him up ahead as he darts around a corner. He runs with a strange, waddling gait, as if he has an injured leg. He is also incredibly short, about the same size as Susan.

"Wait!" I call out. "I'm not going to hurt you! Much," I add beneath my breath.

"Hah!" shouts my attacker. "*You're* not going to hurt *me*! That's funny, that is."

Around another corner, then another. I realize we're simply running around the open square where I'd first been attacked. In fact, this would be the opening where I—

The stick comes swinging out from behind a wall, connecting against my shin with a sharp crack. I yelp in pain and tumble to the ground.

I roll over to find the ugliest man I've ever seen staring down at me, his heavy walking stick raised to strike again. The man's limbs are disproportionately sized, his body pushed forward by a huge bump growing on his back. He looks like what would happen if Yoda and the Hunchback of Notre Dame had a baby together.

"Try it," I snarl. "And I'll take the damn thing from you and ram it down your throat. Understand?"

The small man hesitates.

"I'm not here to cause trouble," I say, rubbing my legs. "At least not for you. We came here to stop people from waking up Cthulhu."

The man finally lowers his stick. "Wake him up? Don't be stupid. If they do that then—"

"Then everything ends. Yes. I know." I frown at him. "What are you doing here?"

"It's my home."

"Your home." I look around. "You could do with sprucing the place up a bit."

"Yeah, sorry about that. When you're the last of your species, dusting and making sure everything smells of flowers is low on the to-do list. You know, as opposed to wailing in madness and staring into the abyss of loneliness and fear."

"Uh . . . last of your species?"

"Well, not species, but . . . job title? I suppose that's more appropriate. I'm the last of the Guardians. We all lived in this city and watched over Cthulhu's prison. To make sure nobody tries to interfere with old octopus-face. Bit of a downer, if I'm being honest. Cthulhu gets into your dreams, you see. Nearly everyone committed suicide after the first couple of millennia."

"But not you?"

"Nah. I just went insane. Much easier."

"You say you're here to stop people from interfering with Cthulhu?"

"Yup."

I stare at him expectantly.

"Oh . . . yeah! I . . . suppose we should go see what's going on with that. See if whoever it is has breached my defenses. The name's Dvalin, by the way."

"Harry Priest."

"Weird name."

§

We make our way back along the streets, finally finding the others lounging up against the wall.

"Thought you were dead," says Graves. "Who's your friend?"

"This is Dvalin. He's a . . . guardian of some kind. He's supposed to make sure nobody messes with Cthulhu."

"Not very good at your job, are you?" asks Graves.

"Hey, bite me, beardy. I haven't seen another living person in hundreds of thousands of years. Forgive me for not sitting outside that great glass erection for my entire life just on the off chance that I get a visitor."

"You *say* forgive me, but I sense you're not being genuine," says Graves pleasantly.

"Are you really one of the Guardians?" asks Winston, his voice an awed whisper.

Dvalin draws himself up proudly. "I am. I was here from the beginning, when the great Cthulhu was brought here by the Elder Gods. That day will long be remembered as one of great import. The skies were dark and bloody. The moon full and gibbous. The Elder Gods were like giants striding against the cosmos, ancient, wise beings who had captured their offspring and—"

"Moving on," says Graves, pushing himself off from the wall and heading along the street again.

The others all follow, leaving a sputtering Dvalin standing in the street behind us.

§

Dvalin, despite muttering and complaining all the time about us intruding in his city, leads us through the dark streets, taking us in the direction of Cthulhu's tower.

I'm not sure how long we walk. The city plays tricks on the mind. One minute we're walking along a thoroughfare, the next we're climbing a set of stairs. But as I look up I see the ground is above us instead of the stars and the night sky is off to my left. I see a group of people on the opposite side of the street and with a sickening lurch of vertigo I realize they're mirror images of us.

"Best not to look around," says Dvalin. "Focus on your feet."

"What's going on?" asks Graves.

"It's something to do with Cthulhu. As we get closer everything sort of twists around. Up is down. Left is right. Just follow me, and you'll be fine."

After a few more minutes of nausea-inducing travel we arrive at the huge plaza surrounding Cthulhu's prison. The tower itself is black obsidian, a massive pillar of volcanic glass hundreds of feet in circumference. There are etchings and inscriptions in the glass, so that as the moon moves or my gaze shifts, I catch glimpses of alien writing that twists and turns in my mind.

But it's the scene playing out in the plaza itself that really draws my attention, a scene of utter chaos. The area is dominated by a Rip, blue light spilling out into the city. And coming through that Rip are hundreds of creatures.

I stare at them, my heart sinking. The outer perimeter of the square consists of thousands of insects, like the ones that made up the wall when I was drawn into all of this. The ground is crawling and writhing with giant maggots and worms, most the size of my arm. There are other insects too: centipedes, millipedes, and spiders. It's like a sea of terror, undulating around the plaza. Every now and then the insects rise up, coming together to form into the shape of a human, striding back toward the tower where they join up with the other creatures. The monkeys move through the insects, occasionally picking a writhing maggot up and shoving it into their mouths.

"Nightgaunts," whispers Graves, pointing.

I follow his finger and see lurching creatures with gray, oily skin standing around the door into the tower. They have horns and tattered wings that flap and twitch as they move.

There are also more of those Shamblers, too many to count. Black-armored hides strike blue highlights, their white tick-heads jerking left and right, sniffing blindly at the air.

There are shoggoths too, those weird, undulating bags of diseased slime. Every now and then arms and legs protrude from the sacks and the creatures take on the human form to move around.

"So," says Anderson. "I hate to be the one to bring this up, but I'm assuming Nyarlathotep is already up at the top of that tower, yeah?"

"Most likely," says Graves.

"And we're getting up there how?"

We all turn to Dvalin.

"We're not," he says simply. "Not unless you want to kill yourselves. There's only one way in." He gestures at the door, guarded by Shamblers and insect creatures. "And we're not getting past them."

"So what do we do?" asks Winston.

"We come up with another plan. Come on."

He leads us back through the city until we're far enough away that we won't be overheard. We turn a corner . . .

. . . and find ourselves facing down ten gun barrels.

"Graves?" says the Inspectre, lowering his gun. "Why the hell am I not surprised?"

Graves throws an accusing look at me. "Seriously?"

"What? I didn't even know! I just thought we could do with some extra manpower."

"What's next?" asks Anderson. "The Stay Puft Marshmallow Man?"

"What the hell is going on here?" growls the Inspectre.

"I can't be bothered to explain it to him. Anderson?"

Anderson strolls across to the Inspectre, and Graves turns on Dvalin. "Well?" he demands. "This is your city. You're the warden. Don't you have any weapons?"

"I have lots of weapons. But they're last resort only. It takes a lot out of me to control them."

"Boo-hoo. Stop being precious and get them armed up. We need to spray that tower with napalm or something."

"It doesn't work like that," snaps Dvalin. "I need to prepare. We're talking a major mental workout."

"I don't give a crap!" shouts Graves. "Do what you need to do and do it now! I for one do not want to vanish in a puff of existential smoke. Do you understand me?"

I walk away, leaving them to argue. Maybe it would have been better if I hadn't called any of them into the Dreamlands with me. Not that I was able to control it, but still. None of them are really helping much.

I spot a set of stairs leading up the side of a building. I start climbing, hoping for a place to just sit in silence. I get past the second story before suddenly realizing I'm walking upside down. The ground is above me again, the sky below. I freeze, wondering which way to go. My instinct is to crouch down and just grab hold of something, but I resist it and keep walking.

Before I make it to the top, I walk sideways, backward and diagonally, and then upside down once again before finally reaching the roof.

I lean over the low wall and stare out over the city. I can still hear the sounds of arguing from below. The Inspectre doesn't sound like he's taking it well. Something about memos and needing to shoot Graves. I know how he feels.

A flare of light catches my eye. I squint into the distance, staring beyond the city walls. At first I think it's just lightning, but then the light flares to life again, and with a sinking feeling I realize it's yet another Rip.

And as I watch, a second army of creatures marches through.

They lope on two, four, sometimes six legs. Some fly through the air, skimming out of the Rip and then soaring over the ocean, flapping massive, leathery wings. There are shantak, the creatures that captured me in the ruined city. Others look like floating octopi, while still others look like huge dragons, covered in black-and-red scales.

In the ten seconds I stand there watching, hundreds of creatures have poured through the Rip to gather on the shores outside the city walls.

I sprint back down the stairs, keeping my eyes focused on my feet so I don't get disoriented. I find the others in the empty square. Graves is sitting on a broken column while Anderson talks to the Inspectre.

"I really can't shoot him?" says the Inspectre plaintively.

"I'm afraid not. At least, not for whatever it is ICD accused him of."

"Army!" I shout. "There's an army coming! Outside the city!" I look around for Dvalin, but the small man has vanished. "Where's Dvalin?"

"He stormed off in a sulk," says Graves. "What are you saying about an army?"

I lead the way back up to the rooftop just as the first of the shantak soars over the walls. I stare at it in fear. I never really got a good look at them when I was clutched in one's claws, but they are massive and black-skinned, creatures from primitive nightmares. Its snout is a black beak dripping bile, and it screeches as its huge wings bring it soaring over the city. It's followed by others of its kind. I count at least fifty of them before giving up.

"Shantak," says Graves. "Nasty things."

The first shantak pulls up and hovers in the air. The others crest the wall in blurs of motion, screaming their hatred as they soar off into the city.

The first shantak flaps its wings slower and slower, sinking to the ground in a cloud of dust. Its beak opens and closes, snapping together with loud *clack-clack* noises I can hear even from this distance.

"I'm not sure standing in the open like this is the wisest thing to do," says Winston nervously.

Before we can do anything I hear an odd noise, a muted thumping, thudding sound that echoes throughout the streets.

"What's that?" whispers Smith.

I kneel down and touch the roof. Vibrations run up through my hands.

Then a furious screech echoes behind us. We run to the opposite side of the building and stare out over the city.

A battle is taking place about a mile from where we stand. The shantak fly through the air, screeching, wheeling and banking to avoid the arrows and spears flying toward them from the ground.

"Who's doing that?" mutters Smith.

Then we see them: the statues. The ones we saw scattered everywhere. They've come to life, all of them gathering together to defend the prison city. All the statues are armed, firing bolts from massive crossbows and hurling spears into the sky.

How the hell did they come to life? Is it an automatic defense system?

"Check it out," says Anderson, pointing.

It's Dvalin. He's standing on a rooftop a short distance from the battle. His hands are raised above his head, and he jerks around as if he's having a fit. Wind whirls around him, making it look as if he is surrounded by a mini tornado. The wind flies briefly in our direction, and I hear him screaming, shouting commands in a language I don't understand. I lean forward. Blood pours from his ears and nose. He calls out again, screaming obscenities into the sky.

He is controlling the statues.

"Huh," says Graves. "He wasn't lying after all. How about that? If we survive I'll have to apologize."

I shift my attention back to the battle. Four bolts slam into one of the flying creatures, bringing it skidding down into the streets with a wet thud. Another takes a bolt through the wing, and it twirls unevenly into the side of a building. It falls to the ground, and one of the statues steps forward and slices its head from its body.

The once-silent city echoes with noise: shrieks of pain. The twang and thunk of crossbows releasing. The wet sounds of shearing flesh. Dvalin's shouted commands.

Some of the shantak swoop low and knock the statues down, but it seems that nothing can stop them. They simply keep getting up until a leg shatters or a head is ripped from a body. And even then they drag themselves across the ground to finish off any creatures that come within reach.

"Shouldn't we help?" I say.

"No need. Those statues have it taken care of."

After another couple of minutes of furious fighting, the last of the flying creatures are shot from the sky. The statues collect together into formation and move along the streets, stepping on the corpses, squashing them into a wet mulch as if they're crushing grapes for a demonic wine tasting.

We watch as they march past below us before we climb down from the roof and follow after them. They carry on through the streets and take the stairs leading up to the top of the city wall. We continue to follow, hesitantly, trying to keep quiet. The statues don't even give us a second glance. Their attention is fixed on the beaches outside the city.

The Rip has closed up now, but every available inch of shore is covered with creatures. They spread away to either side, thousands upon thousands of them.

"What now?" whispers Winston.

"Relax," says Smith nervously. "Look at the size of this wall. There's no way they can breach it."

"All defenses can fall," exclaims Graves cheerfully. "Just a matter of finding the weak spot."

"Even so, we should find a defensive location," says the Inspectre.

"You do that. Maybe somewhere out on the beach."

The Inspectre opens his mouth to argue, but at that moment every single creature suddenly looks up into the night sky.

We follow their gaze. Winston whimpers in fear.

The stars are moving. Slowly at first, but picking up speed, turning in a slow pinwheel across the sky, as if a camera had been left on all night and then speeded up to see the movement of the earth. I fight off a sudden lurch of vertigo.

"He's done it," says Smith in horror. "Nyarlathotep. He's activated the spear. He's using it to unlock Cthulhu's prison."

"We're doomed!" wails Winston. "Doomed! What are we going to do? My God, what—"

Anderson slaps him across the face. He looks at her in shock, and Graves bursts out laughing.

"Blaze of glory time, kids," he says.

Wonderful.

CHAPTER TWENTY~FOUR

I stare up at the spinning stars, and for some reason it takes me back to twenty years ago, lying on the grass verge of Megan's parents' house until four in the morning, just looking up at the night sky and talking about everything and nothing. It was winter, but I wasn't cold. My heart was pumping so hard it kept me warm.

She was the one. I remember thinking that. Megan was the one I was going to spend the rest of my life with. She was kind, funny, had a dark sense of humor, and she seemed to get me. She was perfect.

So what happened? How does something like that, so pure a feeling, just . . . disappear? What happened to that innocence we had? That optimism?

My heart clenches at the thought of all that vanishing. At the thought that it wasn't even real. Maybe *that's* why it disappears. *Because* it wasn't real? Because it was all a dream?

But that's not how it works, is it? If it happened, even in my mind, it's real. If we experience it, it's real. And it's all there for a reason, to bring us to exactly where we are today. I've lost so much, but if I hadn't, I might never have been in the position to join up with Graves. If Megan and I hadn't split, we might never have had this chance to stop something terrible from happening. Megan always said I had to go with the flow. To just stop fighting everything. That there was a reason things happened. Maybe she was right after all.

I look at the others. We're back on the roof now. Graves is sitting with his head tilted back, staring up at the stars and smiling ruefully, his gun across his lap. Winston and Smith both look terrified, and Anderson stands next to them, staring out over the city, holding her shotgun with a determined look on her face. The Inspectre and his men have fanned out around the roof, each covering a different approach.

"Sir," says one of them urgently.

I look across and see that the small army that had been loitering outside Cthulhu's tower is moving, heading toward the walls where the glass guardians are standing watch.

Which means the entrance to the tower is now unguarded.

Fuck it. I suppose if this is going to be done, then I have to do it.

None of the others are watching, so I slip back down the stairs and run through the streets, pausing at every crossroads to make sure there are no surprises waiting around the corner.

The empty plaza isn't quite deserted. There are still two Shamblers standing on either side of the doorway. I walk out of my cover, raise the gun, and shoot them both. They wither and crumble before my eyes, bones dropping into a dusty pile that I kick aside as I enter the tower.

Darkness and freezing cold envelopes me. There's a thick mist hanging in the air. I can barely see my hand in front of my face.

I make my way forward until my foot hits a stair, and then I start to climb, making sure my feet don't slip on the wet glass. A few minutes later I'm on the outside balcony that rings the vast space where Cthulhu is being held prisoner.

I glance out over the city and see that battle has begun. The creatures from the tower are battling with the guardians on the wall. And it looks like some of them have opened the gate, because the creatures from outside are spilling into the city, joining the battle with shrieks and triumphant cries.

The stars are spinning faster now, a pinwheel of white lines moving in a blur. I peer through the closest arch into the huge room. Except it's not really a room. It's a vast floor of black glass, designs etched in silver into the obsidian. It has no roof, the space open to the whirling stars.

The crystal structure is there, just like in my dreams. A multifaceted prison divided into segments that shift into different geometric shapes when I look at it. In each facet I can see an image of Cthulhu. Crouched over, eyes closed, bat wings curled protectively around his body, octopus head pointed at the ground.

He's so big I can't take it all in. A creature larger than the Eiffel Tower, trapped inside a geometric crystal sitting on top of a huge glass tower. It's something out of a nightmare.

Nyarlathotep stands before Cthulhu. The spear has been thrust into a hole in the obsidian floor. The spearhead spins round and round, searching for the combination that will unlock Cthulhu.

I take a deep breath and step beneath the archway onto the glass floor.

And as I do so the stars stop spinning.

Nyarlathotep triumphantly pumps the air. "Yes, yes, yes! Thank you, thank you. Hail to me, everyone. The grooviest person alive."

The prison holding Cthulhu starts to fold in on itself, each segment retreating jerkily back against the next so that it looks like a stop-motion film. I stare in horror as the crystal folds away into nothingness, leaving Cthulhu crouched before us, a monstrosity of a god. It's like being close to Godzilla.

Nyarlathotep giggles to himself and steps toward Cthulhu. That's when I notice he's holding the Jewel of Ini-taya in his hand.

"*Stop!*"

Nyarlathotep whirls around. "By the tentacles of Cthulhu!" he shouts. "You are the bane of my existence, you know that? You're like an unwanted child at a house party. You are the vegan at a barbecue."

"Don't do this," I say. "Please. Think about how many people will die."

"They can't die. They don't exist. *You* don't exist."

"I kind of feel like I do."

"No. You are nothing. You are a blip of thought. A passing dream. Your life is not real."

"It feels real to me."

We stare at each other for a moment.

Then he moves.

I was expecting it. I fire the entropy gun as he leaps forward, black lightning hitting him before he reaches the Old One. He's about ten feet away as black veins start to spread up his body.

I sigh in relief.

A sigh that catches in my throat as Nyarlathotep takes another step.

I stare at him in amazement. He's aging before my very eyes, the entropy gun drawing life from his limbs, withering his legs, sucking the fat from his body. He takes another step. His hair is growing long. His nails, too. His face is sunken and old, like a special effect in an old Spielberg movie. He takes another step, then another. I fire again, but it makes no difference.

I start to run toward him, but even as I do I know I'm too far away. He looks like a desiccated corpse, but he's still moving, sheer determination drawing him on.

His arm sags, the jewel too heavy for his withered muscles. I draw closer. I'm only a few steps away now. I reach out—

And Nyarlathotep falls forward, arm outstretched, and the jewel touches Cthulhu's head.

"G-Groovy," he whispers.

Nyarlathotep collapses, withering up and turning to dust. But I barely notice. My eyes are on the jewel. The skin on Cthulhu's head puckers up and folds around the jewel, then draws it inside.

And the massive god opens its eyes.

"What have you done?" shouts a voice behind me.

I whirl around to find Dvalin staring at Cthulhu in horror.

"It wasn't me!" I shout, staggering away from the god. "I tried to stop him!" I frown. "Why haven't we vanished? I mean, if he's woken up?"

"You ever feel bright and wide awake when you first open your eyes in the morning? Multiply that by millions. Now come on. Something's happened." He looks at Cthulhu in fear. "Something else." He grabs my arm and pulls me back down the stairs.

"Where are we going?"

He doesn't answer. We finally make it out of the tower, and he simply points upward.

I look.

And my mind goes blank.

Creeping globes, looking like diseased planets, are forming from nothing in the night sky, seeming to fade into existence. They're linked to each other by tattered, mucusy tendrils. The globes are impossible to judge in size. They could very well be the size of moons, or just the size of a football field but they all glow from within, lightning flickering inside like light in a pregnant woman's stomach, which I realize is not a great metaphor, but it's what comes to mind.

"See them!" shouts Dvalin. "'The Old Ones were, the Old Ones are, and the Old Ones shall be. Not in the spaces we know, but between them, they walk serene and primal, undimensioned and to us unseen. Yog-Sothoth knows the gate. Yog-Sothoth is the gate. Yog-Sothoth is the key and guardian of the gate. Past, present, future, all are one in Yog-Sothoth. He knows where the Old Ones broke through of old, and where They shall break through again. He knows where They have trod earth's fields, and where They still tread them, and why no one can behold Them as They tread. . . . As a foulness shall ye know Them. Their hand is at your throats, yet ye see Them not; and Their habitation is even one with your guarded threshold.'"

I frown. That sounds oddly familiar. "Are you just quoting actual H. P. Lovecraft short stories now?"

"It is the truth. For the Old Ones are returning."

I stare up again. The globes look . . . alive. Like eggs. As if there is something inside them. As we watch, the globes shift and stretch, pulling apart, yet still staying linked to each other.

"Yog-Sothoth," says Dvalin. "He is the transcosmic one. He is the gateway, the entrance, and the exit. The womb and the grave."

As he speaks the light grows brighter within the globes, a sickly green-and-yellow glow that spreads between the globes and forms a circle hovering against the stars.

"Cthulhu is calling his brethren," whispers Dvalin.

The first to come through the gate is a mass of pink-and-white light, pulling through the gateway into the Dreamlands, impossibly large. Tentacles whip over interstellar distances, knocking the moon aside, slapping it into rubble that flows apart in slow motion.

In the center of the mass are a hideous mouth and yellowed teeth, snapping and grinning, sneering and smiling as it enters the space around R'lyeh.

"Azathoth," whispers Dvalin. "The 'amorphous blight of nethermost confusion which blasphemes and bubbles at the center of all infinity—the boundless daemon sultan Azathoth, whose name no lips dare speak aloud, and who gnaws hungrily in inconceivable, unlighted chambers beyond time and space amidst the muffled, maddening beating of vile drums and the thin monotonous whine of accursed flutes.'"

"Still sounds like you're quoting the books," I say distantly.

Azathoth pulls itself free, and another comes from behind. This one is familiar. Purple lightning flickers around a black, roiling cloud. The cloud grows thicker, and tendrils of cloud reach out, solidifying into oily, black tentacles.

Shub-Niggurath. The Old One the Nazis tried to summon.

The cloud pulls itself through the gate, and the snapping jaws appear, serrated teeth clacking.

Then the night sky changes, rippling like water. The light between the globes turns a deep, primordial blue, and a head appears, a green, scaly head of a monstrous fish-man. The creature slides through the gate, using webbed feet to sail through the night sky as if slicing through water.

"Dagon," whispers Dvalin. "The dreaded fish god. Witnessed by one man who survived, who forever after was haunted by the creature, 'especially when the moon is gibbous and waning.'

"'I cannot think of the deep sea without shuddering at the nameless things that may at this very moment be crawling and floundering on its slimy bed, worshipping their ancient stone idols and carving their own detestable likenesses on submarine obelisks of water-soaked granite. I dream of a day when they may rise above the billows to drag down in their reeking talons the remnants of puny, war-exhausted mankind—of a day when the land shall sink, and the dark ocean floor shall ascend amidst universal pandemonium.'"

I frown and turn on the small man. Just to check he's not actually reciting from an H. P. Lovecraft book. "Nobody's impressed, you know. Stealing someone else's work and passing it off as your own is the sign of a worthless hack."

"I am not stealing anything. If anything, he stole it. Those words are from the Elder Gods themselves. Their work is my bible. My guidebook. I know it all by heart. Now come. There is still a chance we can stop them. It is going to be very dangerous. There's a very good chance you could lose your mind and your soul rent asunder by the sheer power you are about to grasp hold of. Your psyche will more than likely be shattered into a million tiny pieces that will be sucked into the netherworld where you will be aware of the slow onslaught of madness over the next hundred thousand years. So . . . are you keen?"

"Fuck no."

"Tough. We have no choice. I've already told the others. They're going to hold the monsters off while we do this."

"Do what?"

He doesn't answer, instead leading me deeper into the city, away from the walls and the sounds of battle. The buildings drop away behind us, and we arrive at a vast lake easily three miles across. I can still hear the sounds of furious battle raging not too far from us: Screeching and growling. The sharp crack of splintering obsidian guards, the wet rip of skin. The loud crack of guns being discharged, which means that the others are now involved in the fight.

Dvalin leans over next to a small plinth. He glances over his shoulder at me. "Turn around."

"Why?"

"You can't see the combination. It's a secret."

"Goddamn it, Dvalin. Are you serious?"

"Yes! The Elder Gods themselves charged me with this! You don't fuck with the Elder Gods, man. You just don't do it."

"Fine!"

I turn around and fold my arms. A moment later a loud sucking noise starts up, like a toothless hag sucking up a milkshake, but multiplied by a million. I turn back and see the water level dropping, disappearing somewhere beneath us.

It doesn't take long for the lake to drain. The water vanishes to reveal a mud-covered mound about the same size as Cthulhu.

"This is wonderful," I say. "Really. You've drained a lake. Biblical but on a budget. Now what?"

"Wait."

A burst of rain suddenly pours from the sky, falling directly onto the mound, washing the mud and gloop away. I take a step forward, staring in amazement as a massive figure is revealed, lying still on the lake bed.

"What the hell is that?"

"One of the Elder Gods."

I look at Dvalin. "Are you serious?"

"Yes. He sacrificed his life. Sent his mind out into the ether so his body could remain here in case we needed it."

The Elder God looks . . . alien. It's the only way to describe it. Man-shaped, with a beige, bone-like exterior, as if it has a hard carapace instead of skin. Its head is massive and long, misshapen and stretched out.

"What are you waiting for?" I say. I glance up and see that the Old Ones are moving slowly across the sky, coming toward us. "Wake it up."

"It's not like that. I can't just wake it up. It needs a mind to join with. A mind other than my own."

"Wait, what—"

I start to turn, but before I do anything Dvalin jabs something into my neck. "Oh, god*dammit*," I slur.

Then I drop to the ground.

§

You know that feeling when you have a hangover from hell? Your body is all shaky, and it's not obeying you? You feel like you can't control your limbs or anything? I feel like that when I awake.

I sit up, the mud making a loud sucking noise behind me. For a moment I still think I'm going to be looking at Dvalin standing right next to me, but I'm not. For some reason I'm really high up in the sky and Dvalin is far away below me, standing on the shore of the lake.

And I can see me, lying on the ground, my eyes wide and staring.

"Oh for fuck's sake. This isn't cool!" I shout. Dvalin slaps his hands over his ears. "This is the second time I've been drugged against my will! You guys can't just keep doing that."

Dvalin drops to his knees, his hands still pushing hard against his ears. "Stop shouting!"

I push myself to my feet, rising up and up until I'm towering over the city. Everything feels really slow. I'm not used to the weight.

I look around and see Graves and the others are indeed doing their part. They've formed a barricade a few streets away to keep the shoggoths and other creatures away from the lake.

Dvalin points up into the sky. I nod, lumbering into a jog, then a run, then pushing off from the muddy ground. Don't ask me how I knew I could do that. I just did. I sail up into the sky, and I'm flying, moving like Iron Man straight for the closest tentacled monstrosity. I yell with pure, terrified joy. Shub-Niggurath senses something and starts to turn toward me. But it's too late. I grab tentacles and punch it in the snapping, serrated teeth. It cries out in shrill fury as the teeth of a god go flying off into space. I plunge my hands deep into the roiling mass, purple lightning flickering around me, coruscating up along my arms and through my body. I scream with effort, and *pull*, and I'm rewarded with the satisfying sound of ripping and tearing flesh.

I keep pulling, and rip Shub-Niggurath apart. Then I throw the remains back through the gateway that is Yog-Sothoth.

The other Old Ones are now aware they're under attack. Dagon comes toward me, arms outstretched. I lift my own arms and punch out, a jab that snaps the fish god's head backward. He punches me back, and I sail through the sky, stopping myself and going back for more.

But there's something pulling at my mind, trying to get my attention. I ignore it as Dagon and I face off. Trading punches back and forth. Neither of us are gaining the advantage.

Screw it. I whip my foot up and kick the bastard fish god between the legs.

Dagon whimpers and soars back through space, his eyes bulging in pain. He hits the gate and gets stuck there, half of him slipping back though the pink-and-purple mist, the other half trying to come back to me.

Whatever it is pulling at my mind is growing more insistent.

I ignore it and look down. The Shamblers and monkeys are almost overrunning the barricade. Graves and the others have drawn closer together at the mouth of an alley, firing ahead of them as they slowly back up. There are only a couple of the tactical team left. I look around for the glass statues, but they're busy battling the creatures at the wall. Graves and the others won't last long. I have to help them.

The vague tugging on my mind grows even more insistent. I try to ignore it, but it grows stronger and stronger, unintelligible sounds finally forming into coherent words.

Look behind you.

I squeal with fright. Where the hell did that come from?

You are in partnership with an Elder God. Do you seriously not think I can communicate?

Aren't you supposed to be dead?

Death is overrated. It is but a veil, and I am on the other side. Or at least, my mind is. Look, I'm here to help. Just turn around, will you?

I turn just as the top of the prison tower explodes, massive chunks of obsidian soaring into the air to smash into buildings, crushing them and sending plumes of thick dust up into the air.

Cthulhu rises slowly up from the shattered remains. He looks slowly around, then strides away through the city.

And as he does so, I notice something in the sky as he moves.

The stars are winking out.

The dream is unraveling, says the voice. *You must stop him. Before the multiverse catches up.*

I look down at Graves and the others. They're in serious trouble. The creatures are closing in, and the monkeys are above them, using the rooftops to get behind their position.

"I need to help them."

I start to move, thinking I can just . . . pick Graves and the others up and take them to safety before dealing with Cthulhu.

No. Trust me. There is no time. Just let go. Let me control you.

No chance.

I feel a subtle yank pulling me backward. I resist, trying to move in the opposite direction.

Do not fight. This is the only way to save them.

I look down again, every one of my instincts telling me to go and help them. I can do it. I can help.

Then I sigh, and decide to just do as I'm told for once. To just step away from my ego.

I concentrate on releasing control. It's harder than it sounds. Just to . . . let go. To simply be.

But I manage it. I remove myself from the fight and let the Elder God go where he wants to.

I fly over the city. I feel fragmented, as if there is more than one of me. I wonder briefly if this is just because I *am* fragmented. My body back in the Bradbury Building, and my dream body now lying down below. That's some serous *Inception* shit going on.

Either that or it's the whole psychotic break thing that Dvalin was talking about.

My pondering is interrupted because at that moment I feel the burning awareness of a god focused directly upon me.

A flash of yellow eyes, and then Cthulhu roars in fury and moves toward me. Even from this distance I feel a poisonous heat, a horrible, gangrenous stench.

I feel sick. I want to take back control. To run, to flee. How can I stand against something as ancient and terrifying as this? I'm nothing. I'm a microbe compared to the most advanced being in the multiverse. Who am I to even contemplate standing up against such a magnificent creature?

My ears are buzzing, my eyes throbbing. I freeze up, waiting for Cthulhu to snuff me out just as I deserve. To end me as is his right. To do with me as he will.

Just let go, says the voice in my head. *Trust me. You don't have to be in control here. Let me do it. If you don't he will take over your mind.*

I close my eyes. I can't let go. It feels too alien. Like I'm dying. Like I won't come back.

Just trust for once. Don't try and control everything.

And I stop trying to hold everything in. Stop trying to close everything off.

Stop trying to control the world.

Ar'atak, says the voice in my head, and it is like a sudden crack of thunder. I know instantly what it means. It is a first word, one of the words of power that Mad Arin told me about, a word that the Elder Gods used to create the universe.

Except it's not about creating. This word is about undoing. Ending. It is the only word that can end a god, and the only ones who know it are the Elder Gods.

The letters that make up the word, the word itself, is nothing as to the actual feeling-sense it possesses, the true meaning behind the word. *Ar'atak* is a surface guise, like the ant hill that hides the vast colony beneath the ground. I feel the meaning of it radiating outward, like ripples in a pool.

Ar'atak.

I see the past—I see the word used on a mountain and see the mountain crumble to dust. I see it used against an ancient beast of the forest, and the horned creature unravels, its life going backward, undoing itself until it doesn't exist, until it never *had* existed. I see that ancient battle, the Elder Gods against the Old Ones, them using the word of undoing against some of the Old Ones before Cthulhu and the others surrender.

Ar'atak.

The power builds up inside me. It is a maelstrom of heat and energy, a gathering of . . . undoing, of nothingness.

Cthulhu reaches out to me. He grabs my neck, but I let the power burst out of me, a surge of entropy, an invisible heat wave that sucks in and swallows everything in its path.

I direct it at Cthulhu's head, and I reach out, the massive fingers of the Elder God rending through Cthulhu's skin. I feel the fingers curl around the Jewel of Ini-taya, Cthulhu's consciousness, and I unleash the power.

"*Ar'atak.*"

The force strikes Cthulhu. He staggers, his head tilted back as he screams his fury into the Dreamlands. Cracks spread across his skin like corrupted veins, purple light pouring out. I sense the battle down below stopping, all eyes turned to us.

And I pull my hand out with the jewel resting in my palm. The word of undoing surges through it. The jewel trembles in my hand, then explodes, shattering and turning to dust that drifts away on the wind.

Cthulhu's scream breaks off. His eyes close, and he sags.

A moment of weightlessness, and then he falls over backward and drops onto the city, buildings and structures crushed beneath his weight.

The blankness in the sky pulses; then the stars flicker back into view. The Old Ones shriek in the night sky and flee back through the gateway, Yog-Sothoth herself turning inside out and vanishing into nothingness.

I close my eyes and smile—

And when I open them again I'm on the shores of the empty lake, Dvalin peering down at me with some surprise.

"You're still alive," he says. "Well . . . that's good. Didn't really expect that, if I'm honest. Well done."

"Did I do it?" I croak.

"Um . . . if by do it you mean did you destroy Cthulhu's consciousness and force him into an eternal coma from which he will never awake, thus ensuring the survival of the entire multiverse, then . . . yeah. You did it."

I sigh with relief. "Groovy."

EPILOGUE

The polite term for what I do for a living is "supernatural hazard remediation."

That's what I say if anyone asks me at a dinner party. Not that I'm ever invited to dinner parties.

Well, that's not exactly true. I am sometimes. Megan has invited me over a couple of times recently, which is nice. And Graves. I've been to a few with him, but it's best to keep those as a special treat. They usually last for a few days and involve dimension hopping on a grand scale.

Another term for what I do is *Decontamination of Interstitial Crime Scenes.*

Which, basically, means that I clean up stiffs for a living.

All the stiffs. No prejudice in my line of work.

Murder of citizens of a Class D medieval-based society by a space-faring race? Check.

Superhero villains invading a non-magic-based society? Check.

Fairy genocide? Check.

Wizard duels held on hillsides with magic lights and fireballs spitting between the combatants? Check. (Not that I've ever had one of those, but I live in hope.)

The department I work for is called the DDICS. That's not "dicks" by the way, so stop laughing. It stands for the Disposal Department for Interstitial Crime Scenes. My boss is a man called Havelock Graves, and he's a complete ass.

I've been stuck in this dead-end (ha-ha) job for two months now. Not bad, considering it was only ever meant to be temporary. I was assured we would be promoted back to the actual investigative unit after what we did. You know, saving the entire multiverse from destruction.

But no. All that had to be kept super-duper quiet. Even though Graves took great joy in making the Inspectre stick up for him. He said the whole thing was worth it just to have the Inspectre stand before the disciplinary commission and tell them that they had to leave Graves (and me) alone. That more people knew the truth now than could be silenced.

We had to sign a lot of papers promising not to talk about it all. Papers that had scary words like "official secrets act" and "permanent incarceration."

Graves assures me that after a proper amount of time has passed we'll move back to ICD. We just have to keep this up for a little while longer. How long, he won't say. But I did catch him weeping in the toilet a few days ago, so I'm not sure that's a good sign.

"All I'm saying," says Graves, "is that I'm right."

"You're not. You're so wrong it's not even funny."

"It *is* funny. An Elder God miraculously appeared and destroyed the other big, nasty god. It's *literally* the textbook definition of deus ex machina."

"No. Because if I wasn't there, then it wouldn't have happened. See? deus ex machina means the god did everything. But it didn't. I did."

"Only by *inhabiting* a god. Admit it. It was a cop out."

"I saved the fucking multiverse. It was not a cop out. The whole thing since we started out was about gods. Of course the resolution was going to be the same."

"Keep telling yourself that, sport." He yawns and stretches. "What's the job today?"

I check the clipboard.

"Robot war being fought in primitive, Neanderthal alternate. We have to clean up the evidence."

"Of course. And we'll have to stay out of sight. Just imagine what they'll think if they see us."

I don't say anything.

"These primitive people, watching us appear in a flash of light."

I stay silent.

"Why, they'd almost think we were some sort of supernatural advanced being."

I sigh.

"Come on. Say it."

"I'm not saying it."

"Say it!" shouts Graves gleefully.

"I'm not saying it."

"We'll be like gods! It will be—"

"Don't."

"—a deus ex machina."

Then he bursts out laughing. And won't stop.

I hate my job.

ACKNOWLEDGMENTS

Many thanks to my editor, Rene, for putting up with my crap and never losing patience with me. And thanks to my copy editor, Jeffrey Curry, for untangling my many abuses of the English language.

And to Noelle Adams, for being an awesome beta reader/English fixer-upper.

And to time. Just for, you know, passing. And making things easier. Keep on keeping on.

ABOUT THE AUTHOR

Paul Crilley is a Scotsman living in South Africa. He writes for television, comics, and computer games. His previous books have mainly been for children, among them the Invisible Order series about a hidden war being fought on the streets of Victorian London between humankind and the fae. He also wrote *Poison City*, a supernatural thriller set in Durban, South Africa.

Photo by Caroline Doherty